THE BOOK OF MORMON SLEUTH 3

The Hidden Path

C.B. ANDERSEN

DESERET BOOK
SALT LAKE CITY, UTAH

For Seantylle, Jeff, Brandon, Megan, Chelsey, and Dallin—
extraordinary children who inspire me in countless ways
It is genuinely humbling to be the father of such valiant souls

Library of Congress Cataloging-in-Publication Data

Andersen, C. B. (Carl Blaine), 1961-
   The Book of Mormon sleuth, vol. 3 : the hidden path / C. B. Andersen.
     p.   cm.
   Summary: When Shauna, Jeff, Brandon, and Meg Andrews inadvertently stow away on a yacht carrying the creepy Dr. Anthony and his associates to Russia in search of the tribe the Andrews family met the previous year, they find hope and courage through prayer and the Book of Mormon.
   ISBN 1-57008-988-4 (pbk.)
   [1. Robbers and outlaws—Fiction.   2. Brothers and sisters—Fiction.   3. Mormons—Fiction.   4. Book of Mormon—Fiction.   5. Russia—Fiction.]   I. Title: Book of Mormon sleuth volume three.   II. Title: Hidden path.   III. Title.
   PZ7.A51887Br 2003
   [Fic]—dc21   2003006742

Printed in the United States of America   7973-7103
Bang Printing, Brainerd, MN

10   9   8   7   6   5   4   3   2   1

Contents

Acknowledgments

Now that the third book in this series is available, I must acknowledge the outstanding efforts of both Emily Watts and Richard Peterson of Deseret Book Company. Their guidance has been invaluable in bringing about each of the three novels. Richard was able to persuade the powers that be that he could craft something worth publishing from the unsolicited manuscript by an unknown author—the manuscript that became *The Book of Mormon Sleuth*. Emily's patience has been immeasurable and our phone conversations innumerable as she has encouraged and supported me through each of the manuscripts. These are people of the highest caliber whom I am pleased to call friends.

Preface

This is a work of fiction. Its purpose is to entertain but also to help young readers become more familiar with scriptural teachings. In this case, I have focused on peoples of the world, past and present, who have dedicated themselves to living by these teachings.

Do I believe the lost ten tribes of Israel are in northeast Asia? There are at least ten separate references in the standard works of The Church of Jesus Christ of Latter-day Saints that speak of the gathering of Israel. Third Nephi 5:24 states: "And as surely as the Lord liveth, will he gather in from the four quarters of the earth all the remnant of the seed of Jacob, who are scattered abroad upon all the face of the earth."

Other references specifically mention "the isles of the sea" (1 Nephi 19:16) or "the north countries" (Ether 13:11). Rather than gathering an entire group or nation, which has been hidden from the knowledge of the rest of the world, perhaps part of this gathering will proceed as Jeremiah prophesied: "I will take you one of a city, and two of a family, and I will bring you to Zion" (Jeremiah 3:14; see verses 12–19).

More important than the *location* of the lost tribes, is this: if we will seek to understand the prophesies found in the scriptures, we will develop a deeper appreciation for the sacrifice of our Savior, Jesus Christ. May we exercise as much faith in that unparalleled event as did so many who lived before it even happened.

CHAPTER 1

A Blast from the Past

Jeff just doesn't get it. He's my big brother, and I think he's great and all—but he just doesn't get it. Yeah, I know, he's a year older than I am, but in this case, older and wiser don't go together, even if he is starting high school next month and I'll just be a ninth grader.

You see, Jeff thought that after we had a horrific experience trying to claim our free Alaskan cruise the first time, that Dad would be smart enough to stay away from any more situations with such obvious and proven disaster potential. *Hello-o-o!* Where's Jeff been? What did he miss in the last 15 years? I can't remember a single time that Dad missed out on purpose on anything that included the word *free.* (I'm sure we must hold the world record for the number of Saturdays in a row an entire family has eaten free hot dogs at the furniture store. Dad would always ask me, "Aren't you hungry, Brandon?" Well, truthfully, hot dogs were never something I was that big on—even before we had to all pile into the car together and drive five miles to go get them.) I guess when you have six kids, you have to take advantage of free stuff whenever you can.

But aside from Dad's being basically cheap, what's my point? Well, the fact is, just one year and one month after we spent a luxurious night spread out across three rooms on the top floor of the Marriott Hotel in downtown Anchorage—all paid for by the airline company that never managed to get us anywhere near the ship for our free cruise—we were back. It was the end of July, and we had returned to once again attempt to claim our "free" Alaskan cruise. The cruise was free, but the hotel wasn't. So instead of three rooms on the top floor, we were now crammed into one large room on the second floor of a two-story, who-knows-what motel, half a block from the dock in Seward, Alaska.

That's right: Seward. No one that I know has ever heard of Seward, Alaska. That's probably because, according to the map we got, it has a whopping total of *thirty-five* streets in the whole town . . . and no Marriott.

It turns out that cruises that claim "Anchorage" as a port really mean "Seward," which is a 120-mile, three-hour, shuttle-bus-ride away from Anchorage, a trip that was made bearable only by our living, breathing, tour-guide-Barbie—a doll named Brittany, who had long, curly, blonde hair, a dazzling smile, and the incredible ability to speak glowingly about every possible thing visible through the bus windows for the entire three hours—nonstop.

But being in Seward instead of Anchorage had its advantages: there they were a little less strict about how many people we could put into one room. Instead of making us pay for two or three rooms because we had eight people, we were allowed to pay only slightly less for the privilege of sharing one "deluxe room," with two queen-size beds, three single roll-aways, and a private balcony with a great view of the bay, the dock, and the mountains.

Two queen-size beds and three single roll-aways gave everyone a place to sleep, but nowhere to walk. The roll-aways were squeezed in on either side of the big beds, so it looked like we actually had only one bed that was about 20 feet wide. I saw a show once where someplace out in the middle of nowhere—somewhere in Asia— they had an inn where travelers could stay. And in the wintertime everybody staying there slept in the main room in one huge, community bed on the floor so they could all stay warm. At least *our* community bed was shared only by members of our family, and as

far as I knew none of them came with any tiny wildlife. I was starting to feel grateful for simple luxuries like hot and cold running
water—even if there was only one bathroom. These were luxuries
that I should have appreciated more while I had the chance—but
I'm getting ahead of myself.

We arrived Saturday at the airport in Anchorage without any
problem, improving the airline's record for getting us safely to
Alaska to a whopping 50%. (Which, in my book, was a significant
improvement over the previous 0-for-1 mark.) We immediately
hopped onto the shuttle bus, leaving civilization well behind us and
arrived in Seward late Saturday night with just enough time to
stock the refrigerator in our room with enough food to get us
through till Monday morning, when we were scheduled to board
the cruise ship.

Amazingly enough, Seward actually has a branch of the
Church, so Sunday morning we attended all three meetings.
Because the branch was small, Jeff and I both got to help pass the
sacrament, which neither of us had done since the time we were
deacons. For Jeff, that had been about a year and a half and for me,
just a few weeks. After church, we headed back to the motel. After
a do-it-yourself lunch of homemade sandwiches and fresh fruit, followed by a family devotional using the latest conference *Ensign,* we
spent most of the afternoon playing games that we had brought
with us.

At one point I asked Dad, "Why are we here? I mean, I thought
our free cruise tickets expired in June."

Dad smiled broadly and said, "Ah, you lucky boy! The airline
extended the deadline until September 26th, giving us the whole
summer to use them." I had no response to that. Later, we had just
finished a dinner that looked shockingly similar to lunch, when we
discovered that Mom and Dad had nothing else planned for the rest
of the evening.

"Me and Jeff are going for walk," I announced to Mom and Dad, as we headed for the door.

"Jeff and I," Mom corrected me.

"Right. Jeff and I are going for a walk."

Dad stared at us blankly. "You might also like to change that statement into a question."

I thought for a minute, then asked, "Did you *know* that Jeff and I are going for a walk?"

Dad didn't look even mildly amused, but Mom burst out laughing. "Try again," Dad said without a hint of a smile and one eyebrow raised.

"Is it okay if we go for a walk?" I asked.

"We want to go down and look at the cruise ship," Jeff added.

The one nice thing about our motel was that it was close to the harbor. We would only have to walk a couple of minutes to get down to where our cruise ship was docked, ready to leave the next morning. Earlier, from our motel balcony, we had seen the ship as it arrived.

"Sure," Mom answered.

"Don't be gone too long," Dad added.

"We'll be back before dark," I said, opening the door.

"What?" Dad gasped. "You'll be back long before that, thank you!" Jeff and I both turned to see what he meant. He asked, "Did you forget that the sun stays up half the night here?"

"Oh, yeah," I said, looking at my watch. "We'll be back in an hour or so, okay?"

"I want to come," Shauna said, bouncing to the edge of the mega-bed before Mom or Dad could answer me. Shauna is the oldest. She had just graduated from Orem High and was going to be starting college in a few weeks. We wouldn't have really minded her coming with us, but once she bounced across the beds and headed toward the door, she got everyone else's attention (read: little people) and then they all wanted to come, too.

"Can I go?" asked Meg, who (as I had recently begun to discover) communicated with the world almost entirely through questions. She had just finished fourth grade, which seemed to cause her to ask even more questions than ever before. I was thinking that maybe they ought to be teaching her at least a few *answers* by now—to go along with all of her questions. She was already reaching for her new, pink, flowered backpack before the question had even escaped her mouth. The backpack was supposedly for the new school year, but she was so in love with it from the time she first saw it in the store, you would have thought it had been surgically attached. She wouldn't even take it off to be scanned so Mom could pay for it, choosing instead to pull it part way over her head and twisting one arm behind her so the checkout girl could reach the tag. I think Meg had actually slept with it on her back every night since.

Of course, then eight-year-old Chelsea and five-year-old Danny immediately jumped to their feet as well. Neither of them had any idea who was going or where, but they never wanted to miss out on anything that involved the word "go." Luckily, this time, Mom and Dad had pity on us and didn't make us take them with us, but they agreed that "Meg wouldn't be a bother."

"Oh-h-h!" Chelsea pouted at the news that she wouldn't be going. She has an amazing ability to stick out both lips clear past the end of her small nose whenever she thinks life is unfair—which turns out to be pretty often. Danny was just as happy to stay behind with Chelsea as he was to go with us, so he quickly took the opportunity to practice high-jumping back up onto the community bed. Dad helped Chelsea get over the disappointment of being left behind by offering to play a game with her.

"Be back at nine for prayers," Dad said. This was no surprise. Nine o'clock had been the magic, evening family-prayer time for as long as I can remember. Unless something unusual was going on, everyone was expected to be home at nine for family prayer. If you were at a friend's house doing homework or anything else, you came home long enough for prayer—even if you had to go back again right after. Any friends that came with you or happened to be any-where in sight were also expected to join the circle. Our prayer circle often had at least twice as many people as there are in our family.

"I don't have a watch," Shauna said. She glanced about the room as if trying to find one. Shauna's great at just about everything except keeping track of things. She had lost practically every watch she had ever worn (whether it was hers or not), so I can't imagine that she really expected to find one that belonged to her in a motel room—or one anybody would be dumb enough to let her borrow.

"I have mine," Jeff said. Turning to Dad, he added, "We'll be back on time."

"Take your coats, please," Mom said. "It can get chilly pretty quickly in the evening near the water." Before we had even found our coats Mom was already being distracted by Danny's repeated "jostling" of the community bed with each new high-jump record attempt, and Dad was listing off the game options to Chelsea. With coats under our arms, we closed the door behind us as quickly as possible, before any more random, overprotective comments were tossed in our direction. Meg wanted to wear her coat under her backpack, but we didn't let her take the time to rearrange herself until we got to the lobby.

"Meg, why are you bringing your backpack?" I asked, hoping for a response that wasn't in the form of a question.

"Can't I bring it if I want to?" she asked.

"Sure you can," Shauna smiled as she stepped in between Meg and me. I think my voice must have given away how annoyed I was. "What do you have in it?" Shauna asked.

"Can I show you?" replied Meg.

"Why don't you show me when we get back to the room?" smiled Shauna. "That way we can spread it out all over the bed and

6

make sure you show me everything!" That sounded fantastic to Meg, whose eyes twinkled at the thought.

Jeff looked at his watch and announced that we had an hour and a half before we had to be home for family prayer. The sun was low in the sky, but we had learned the previous year that this far north in the middle of the summer, the sun almost made a full circle around us before going down below the north horizon for just four or five hours.

"Are we going to see the boat for our cruise?" Meg asked.

"That's where we're going," Shauna answered.

As we walked toward the dock we started talking about all the fun things that we had been told about this ship. We were going to be on board for five days and apparently everyone could have as much food as they wanted, whenever they wanted. There were free movies, free video games, several swimming pools, and all sorts of other things to do. It really did sound like it was going to be a blast. And it was finally looking like it might really happen. It's amazing how fast things can change.

"There it is!" announced Shauna to no one in particular as we turned the corner at the dock.

"That thing is humongous!" Jeff gasped.

My thoughts were the same as I began to count the number of rows of windows up the side of the ship—there were *seven!* The lowest two rows had smaller, round windows and were below the main deck. On the other five rows, the windows were large and square, making it look almost like an office building. I didn't even bother to try counting how many windows were in each row, but I'm sure there were fifty or sixty.

"How many people can fit on that thing?" I asked, leaving my mouth gaping open.

"Dad said it was more than a thousand," Shauna answered.

As we continued to talk about the number of levels and windows and people and swimming pools and everything else we could remember or figure out about the ship, I noticed that Meg was frozen in her tracks with wide eyes and sunken cheeks.

"What's the matter?" asked Shauna after we had all watched Meg for a moment.

"Is it real?" Meg questioned slowly.

"Yep," answered Shauna. "Cool, huh?"

"Does it move?" Meg asked.

"Of course it moves," laughed Jeff. "It's not a cruise *anchor*, it's a cruise *ship!* That means it goes places."

Meg's eyes started to get tears in them. "It's going to be really loud, huh?" she asked. She was trying her hardest not to cry. For as long as I could remember, Meg had absolutely hated loud noises. She jumped at anything and everything that was the least bit unexpected. And loud noises were the worst. I admit I probably took a little too much delight in "forgetting" that fact and "accidentally" scaring her by slamming a huge school book down on the kitchen table when she was sitting there or slapping my hand against the bathroom door while she was brushing her teeth.

"Oh, no, Meg," Shauna comforted her, stooping down to put her arm around Meg's shoulders. "You won't even hear it," Shauna said. "The engines are all at the back and underneath, see?" As she pointed to the rear of the ship she added, "And we'll be up on top or inside or someplace else where we won't even hear them at all."

Meg's expression immediately got hopeful as she looked up at Shauna and asked, "Are you sure?"

"I'm sure," Shauna smiled.

Without another word, Meg just grabbed Shauna's hand and held on tight.

"Let's go over close and see what those guys are doing," Jeff suggested.

There were two long ramps that ran from the dock into a large doorway in one of the lower levels of the ship. Men and women were loading cart after cart of who-knows-what onto the ship. They rolled the carts down steep ramps out of the back of semi trailers and rolled them up one of the gradually sloped ramps into the ship. They would return a few minutes later, rolling empty carts down the other ramp and lining them up at the back of the semi trailer. When the trailer didn't have any more carts in it, they started loading all the empty carts back inside it. Another semi pulled up to be unloaded after the first one drove away. We watched this for so long that I lost track of both the time and the number of semis that came and left.

Near the front of the ship was a large building that was several stories high. There was a walkway from the top level of the building that ran pretty much straight across to the top level of the ship. We figured that was probably where the passengers got on.

After a while we decided to walk farther down the dock where there were some much smaller boats. As we got closer we found that they were still pretty big. Shauna said that they were called "yachts" and were probably owned by people who are really rich. They were different sizes, but most of them were as big as the houses where we lived. We were amazed as we thought about what it must be like to be on a yacht that was as big as our house.

After a few minutes we decided that our time was about up and began walking back toward the cruise ship and our motel. As we were passing one of the yachts, we heard a man call, "Good luck!" to some unseen person on the yacht and then climb the ramp to the dock a little way in front of us. Once on the dock, he turned the same direction we were going and continued walking. I didn't really think much about him until Jeff whispered, "Is that John?"

"That's what I was thinking, too," Shauna said with a half smile.

"Who's John?" Meg asked.

"Yeah," I joined in, "John who?"

"John the co-pilot," Jeff said. "You know—the one who was in Russia with us last year."

"Yeah," Shauna agreed.

"*That* John?" I questioned.

"Why is he here?" Meg asked what we all were wondering.

"Let's find out if it's him first," Shauna said, "and then we can ask him."

"John!" Jeff called, taking Shauna's suggestion.

The man immediately turned around to see who had called to him. He stood waiting as we continued toward him.

"Jeff!" he called back after a moment. "Shauna, is that you? And Brandon! And Meg, right?" As we got closer he said, "It *is* you! What are you doing here?"

"Hi, John!" we called back. He grabbed us each by the shoulders and shook us gently, looking into our eyes one at a time. His smile was wide, but his eyes glistened slightly as though he was trying to keep from crying. It was as though he was trying to assure himself that we were real people and not just part of some horrible nightmare he had had more than a year earlier. We were living proof that it wasn't just all in his mind. I knew the feeling. The entire experience seemed completely unreal to me, too—and probably to every one of us.

I guess I ought to explain what happened. The truth is, the last time we climbed onto a plane to go to Alaska, we never actually made it. Just as we were getting close to landing, we were told there was a volcano that had erupted in the area a few minutes earlier. The eruption created a cloud of dust that was floating right toward us. Apparently radios won't work from inside a volcanic cloud like that, so the pilot didn't want to fly through it. Just as the plane was turning to get away from the cloud, there were several loud thumps somewhere that broke the navigation system. We learned after we finally got back that another volcano had erupted much closer to where we were flying, and the airline people figured that we could have been hit by rocks from the second volcano. They had some other ideas, too, but since they never recovered the plane, we would probably never know for sure.

Anyway, after the thumps, the pilot and copilot decided to just fly straight ahead instead of continuing the turn because they couldn't tell how far to turn. We ended up flying right through the volcanic cloud, which made the radio not work. They kept telling us that the radio should work again as soon as we were through the cloud, but it never did. And the backup radio didn't work, either. So we ended up flying for several hours through clouds without radio or navigation. The cloud from the volcano wasn't that big, but there were lots of other clouds, and so we couldn't tell where we were for a long time.

Finally, when the clouds cleared, the pilot and copilot were able to see well enough to land the plane along the shore of what they figured was the Arctic Ocean. We were in Russia. I could never figure out how we ended up in Russia when we were flying from Portland, Oregon, to Anchorage, Alaska. When we got home I actually looked at a globe and found out that if you draw a straight line from Portland to Anchorage, that only a slight turn to the west will take you right along the northern coast of Russia! It doesn't look that way on a map, but you can sure see it on a globe.

Well, we ended up meeting these people that apparently nobody in the world knew anything about. They had ancient writings from the Bible and were still following the rituals and sacrifices from the Law of Moses. Some of them were really mad that we were there. They were afraid that we would go back and tell others where to find them. They wanted to remain hidden from the rest of the world. There were some nice people there, too, though. There had been a man from the United States who had lived with one of the families for more than fifty years and who had given them a Bible and taught them English, so we were able to communicate with them. The man had died not long before we got there, but the family that he had lived with turned out to be good people and good friends. But after a year, the whole experience seemed totally unreal. Actually after being home for only about three days it had already seemed unreal.

"What are you doing here?" John asked. Before we could answer he also asked, "Are your parents here?"

"Yeah, they're here," Shauna answered. "We're staying in a motel just around the corner down there." She pointed as she spoke and John turned to see where she was pointing. "They stayed at the room with our little brother and sister."

John wanted to know the name of the motel and room number. He wrote it down on a small notepad he had in his shirt pocket. "That's great!" said John as he put the paper away. "So why are you here?"

"We're trying one more time to make it on our free cruise," I said, rolling my eyes slightly.

John laughed. "Oh, that's right!" he said. "That's how you ended up on the plane last year! I had forgotten." Then he asked, "Do you think you'll make it this time?"

"We're hoping!" Shauna smiled.

"That's our ship down there," Jeff pointed as he spoke. John turned to look again. "We leave in the morning," Jeff added.

"You look pretty excited for it," John smiled as he turned back around. He looked down at Meg and said, "Except for you. Aren't you excited to be going on a cruise in the morning?"

I listened carefully to see if my theory about Meg always using questions still held true even when she was talking to people outside our family. "Do you think it will be too loud?" asked Meg. "Shauna and Jeff and Brandon said it won't be too loud, but do you think they're right?"

John smiled as he replied, "Oh, I think your sister and brothers are quite right! Airplanes are much louder than cruise ships. Did you think the airplane was too loud?"

"What airplane?" Meg asked.

"The airplane that brought you here," John said. "Did you think it was too loud?"

Meg thought about this for a moment before turning to Shauna and asking, "Did you think the airplane was too loud?"

"No," Shauna said. "It was pretty loud, but not *too* loud."

Meg just looked at her for a moment before asking, "Did *I* think it was too loud?"

"I don't know what you thought," Shauna answered, "but if you don't *remember* thinking that it was loud, then it was probably okay." Meg thought about that as Shauna continued. "So if the airplane wasn't too loud and if John is right about the cruise ship not being as loud as the airplane, then it should be just fine."

"Do you think John is right?" Meg asked hopefully.

"Yes," Shauna nodded. "I'm sure he's right."

That was good enough for Meg: she just smiled slightly as she lifted her shoulders up almost to her ears and let them drop with a contented sigh. Her pink, flowered backpack bounced against her.

"So why are *you* here?" asked Jeff.

"Oh!" smiled John excitedly, as if he had just remembered something wonderful. "You will not *believe* the great thing that has happened!" He pointed to the boat that he had just left and said, "The man who owns that yacht wants to help us make up for that terrible thing that happened last year!" He paused and looked at each of us in turn before slowly adding, "He's taking this whole boat full of salt to the tribe!" He smiled triumphantly as he gave us the news.

"Wait, what?" asked Shauna.

"You're not serious!" I said.

"*What* did you *tell* them?" asked Jeff.

John's confident look began to fade just a little as he stammered, "I-I-I told them that we had . . . ruined a . . . their major source of salt when w-w-we dumped the jet fuel before our emergency landing."

We all continued to stare with mouths open and wide eyes. His smile was completely gone now. He continued with, "I know how much you cared about those people! I thought you'd be as pleased as I am!"

"They want to be left alone!" said Jeff.

"What did you tell that man?" I asked. "How is he going to find them? Are you going with him?"

"Is he by himself?" asked Shauna before John could answer any of the other questions.

John looked back and forth between us as if he couldn't decide whose question to answer first. "They . . . ," he began. "There are three of them," he said finally. "No, I'm not going with them. They came to me a few months ago and just wanted to know what I could remember about how we got there and how we got home. I didn't want to tell them anything at first, but they already knew about the salt and said they were hoping to take some to them. I guess they had already talked to others who were there with us, but they all said that I had taken notes and made drawings about how to get there. One of them is a famous historian who just wants to meet them and see them. They're not going to do anything bad! They promised me that they wouldn't tell anybody where they are! They . . . they're going to *help* them . . . and they promised to protect them. They'll keep it *all* a secret!"

"I thought you *lost* all your notes," I said, looking at him narrowly.

"W-well," John stammered some more, "I did! Yes. Of course I did. You all saw that, but I remembered some other things like how long we floated down the river to get back to the ocean and things like that . . . but they already knew all that! Someone else had told them, and so there's this other guy here who's from Russia and I guess he travels the river a lot and thinks he knows where that mountain pass is that we came through to get home. So . . . it's not really my fault they know how to get there. But I only told them things after I found out that they want to take them some salt."

"So there are four guys?" asked Jeff.

"What?" said John.

"You said there's a Russian guy now, too," Jeff explained.

"No," said John, "the Russian is one of the three. Well . . . , unless you count the other guy's bodyguard. If you count him then I guess there are four all together, yeah."

John seemed completely frustrated.

"They paid you, huh?" I said.

"No!" John said. He acted offended. "Of course not! They're not after anything for themselves! They just want to be good citizens—good citizens to the whole world! I told you they want to take the people some salt—huge boxes of it! That whole boat is full of salt! Come with me! I'll show you!" With that John walked briskly back toward the yacht and motioned quickly several times with his hand for us to follow. "Come see this," he said. "And come meet these men. You'll see that they are good men who only have the welfare of these people in mind!"

We each looked at each other, trying to decide what to do.

"*I'm* not going on that boat!" hissed Jeff. "Meeting them is not going to change their plans or change my mind."

"Well, *I* am going," I said. "I want to see this for myself."

"Yes, yes!" encouraged John. "Come with me! All of you come with us."

"Brandon," Shauna said firmly, "we need to be getting back. Let's just go."

"This will just take a moment, I promise," John assured us.

Personally, I didn't need any assurance. I was right there with him. I wanted to see all this salt they supposedly had loaded onto this silly boat. Reluctantly, Jeff took a couple of steps toward us. Shauna put her arm around Meg's shoulders and followed.

"Are they going to turn the boat on?" Meg asked. "Will it be loud?"

"No and no," answered Shauna. "We'll just be a minute. Then we're going back to our motel."

We all followed John on board the yacht and down a spiral staircase to a lower level that had round windows along the top of the outer walls. As I looked around at the inside of the huge boat, I thought, *Someone could live on this thing.*

"This way," John said. "The salt is right in here. I'm glad we all found each other just now, because these guys are leaving tonight." He stopped at a door and then heaved a frustrated sigh as he said, "Oh, they've locked it!" There was a large bolt mounted to the door jamb that slid into a thick metal loop on the door. Hanging through a hole in the bolt was a large padlock with a number dial on it just like the lockers at the junior high school. Just then we heard voices coming from around a corner some distance away. "Oh, good," John said. "Come with me and you can meet these fine men and we'll get them to unlock the cargo hold so you can see for yourselves!"

John headed down the passageway and around the corner. I was right on his heels. Shauna, Jeff, and Meg were right behind me. As we walked past a couple of small windows, John glanced through them and said, "There's one of them now."

I glanced through the window as well, then stopped short as I realized that the man looked shockingly familiar. Everybody else sort of bunched up behind me because we had been walking so quickly and I had stopped so fast. Shauna, Jeff, and I all stared at the man. He was turned sideways so we had a perfect view of his profile. He was tall and skinny, with stringy hair and glasses. When I realized who it was, my stomach immediately twisted into a knot and my heart jumped into my throat.

John stopped in the doorway and announced his presence by saying, "I'm glad I found you!" As he entered the room ahead of us we heard him say, "I have some children here that you should meet, Dr. Anthony."

CHAPTER 2

The Doctor Is In

Still standing at the window, I immediately dropped down below the level of the windows. Shauna and Jeff did the same. I grabbed Meg by the arm and was ready to yank her down next to us when I realized that she was too short to be seen through the window. It was a good thing that I figured it out when I did, too, because as scared as I was, I'm sure I would have practically pulled her arm from its socket.

Meg was staring at my hands wrapped around her wrist when Jeff hissed, "Let's get out of here!"

Without another word we all turned and scurried back down the passageway and around the corner, crouching next to the locked door where the salt was supposedly stored.

"What are we doing?" asked Meg.

"Being scared," Shauna panted, her eyes darting toward Meg and then flashing back toward Jeff and me. "Please tell me that wasn't who I think it was," she said.

"Who?" breathed Meg, her eyes getting wider. I think Shauna wanted to hear it from Jeff and me first, before telling Meg the truth. She waited impatiently for our response.

"It *can't* be him," gasped Jeff.

"Who?" breathed Meg, a little softer this time, but more intense. Her eyes continued to widen.

"It's him," I said soberly. "I'll never forget that greasy hair and that creepy face." I shuddered as I imagined him sitting there.

"Who-o?" whispered Meg, begging to know the truth. I turned my attention to her and saw that she was petrified. My answer wasn't going to make her happy, but I always felt like if you're going to be scared either way, then it's usually best to know exactly what there is to be scared of. Personally, I had discovered that I had an amazing ability to *imagine* things far more frightening than reality.

"Dr. Anthony," I admitted. "He's here."

Meg's lips scrunched together and immediately began to quiver. Her eyes filled with tears, but she didn't make a sound.

I suppose now would be a good time to explain who Dr. Anthony is and why we each were horrified at seeing him—or in Meg's case, even the thought of him. More than two years earlier, this same man had broken into our Aunt Ella's farmhouse with a gun and threatened the four of us if we didn't tell him where to find Aunt Ella's copy of the first edition of the Book of Mormon. We kids were there alone because all the adults were out for the evening, and they had taken our youngest brother and sister with them. When we wouldn't tell Anthony anything, he locked us in the cellar as he searched the house. We had never really talked about it much, but as for me, I had always felt pretty lucky to get out of there without getting hurt. The man was a complete lunatic—on top of being totally slimy. Meg was only eight at the time it happened, so I'm sure for her the memory was still terrifying. Her silent tears said it all. We all felt pretty much the same way.

"But I thought he was in prison!" hissed Jeff. "He's *supposed* to be in prison!"

"Looks like he's out," I responded with disgust.

Just as I finished speaking, we heard men's voices. Afraid of what might happen when they came around the corner, I quickly checked out the door on the opposite side of the passageway. Unlike the other doors we had seen so far, this one had a large wheel in the center of it that looked like the steering wheel of a car. It wouldn't move in one direction, so I quickly spun it the other way. I heard a soft click that made me think it had unlatched, but I still couldn't pull it open.

"Open the bolt!" whispered Shauna. Before I had time to figure out what she was talking about, she reached up about a foot above the wheel and slid a thick, six-inch bolt out of its latch on the door jamb. The bolt was just like the one on the room across the hall, except there was no padlock attached to this one. I pushed on it, and the door opened. It was spring-loaded and wasn't like a normal door, because it didn't go all the way down to the floor. It had an edge of thick, black rubber all the way around it that made a tight seal when the door was closed and latched. Stepping over the ledge at the bottom of the doorway, I quickly slipped into a darkened room, then held it open as everyone stepped in after me. I still held the handle as I let the door slowly close, keeping the springs from banging the door shut and giving us away. After it closed I spun the wheel a couple of times.

Still shaking, we stood huddled together in a small room with a low ceiling. The only light came from an electric light bulb glowing dimly in a metal cage on the wall next to the door. I was afraid Meg would complain about the darkness, but she didn't say a word. We all listened intently for any sounds through the door, but all we could hear was our own breathing. Gradually my eyes adjusted enough to barely see the rest of the room.

"What are we *doing* in here?" asked Jeff softly, but firmly.

"Hiding!" I whispered in a breathy voice.

The look on Jeff's face said that he'd rather be running than hiding. "Well, how long are we going to stay in here?" he asked.

"Until we can hear that they're gone," I hissed.

"I don't think we'll be able to hear *anything* through *this* door," Shauna said. "This room must be really well insulated. That's probably why the door seals the way it does. They could be standing right outside this door!"

The rest of us instinctively leaned away from the door. I quickly moved deeper into the room with Meg right behind me. If that door opened suddenly I didn't want to be anywhere near it.

"What is all this stuff?" squeaked Meg, surveying the room with wide eyes. I think she was trying to decide if she should be more afraid of Anthony, or all the strange things in this room. For the first time I began to check it out myself. Everywhere I looked there were pipes and tubes and vents and hoses. Every wall in the room and most of the floor space was covered with large tanks or containers of various sizes and shapes. It looked really freaky in the dim light.

The pipes and tubes ran in every direction along the walls, and either connected the various tanks to each other, or else one end would disappear into holes in the walls or ceiling. I couldn't imagine how anyone would be able to make any sense of it. It looked sort of like our furnace room at home, but it had to be five times the size and ten times as complicated. There was a small, metal workbench in the center of the room that pretty much filled up any extra space, leaving just enough room to walk between the bench and the equipment along the walls.

"I think this is what they call the engine room," Shauna answered as I continued to move farther from the door and tried to figure out what everything might be for.

"I don't see any engine," I said, walking slowly around the workbench.

"Aren't the engines outside at the back?" asked Jeff. "Wouldn't it be bad to have an engine inside? Wouldn't you die from the exhaust and smoke?"

He was starting to sound like Meg. "Maybe that's what those are for," I suggested, pointing at a couple of aluminum pipes coming out from under what looked like two upside-down bathtubs that were latched to the floor. The pipes went up to the top of the wall and out what we figured was probably the back of the boat.

Shauna looked at where I was pointing, but seemed uninterested as she said, "Can we just get *out* of here!"

"Hey!" I replied, turning back around to face her. "Have you forgotten about Dr. Creepy out there? Let's just wait here for a minute!"

"But we *have* to get off this *boat!*" Shauna said.

"Not yet!" I insisted. "In a minute! That guy is psycho. We can go in a minute."

"I don't like this," admitted Jeff, shaking his head slowly and glancing toward the door. Crouched behind the workbench, we argued for what must have been several minutes about why we were hiding and how long we should stay there until we tried to get off the boat again. Just as we agreed that it was time to get out of there, the upside-down bathtubs suddenly began to roar and Meg screamed. Everyone one of us jumped. That was where the engines were all right.

"Let's move!" Jeff called as he lurched toward the door. I instantly followed Jeff. While he was spinning the wheel to open the door, I looked back to see that the girls hadn't moved yet. Meg, who was torn between the horror of her memory of Dr. Anthony and the noisy rumbling of the engine, simply huddled in the corner, petrified by fear. Shauna was trying to convince her to come with us when the boat suddenly began to move.

"We've got to tell someone to let us off of this thing!" Jeff yelled as he pulled the door open. The door slammed shut behind us as we ran to the spiral staircase that led to the upper deck and quickly climbed up. The boat was moving, and we could see John standing on the dock, which was already twenty or thirty feet away, with the gap quickly widening.

"*John!*" I yelled. Jeff was beside me almost immediately and both of us waved our arms frantically. John saw us and lurched forward as if he were going to do something but then suddenly realized that there was nothing that he *could* do—except yell.

"Stop!" yelled John. "Come back! Wait!"

I assume he was trying to get the attention of whoever was driving the yacht, but as far as I could tell, he wasn't having any effect. Still waving his arms wildly with an occasional yell, John began running along the dock trying to stay as close to us as possible.

"Maybe we should jump," I suggested without thinking, looking over the edge into the black water.

"Are you nuts?" said Jeff. "That water's got to be freezing!"

"Well, then, go find somebody to let us off this thing," I said.

Jeff immediately started shaking his head back and forth. He held his hands up as he said, "I'm not going *anywhere* on this boat by myself with that weirdo around!"

"Fine!" I said with disgust. I was about to say that I would do it instead, but the thought of running into Dr. Anthony by myself twisted my stomach into a knot again. "Let's go together," I suggested quietly after a brief pause. I glanced back again at John on the dock. He had quit running and was standing, holding both arms out at shoulder height, palms up, like he couldn't believe what was happening. The last thing I saw him do was to pull out the notebook where he had written down our family's motel and room number and then, still facing us, he pointed dramatically with both arms a couple of times in the direction of our motel. All I could figure was that he was going to go tell Mom and Dad what had happened. I was hoping that maybe there would be "dock police" or something that could stop the boat.

Quickly, but cautiously, Jeff and I went back down the spiral staircase to the lower level and checked the kitchen where we had last seen Dr. Anthony. No one was there. We checked every room on that level without success. We found three bedrooms: two that were obviously being used and one that wasn't. Finally, Jeff suggested that we ought to see if Shauna and Meg were still in the engine room. With the door closed behind us, our eyes had trouble adjusting to the dim light again, but Shauna and Meg were in there all right. Meg was still huddled in the corner and Shauna was begging her to get up, promising her that there would be a lot less noise outside.

Feeling around on the wall for a moment, I eventually found a light switch and flipped it on. Then Jeff and I went over to help Shauna persuade Meg to move.

"C'mon, Meg!" I pleaded over the roar of the engines. "Let's get out of here!"

"Yeah," agreed Jeff. "I don't want to get stuck here!"

After almost a full minute of the three of us threatening to drag her out of there or just leave her behind—whichever she preferred—Meg finally stood and inched slowly toward the door. Personally, I didn't think the engines were really that loud, but she held her hands tightly to her ears, leaning over so far that her pink backpack was actually resting on top of her back. Shauna kept her hands over the top of Meg's hands in an attempt to muffle the noise even more. It didn't seem worth the trouble to me, but I guess that's what makes Shauna such a great sister.

When I got to the door I took hold of the wheel and pulled on it. But instead of coming open, the door wouldn't budge. Frustrated, I grabbed the wheel with both hands and pulled on it several times as hard as I could, but the door was sealed shut.

"Spin it!" Jeff suggested.

I tried to turn it, but it was already as far as it would go in that direction. I pulled on it again and it still wouldn't budge.

"Try the other way!" said Shauna, sounding a little frantic.

I spun it back until it had made several revolutions and came to a stop. I pulled as hard as I could, but it was no use.

"What happened? Is the bolt on the outside locked?" Shauna yelled over the muffled roar of the engines. "It's only on the outside, isn't it?" She desperately ran her hands along the edge of the door, searching to make sure that the latch really wasn't there and that her eyes weren't playing tricks on her. "How did it get locked, you guys?" Her face looked pained as she said, "How could this happen?"

Jeff raised his hands in disbelief and said, "Somebody must have locked it from the outside!"

"No way!" I breathed, looking back and forth between the two of them.

"Why would they lock it right now?" asked Shauna. "Did someone see you? Do they know we're in here?"

"We couldn't find *anybody*," Jeff said. "We checked every room on this level."

Shaking my head back and forth, I grabbed the wheel and spun it all the way the other direction again, but it still wouldn't open. "No-o-o!" I moaned, hanging my head and squishing my eyes shut. I couldn't believe it. I couldn't think of anything in the world worse than being trapped with Dr. Anthony. After everything he had put us through before, I had absolutely no interest in ever coming face to face with him again.

I opened my eyes and looked at Shauna who was still paralyzed with that look of disbelief on her face. Meg had one arm wrapped tightly around Shauna's waist, the side of her head squished into Shauna's stomach, and her other hand held tightly over her exposed ear. Jeff began pounding on the door and yelling, "Help!" over and over again at the top of his lungs.

I felt myself stumbling slightly backwards as I thought about the horrible possibilities of this situation. We didn't have anything valuable that Anthony wanted from us anymore, but the guy had ended up in prison because of that little incident, along with a few other things he did trying to get the book. Would he take that out on us now? My mind kept spinning with possibilities. Overcome with the combination of fear and despair, I leaned quietly against the workbench and just watched as Jeff continued to pound and yell for at least a couple of minutes. Shauna and Meg snuggled in together not far from me. Meg kept one hand over her exposed ear and her eyes tightly shut. Her arm was looped through one of the straps of her backpack on the floor in front of her.

"Didn't they check the wheel when they locked the door?" yelled Jeff at no one in particular in rhythm with his pounding on the door. "Somebody's *in* here, you idiots!" More pounding. "Help us!" he called again.

When Jeff finally gave up, he turned around and slid his back down the doorjamb and settled into a heap on the floor. Shauna said something that I couldn't hear.

"What?" I called back, without enthusiasm.

"Maybe they're not going very far!" she repeated. Then she added, "It's late! Maybe they're just going for a quick ride somewhere and coming right back!"

Jeff shook his head and called back, "John said that they're leaving for Russia *tonight*, remember?"

Shauna's hopeful look immediately fell as she remembered that that was indeed what John had told us.

"I think John was going to find Mom and Dad, though!" I said loudly. I described for Jeff and Shauna what I had seen John do with his notepad. Neither Jeff nor Shauna really responded, they just nodded their heads as if they were hopeful, but still concerned. Meg had seemed to be just ignoring our conversation, but just then she sat up with an intent look on her face.

"Shouldn't we say a prayer?" she asked.

"Yes, we should," Shauna agreed. "You're absolutely right."

Jeff and I each nodded our agreement and we each worked our way into a kneeling position.

"Who wants to say it?" asked Shauna.

Jeff and I just looked at each other and then back at Shauna. I didn't think they'd want me to pray because all I could think about was making Anthony disintegrate. I was sure that one of them would have a clearer head than I did.

"How about if I say it?" said Shauna.

Jeff and I nodded in agreement and bowed our heads. I was right. Shauna came up with a much better prayer than I would have. First, she thanked Heavenly Father for keeping us safe. Then she thanked Him for quite a list of blessings, including our parents, our family, and our home. That's why it was a good idea for her to say the prayer: I think I would have probably just saved the "thanking" part for some time after we were rescued and I would have just jumped straight to the "please get us out of here" part.

When she was done thanking Him for things, Shauna asked that we would be able to be calm and not afraid, but have trust that we would be protected. To this point, the calm thing wasn't working for me. Then she asked that John would be able to get to Mom and Dad quickly and tell them what had happened. She asked that they would be comforted and not afraid of what might happen to us. I'm pretty sure I wouldn't have thought about praying for *that*. She also asked that Mom and Dad would be able to learn from John that Dr. Anthony was here, so they would better understand what we were dealing with. That seemed like a good idea, too.

Then Shauna asked for something that I definitely never would have come up with, but that I thought was a fantastic idea. She asked that Anthony's "heart would be softened." The words she used made me think of how people in the Book of Mormon prayed about their enemies. I realized that that was exactly what we were dealing with here: an enemy. Two years before Anthony had chased us through four different states, tried to kidnap us, and threatened us more times than I wanted to remember. He was not the type of guy you'd invite to a party.

Lastly, Shauna prayed for our protection. She prayed that we would be able to get out of this as soon as possible and that all would be well. She said that if this was something that we *had* to do, then to please give us the courage to face it and be true to our testimonies and our covenants. Wow! That sounded like something that Mom or Dad would pray for in our family prayers, but not something I'd ever heard from Shauna before. She closed the prayer in the name of Jesus Christ. The warmth and the calm that came over me when I heard her say the name "Jesus Christ" was amazing. I didn't see how we would be able to get out of this anytime soon, but it was okay. I just had the feeling that things would turn out all right.

"Thanks," I said, just loud enough to be heard above the noise of the engines. Suddenly we felt the boat start going quite a bit faster. We just looked at each other. The engine didn't really get louder, the pitch just went quite a bit higher, so we still could have talked with each other okay, but I couldn't think of anything to say. I got the impression that Jeff and Shauna felt the same way. I felt peace, though.

Shauna took off her coat and wrapped Meg up in it, trying especially to keep her ears covered. It started getting hot after a few minutes, and I was starting to feel tired, so I took off my coat and made a pillow out of it, stretching out on the metal floor. Jeff gave me a look that said he wasn't going to give up yet. I almost had the urge to defend myself, but it wasn't worth it; he already knew as well as I did that there was nothing we could do.

I don't remember anyone else saying anything as I snuggled into my coat-pillow. The anxiety created by this whole thing must have really worn me out, because I felt really tired. Soon I felt myself drifting off to sleep. I did nothing to try to stop it, either.

A long time later, I woke up. It took me a minute to remember where I was. Without lifting my head, I glanced around to find everything pretty much the same as before I went to sleep, except that everyone looked like they were asleep. It felt like I had been asleep for several hours. As I lay there with my eyes closed again, listening to the droning of the engines, I realized that I had had a dream. I had dreamed about Aaron and our vacation the previous summer.

Aaron was one of the people who had learned English. He and his family and a friend of his had been very good to us. Aaron and his father and Aaron's friend, who was a couple of years older than Jeff, were the only ones that had learned English. Aaron was about Jeff's age. He had an amazing commitment to God and to living righteously. I dreamed that we found him again. I dreamed that Aaron's father, Levi, who was the leader of the tribe, was teaching all the people from the copies of the Book of Mormon that we had given them. It was a great dream.

As I lay awake thinking about the dream, I found myself wishing that we had a copy of the Book of Mormon with us now. I always felt such peace when I read from it. Just then the boat began to slow down dramatically. Then I heard a sound that made my heart jump into my throat: the engines came to a complete stop, and we were suddenly drowning in silence. Before I could even decide what this might mean or what to do or think next, I heard the bolt on the outside of the door being released. Immediately, the door was pushed open about six inches. Apparently, both Jeff and Shauna were awake, too, because I saw their muscles tighten just like mine did. But neither of them moved.

"Who is leaving the light on in engine room?" came a deep voice with a thick accent. It reminded me of our Russian rescuers from the previous summer. I figured this must be the Russian that John told us about. Without opening the door any wider, a strong, weathered hand reached through the opening and began to feel around for the light switch.

"Why are you unlocking *that* door?" came another voice. I knew who belonged to this voice: Anthony. I just watched the hand. It quit feeling around when Anthony asked his question.

"I am already telling you this," said the Russian. "I am knowing from experience that the men of the Coast Guard of Russia are wanting to be searching every room on vessel that they are finding locked. I am unlocking every room on vessel so perhaps they might not be searching so many rooms and we are moving again much quicklier."

I was stunned by the mention of the Russian Coast Guard. Had we gone so far already? Hadn't John gotten to Mom and Dad? What about the police, or better yet, the U. S. Coast Guard? Where were *our* guys?

"Why do they have to search at all?" Anthony practically yelled in frustration.

"This being because of smuggling," the Russian replied. "The men of the Coast Guard of Russia are liking no surprises."

"Are you sure you have everything arranged with the Russian authorities?" asked Anthony. "I mean, they know that we're coming into the country with you on this yacht?"

"Naturally," laughed the Russian. "The last time they are finding me entering Russian waters with people not being on their list, they are calling these people *spies* and storing them in jail for six months with I, myself, being stored in jail for two weeks before even they are asking any questions of me!"

Shauna looked over at me to see if I was listening. Her eyes were open wide.

The Russian continued by saying, "Jail in Siberia is not being a place where anyone is wanting to be spending any time. I am happily being confident that all is in order for our entering into Russia. I unlocking every room on boat because they are perhaps searching every room on boat. Always thoroughly and completely are they searching every room that is remaining locked and also many rooms that are unlocked."

"Yeah," grunted Anthony. "You mentioned that."

With that, the Russian's hand quickly found the light switch and turned it off. Pulling his arm back out of the room, the door banged shut again, leaving us in the near darkness, broken only by the dim bulb by the door. From what the Russian had said, I was sure that the door would be left unlocked. I knew that Shauna was awake, but I wasn't sure about anyone else.

"Did you hear that?" asked Jeff in the silence. I didn't respond because I was waiting for Shauna to say something. But it was Meg who spoke first. Her voice was trembling.

"Will they make me be in a jail room all by myself?" she asked.

CHAPTER 3

Prisoners at Sea

"No one's going to jail," Shauna reassured Meg. "But I want to see where those two bozos are going, so can you please lean on Brandon for a minute?" At the same time that Shauna was saying this, she was lifting Meg's head off of her lap and pushing her over toward me.

"Will you be right back?" Meg asked Shauna as she leaned on my shoulder.

"I promise," Shauna said as she scampered to the door. "Now everybody quiet." Still on her hands and knees, Shauna slowly opened the door just enough to get her head part way through the opening and peer with one eye into the passageway. Her head was moving slowly until she jerked to a stop, frozen in place for several seconds. Then she drew her head back inside the engine room and allowed the door to slowly close.

"What's going on?" asked Jeff.

"That Russian guy was unlocking the room across the hall," Shauna said.

"The cargo hold?" I asked. "So it's open now?" Before waiting for her to answer, I added, "I still want to see what's in there."

I started pushing Meg off of me so that I could get to my feet, but Shauna quickly said, "Not now, Bran!"

"Why?" I asked indignantly.

"Because we have a much more important problem," Shauna answered. She said it as if that should be obvious to anyone.

"But this might be our only chance," I protested.

"I wish that were true," she said.

"Didn't you hear what they were talking about?" asked Jeff. "We're about to be boarded by the Russian Coast Guard. We're not in Kansas anymore, Dorothy."

I grunted. "I'm aware of that, thank you," I said. "But if they lock that room again we won't be able to get in later. *Now* may be our only chance!"

"I watched him do the combination," Shauna said. "We can get in there any time we want to."

That was something that was amazing about Shauna. She had a way with numbers. She couldn't remember where she put her watch five minutes ago (or anyone else's, for that matter), but she could remember every number that had crossed her path since the day she realized she was a conscious being. She knew every locker combination she'd ever had. She remembered every phone number of every friend she'd had since she was six years old. And here's the one that's truly amazing: when we would walk through the grocery store she'd say things like, "That laundry detergent was 21 cents cheaper two weeks ago." Excuse me—laundry detergent? I could see tracking the price of your favorite candy bar—but *laundry detergent?*

So when Shauna said that she had watched the Russian do the combination, I had absolutely no doubt that she would remember it until the day she died. But there was something else that she had seemed to forget.

"What if they lock us back in here again?" I asked. "It won't matter how many locker combinations you know as long as we're stuck in here!"

Even in the dim light I could tell that she was perplexed by the "locker combinations" comment. She got the point, though.

"That's just a chance we're going to have to take," Shauna said.

"I don't have to take *anything*," I said defiantly.

"Didn't you *hear* what the Russian said to Dr. Anthony?" gasped Shauna. "If we get caught . . ."

I think she didn't dare finish because she had just promised Meg that none of us would go to jail.

"Well, maybe if the Russian knows that we're here," I argued, "then maybe he'll just turn us over to the Coast Guard instead of trying to hide us. Maybe that's why he got in trouble last time."

"But we don't *know* that," said Shauna.

"I want outta here," I said firmly, "and I'm willing to take my chances with the Coast Guard. Those Russians were really nice to us last summer, when they picked us up from our raft."

"And I'm starving," said Jeff. "If we get locked in here again, who knows how long it will be until we get another chance to get out!" He paused dramatically before adding, "I'd rather spend six months in a prison in Siberia than starve to death in here."

I had never thought of Jeff as an actor—after all, he'd never shown any interest in trying out for any school plays. But, honestly, I was quite impressed with his delivery of that line. Personally, I thought it was very well played. I was sure that Shauna would have to give in. Before she responded, though, the silence was broken by Meg.

"Is there a bathroom on this boat?" she asked.

"Probably," said Shauna, "but how do we find it without getting caught?"

"Easy," said Jeff. "We found a big bedroom just around the corner and it had a bathroom inside it."

"A bedroom?" asked Shauna, sounding a little uneasy. "Did it look like someone was using it?"

"Nope," Jeff answered.

"Uh-uh," I agreed, shaking my head back and forth. "The beds were all made and there was nothing laying around in it."

"It looked like a motel room when you first open the door," Jeff added.

"Except for the time that we got to that one motel, remember?" I said, getting slightly off the subject. "They forgot to finish cleaning it or something, because there were still piles of sheets and towels around."

"Are you going to let me go potty?" Meg winced. It was like the act of allowing the word "potty" to escape her mouth suddenly multiplied her need for it by about twenty times. Or maybe she just felt like a discussion about a motel room that wasn't clean yet didn't really need to take place at this particular time. Either way, we all crawled out of the engine room and headed out with Jeff in the lead.

Sneaking quickly down the passageway and around the corner, we made it into the only bedroom on that level that looked like it wasn't being used. The bedroom was along the side of the yacht where we had first gotten on. It was getting light outside, and from where we were we could see that we were moving quickly and that there was nothing but water in all directions. Once inside the room, we *all* realized that a bathroom seemed like a pretty great idea, so we each took a turn. There were two single beds, one on each side of the room. I was happy for the chance to stretch out on something soft for a minute or two.

"Now let's get some food!" said Jeff with excitement.

"I think we'd better stay put," Shauna suggested. "And we need to decide something before we do anything else."

"Like what?" asked Jeff.

"Yeah, what?" I agreed. "Like you want to know what we want to eat or something? Do you want to take our orders?"

Shauna was not amused. "No," she said firmly. She waited a moment before continuing. "We need to decide if we're going to try to keep hiding from everyone, or if we're going to go tell the Russian Coast Guard that we're here while they're searching the

34

boat, or if we're going to wait till we start moving again and announce to the Russian and Anthony and whoever else is on this thing that we're here—and then take our chances with them."

"We're taking our chances no matter what we do," I said, sitting up slightly.

"Yeah," Jeff agreed. "But it all started with taking the chance of trying to find out what was going on on this boat." I was surprised to see that he was glaring at me like it was all *my* fault. "We shouldn't have done that," he added.

"Hey!" I said, ready to defend myself. "You guys didn't have to come. In fact, if you hadn't, you probably could have gotten to Mom and Dad a lot faster than John obviously did and then this whole thing would be over already for every one of us."

"Guys!" interrupted Shauna. "We're not doing this." She was slowly shaking her head back and forth. "It doesn't matter who did what or who said what or what we think might or might not have happened if this thing or that thing were different." She looked slowly back and forth between me and Jeff before continuing. "We're here, and we just need to decide what we're going to do *now*. And the biggest mistake we can make is to argue about it." She paused again. "Besides," she sighed, looking directly at me, "if we hadn't come with you, Brandon, then you might be stuck here alone right now, and we would all feel terrible."

We all remained silent for a moment. I thought about what she had said and I had to agree that I would probably feel a lot differently about things if I were here by myself. I was glad we were together.

"You're right," Jeff said. "It's good that none of us is alone. And we need to stay together and not argue or blame each other." He looked at me and said, "Sorry, Bran."

"It's okay," I said. "I know I need to be more careful."

"Okay," Shauna said with new energy. "Let's all just forget about what's behind us and decide what we're going to do."

"Well, if they just walk in on us," Jeff said, "then our decision is made, right? So maybe we should at least hide until we decide what we *want* to do."

"Shouldn't we say a prayer?" asked Meg, breaking the silence.

It was funny how that question was her answer for everything. (Can a question be an answer?) I guess when I was ten, prayer was probably my answer for everything, too. But what's even more funny is how when you get older you start to come up with your own ideas and want to try those first and then you finally decide to pray after nothing else works. I guess that's when you're just one step away from not praying at all; you just depend on yourself because you think you're smart.

"Good idea," I said to Meg. I looked at Shauna and asked, "Do you want me to say it?" I was feeling pretty prayerful at this point—not to mention the fact that I was feeling dumb for being the one that got us into this mess. Shauna was nice enough to not let Jeff beat me up about it, but we all knew that he was right.

"I think it's my turn," said Jeff quietly. I couldn't remember the last time he had volunteered to say a prayer, but since Shauna had said the last one, that did make it Jeff's turn. Dad pretty much tried to give everybody equal chances saying family prayers and blessings on the food by rotating in age order. We rotated except for our morning prayer at the end of devotional, that is; Dad almost always gave that prayer himself.

"Whoever wants to is okay with me," said Shauna.

"Go ahead, Jeff," I nodded, as I knelt down. "It's your turn." Everyone else got on their knees, too.

Jeff gave a good prayer. He prayed that we would all be smart enough to be nice each other and stay together and help each other. He prayed that we wouldn't be afraid and that we would be protected from harm and that we would have the Spirit with us so that we would know what we should do. He asked for protection for the rest of our family, too, and that they could help us get out of here as soon as possible. The last thing he asked was that if we had to be away from the rest of our family for awhile, that we hopefully could learn something valuable during the time and that God's "power could be made manifest."

I smiled when Jeff said that last part, because it reminded me about the previous summer. Dad had talked a lot about a scripture in the New Testament that said that sometimes things that you don't like just happen so that God's power can be made manifest. He told us that blessings can come from any experience, if you look for them.

"Thanks for the prayer, Jeff," Shauna said. She was starting to sound like Mom and Dad. It was funny how she was just sort of taking over as the one in charge. That was just fine by me. Apparently Jeff and Meg felt the same way.

"So what do you think we should do?" asked Shauna. "Do we have any more choices besides the three I already said?"

I was trying to remember what the three choices were when it became obvious that we were suddenly down to only two: the boat engines started up again and the boat immediately jolted forward and began picking up speed. It was now too late to go out and introduce ourselves to the Russian Coast Guard. We were still kneeling in a circle, and I quickly looked from person to person trying to decide if we were in agreement about whether to panic or not. Apparently I was the only one who felt like that was a good option.

"Do you think the men already searched the boat?" asked Meg.

"I don't know," admitted Shauna.

"They took off really fast," said Jeff. "A lot faster than before."

"Well, maybe," Shauna said, "that was because *before* we were in a harbor next to lots of other boats, because I know that's when you're supposed to go slow. And so maybe now they just met up with the Coast Guard out away from everything else and now that they're done with their inspection that's why they can go fast."

"Or maybe these guys are in trouble for something else!" I

suggested with excitement. "And now they're trying to outrun the Coast Guard! Let's go see! C'mon!"

They all just stared at me. I wondered how they could all stay so calm. Obviously we weren't going to go see anything just yet. Finally, Shauna looked at Jeff and asked, "Would you feel safer if we kept hiding and didn't have to worry about what Dr. Anthony or anyone might say or do until they happen to find us . . . or should we just take our chances with letting them know we're here—whoever *they* are?"

Jeff acted as though he wasn't sure how to answer. I think I know what the problem was. Shauna's question was one of those questions like what Dad asks. It was the kind of question that is filled with enough descriptions of the options that you have the impression he is trying to lead you to the answer he wants, so you don't even try to answer what you really think. That part is bad enough, but there is also enough detail in there that you're not really even quite sure what the real question is anyway. So you end up just staring at him with a blank look on your face. You also leave your mouth half open just in case the right answer happens to stumble onto your tongue and might need a way out.

"I *really* need something to eat," Jeff said finally. "So we can either go find it ourselves—since we happen to know right where the kitchen is—or we can tell somebody we're here and leave ourselves at their mercy and perhaps still not eat for who knows how long."

I thought Jeff was just as good as Shauna at leading you to the idea he thought was best. He certainly had *me* convinced. I hadn't really noticed it before, but the thought of food was sounding actually pretty good right about now. First priority for me, though, was still finding out what was really in the cargo hold. I just couldn't believe that Anthony could be involved in anything honest.

"Okay," said Shauna, "how about we go to the kitchen first and see what we can find to eat and then we go find out who's driving this thing."

"So what are we going to say to them?" asked Jeff.

"We're going to ask when the next stop in the United States is, that's what," I said.

Shauna just looked sideways at me before saying, "We'll just tell them the truth: that John invited us on board and we hid when we saw Dr. Anthony and the boat left while we were still hiding and then we got locked in the engine room before we could tell anybody that we were here."

"Are we going to tell them *why* we were hiding?" Jeff asked.

"You mean because Anthony scares the living daylights out of every one of us?" I asked. "Well, what if everybody else on this thing is even scarier than *he* is?"

"Bran," Shauna said, "Jeff asked in his prayer that the Spirit would be with us. The scriptures tell us that God doesn't give us the spirit of fear." As she said the word *fear* she glanced quickly at Meg. I immediately saw that Meg's eyes were wide and her cheeks were sunken.

"Sorry," I mumbled. "You're right. We need to just follow the Spirit and have faith." Turning to Meg I asked, "Are you hungry? Do you want to go get something to eat?"

"Do you think the men will be scary?" Meg asked.

"No," I said, shaking my head. "I was just being dumb. Let's go get some food."

"Are the men in there?" Meg asked.

"I don't think so," said Shauna. "But even if they are, everything will be okay. Right, guys?"

"Yep," Jeff and I both agreed.

With that, Meg hopped to her feet and acted ready to go. She was still wearing her pink backpack and the things inside it jostled as she jumped up. It didn't sound like she had much in there at all. With Shauna in the lead, we all crept into the passageway and headed toward the kitchen. We went right past the engine room and cargo hold on the way. The padlock on the cargo hold door was still open.

"Let's check it real quick," I suggested. Not waiting to be talked out of it, I immediately opened the door and stepped inside. I heard Shauna hiss my name in obvious frustration, but I kept going anyway; I knew it would just take a minute. They followed, but just far enough to see inside. Jeff held the door part way open, not wanting to take another chance at accidentally getting locked inside a room again.

The room was long and narrow. The walls were lined with shelves that went all the way to the ceiling. They were full of all sorts of stuff. I found a few cleaning supplies at the back, but mostly we were looking at shelf after shelf of bags and boxes of food of various kinds. There was brown sugar and honey and powdered milk and crackers and all sorts of stuff. It looked like a grocery store in there. The floor under the lowest shelves was stacked about three feet high all the way around the room with large, plastic, see-through containers that were filled with something white. There had to be at least 50 containers and every one of the them had the word *SALT* written on it by hand with a thick, permanent marker.

"Looks like you're wrong," Jeff smiled. "So can we go get some food now?" He moved out into the passageway as he spoke.

"It sure looks like a lot of salt," Shauna agreed as she moved in for a closer look at one of them.

"Not enough to replace everything that got ruined last year," I said.

"But something's funny about it," Shauna said as she looked around at the various salt containers. "They don't all look the same. See, this one looks more grainy and that one over there looks more like a powder."

She was right. I quickly pulled out the last one she had pointed to. Twisting the lid off from one corner I soon discovered that this "salt" container actually held flour. Shauna opened the first one she had pointed at and found that it contained white sugar.

"Why does it say 'salt' on the front," asked Meg, "and 'sugar' on the back?"

Shauna quickly looked down at where Meg was reading. "You're right, Meg! It does say sugar."

I immediately turned around the container that I was holding and found that it had the word 'flour' written on it. Soon we were pulling all the boxes out and reading the backs. It turned out that most of them had flour inside, and a few held either sugar or powdered sugar. We found a single box that had "SALT" on one side and nothing on any other side. That one actually did contain salt.

"I can't believe John fell for that!" Jeff sighed, rolling his eyes.

"I *knew* it!" I exclaimed. "I just *knew* it couldn't be true. Anything involving Dr. Anthony *has* to be a lie!"

Just as I finished speaking, I heard a voice that made my whole body tighten.

"Well, well, well," sneered Dr. Anthony. I immediately spun around to see Jeff stumbling backwards into the room and Anthony standing in the open doorway with his hands on his hips. In a sicky-sweet voice and with a smirk on his thin face, he said, "How *nice* of each of you to come visit me on vacation." His sneer immediately returned when he said, "Too bad you never made it to visit me in prison."

We all just stared at him. I immediately thought, *I was right; he thinks it's our fault he went to prison!* Meg was clinging to Shauna again, with her face buried somewhere in Shauna's coat. Jeff was on his rear end, inching backwards with his hands and feet.

"Just what do you think you're doing here?" asked Anthony.

None of us seemed to know what to say. Finally Shauna managed to say something.

"We didn't know it was you," she squeaked.

"You didn't know *what* was me?" Anthony asked.

"We just happened to see John on the dock," Shauna explained quietly, "and he told us that some men were taking lots of salt to the tribe we found in Russia." She paused and Anthony just waited for her to continue. "Salt to make up for the salt we ruined when we landed there, because they're such religious people and use salt for all of their ceremonies. He was excited to have us meet the men who were going to deliver the salt. He said they were good men."

She stared directly into his eyes as if challenging him to a duel or something.

"So did you meet any of these *good* men?" Anthony asked with obvious disgust.

"No," I said flatly. "We just saw you." He turned his head quickly in my direction and gave me a look as if to dare me to say what I was really thinking. I was tired and hungry and lost and I didn't feel much like beating around the bush. So in answer to his daring look, I added, "So we imagine the others are all slimy, too."

I don't know who was more shocked at my statement: Shauna or Jeff or Dr. Anthony. Jeff whipped around and gave me a look that said he thought I had just signed our death warrants. His eyes were wide and his face was white. Shauna gave me a look that showed that what I had done was just about the dumbest thing she could have imagined anyone doing in this situation. And Anthony looked like he had just discovered the most hideous creature known to man: me.

At first I was sure he was going to lunge straight for me. Out of the corner of my eyes I looked for anything that I could quickly grab to defend myself. Before I could find anything, though, I saw Anthony take a deep breath as if trying to force himself to relax. He closed his eyes and slowly forced his clenched fists to open as he took two or three more deep breaths. I noticed that his jaw continued to clench and flex.

When he opened his eyes, he said, "Perhaps you should meet them." Before any of us could respond or even think about what he had said, he stepped backwards out of the doorway, slammed the door shut, and locked us inside. We were all too stunned to move.

"Brandon!" growled Shauna. "Just *what* are you trying to do!"

"We're in a bad enough situation as it is!" agreed Jeff.

"The only hope we have of getting out of here safely is not to make these guys mad," Shauna continued. "And for all we know, *he* might be our best chance! We have no idea what the other guys are even like!"

Jeff didn't say anything, but his lips were scrunched together and his eyes were hard as he vigorously nodded his head up and down several times. I could see what they were saying, I guess, but I wasn't sure I agreed with them. I always thought it was best to take matters into my own hands whenever possible.

"I saw this show once," I said, "where these kids were locked in a barn or something and when the guy came back they took a handful of dirt from the floor and threw it in his eyes and then just ran over the top of him to get away."

Jeff just stared at me like I had three heads.

"Where are you going to get dirt?" asked Meg.

"We could just use the salt!" I said with excitement. I was glad that I had gotten somebody thinking with me. "Or the powdered sugar! But the salt would probably sting more. What do you think?" Before anybody answered, I went for the powdered sugar container and began to open it. "Hurry!" I encouraged them, "get the salt open! He'll be back soon!"

"Yeah," agreed Shauna without moving. "He'll be back all right—with three other guys! Do you think you can get salt in all of their eyes? And do you think the four of us can all get past the four of them? And even if we did, where would we go? We're sort of stuck on this boat, you know? Did you take a look at all that water out there?"

"Don't worry about details," I said. "Let's just go with it."

"You're just going to get us in more trouble," said Jeff. "I won't let you do it."

Just as he said that, we heard the bolt being pulled back and the door starting to open. I reached into the powdered sugar bin, grabbed the biggest handful I could manage and started running for the door with my arm up like a pitcher ready to throw his very best fast ball. True to his word, though, Jeff tried to stop me by lunging in front of me and grabbing for my arm. I swung as hard as I could anyway, and we collided in a cloud of powdered sugar that got in my ears, eyes, nose, and mouth. I fell flat on my back with a dull thud, where Jeff and I ended up in a tangled heap as the powder slowly settled around us. Jeff looked like he was wearing a seventeenth century powdered wig.

"Je-e-eff!" I said in disgust.

He didn't bother to respond, but instead began rubbing his eyes with one hand and wiping his mouth on his coat sleeve. I looked up at Shauna to see a look that I've rarely seen on her face. Her look clearly said that she thought she had the dumbest brother in the history of brothers. I agreed with her—why would Jeff get in my way like that? That's when I realized that she might be giving that look to me and not Jeff, but I never got a chance to find out.

"Gentlemen," said Dr. Anthony, after clearing his voice. "I'd like you to meet the Andrews children."

We all looked up to see three men just inside the room and another standing in the doorway behind them. It was obvious which one was the Russian. He looked like a sailor from a hundred years earlier. He was wearing a striped shirt, canvas pants, and funny hat. His skin was tanned and leathery, and his mouth looked like it had worn nothing but a scowl for many years.

Standing next to the Russian was a man that looked really weird. He had not a hair on his head, not even eyebrows and eyelashes. His skin was white and pasty, but he was smiling widely with wet, pink lips. All his teeth appeared to be intact, but there were gaps between them all around.

The man in the doorway behind them was the only one who looked young. He stood at least six inches taller than the bald man and three or four inches taller than Anthony and the Russian. His hair was long and wavy down to his shoulders. His big arms were folded across his chest, and his face said, "Don't mess with me," but he seemed completely disinterested in what was going on.

The Russian was the first to speak, "I am wanting to be knowing what are you doing on my ship!" he said. When he said *ship* it sounded more like *sheep*. "This is being valuable cargo you are destructing here!" He spoke with way too much spit in his mouth and not all of it stayed there. I found myself hoping that he had just been eating something really juicy and that he didn't always talk this way. It was slightly nauseating.

"I must point out," said the bald man to the Russian, "that the boat is not yet yours. You still have an obligation to fulfill."

"I am delivering you as I am promising to you," said the Russian. "You will not be worrying about this anymore." Turning back to us he said, "These children are bringing much danger with them. We are all perhaps spending many time in jail if they are being found by the Coast Guard of Russia!"

"They were not found," said the bald man calmly. "And we will not be meeting the Coast Guard again. At least not until we return. So, now that we know of their existence we can ensure that they will not be found on our return trip, either."

"But what will we be doing with these much children?" asked the Russian.

The bald man smiled again. "We can burn that bridge when we come to it."

"What?" I exclaimed, spitting powdered sugar from my mouth— it was sweet, but it had turned into a gooey mess. "Don't you mean we'll *cross* that bridge when we come to it?"

"Yeah," agreed Shauna. "People say that they 'burn a bridge' when they are leaving something that they never plan on coming back to. So you meant to say *cross*, didn't you?"

The man just smiled at her as if to say he had all the time in the world for her to figure it out.

"So," Shauna continued, "you're trying to say that you'll worry about what to do with us when it's time to go back, right?"

"And when will that be?" I asked.

Jeff laughed just a little and then said, "What would that mean? *Burn the bridge when we come to it?*" He chuckled again and added, "I guess that would mean that you would completely avoid the problem and never have to deal with it, huh?" Realizing what he had just said, Jeff's face suddenly changed from half a smile to complete fear. The bald man's smile widened just a little bit, and he began to nod his head, as if to say that Jeff had figured out what he meant from the start. He had obviously said exactly what he wanted to.

Turning to me, the bald man answered my question, "We will be going home as soon as we have what we have come here for." I waited for an answer that was a little more helpful. "A couple of weeks," he said finally.

"I say we are dumping them somewheres," said the Russian, returning to the *burn the bridge* idea, "and we are speaking of them to no one. And then nobody is asking much questions which will be putting us into jail."

"John saw us when the boat was leaving," said Jeff quickly, fear still in his voice. "They'll know *you* did it."

"Hhumphff!" was all that came out of the Russian's mouth. I wasn't sure if it was supposed to be English or not.

"Can you just take us back now?" asked Meg with blinking eyes and a pitiful frown.

"Out of the question," said the bald man. "We have a tight schedule to keep."

Jeff's comment about John reminded me that they had tricked

him with the salt. "So what exactly did you come here for?" I asked. "Obviously, it's not to deliver salt!"

"Evidence!" said Anthony with a smile. "We've come to gather evidence of the existence of this *ancient* tribe that we've heard so much about. I'm sure the rest of the world will be absolutely fascinated by them." He smiled contentedly as he rocked his skinny head from side to side.

"What kind of evidence?" I asked warily.

"Who knows?" smiled Anthony. He was enjoying this way too much. "Perhaps these ancient writings that we've heard so much about." He paused. "Or perhaps something even more convincing: something that speaks for itself, . . . should we say?"

CHAPTER 4

The Three Stooges

"What do you mean?" I glared at the gloating Dr. Anthony.

"Your friend John has given us so much information, that we have many options," said Anthony. "Who can say for sure? The only thing that *is* sure, is that you would all be rich if you had only looked around long enough to realize the value of what you had found!" He sighed with a dreamy look on his face. "I guess that's the value of a trained mind like mine," he said.

"Oh, come, now," interrupted the bald man, "we have plenty of time to talk about that later. We need to get you two cleaned up."

"They will be cleaning up this room as well," interjected the Russian. "And they will be paying for the sugar powder."

"Yes, yes," said the bald man, impatiently to the Russian, "all in good time." Turning back to us, he said, "And I would really like to know where you've been hiding all this time."

"When John brought us on board to meet all you," Shauna explained, "we hid in the engine room when we saw Dr. Anthony because we didn't want him to see us."

"But you guys took off before we could get out," added Jeff, "and we got locked in there before we could tell anyone that we were here."

"It is being something I am always doing," said the Russian, "to be closing and locking doors that might be coming open during our traveling."

The bald man threw his head back and laughed as if he thought this was all great fun. "How delightful!" he exclaimed. "It will be wonderful to have someone else to talk to besides these absolutely boring gentlemen."

Both the Russian and Anthony glared at the bald man as he continued. "Vladimir is always worried about the authorities or messes or doors bouncing open and making unexpected noise. And Larry, here," he said, tipping his head toward Dr. Anthony, "seems to always have some twisted plot brewing in his tight, little brain. Which is why we're here, I suppose: he's convinced that we'll be rich and famous when this is all over."

Dr. Anthony's eyes narrowed as he listened. The bald man continued by saying, "I'm already rich, of course, but I wouldn't mind being famous. Mostly, though, the adventure seemed just too juicy to pass up. Larry definitely sold me on *that* part of his plan!" He smiled at Dr. Anthony again.

"By the way, my name is Mr. Omni," said the bald man. "It's very nice to meet you." He didn't pronounce "Omni" with a long *i* sound at the end, the way we say the name of the book in the Book of Mormon. Instead, he used a long *e* sound. It seemed like a strange name to me.

We all nodded and said, "hello" or "hi."

"And this is my bodyguard, Leonard," said Mr. Omni, indicating the large man behind him with a flick of his head. "I probably do not really need a bodyguard, I suppose, but that is just what rich people do." He smiled again, showing his gapped teeth. He asked our names and we told him.

"Now, we need to make better accommodations for you than the engine room," Mr. Omni said. "There is a servants' stateroom on this level with a bathroom and sleeping arrangements for four. I am sure no one will object to letting you use that room while you are onboard. Is there anything else we can do for you?"

"Yes," said Shauna, firmly. "You can take us back to our parents."

"Oh, I'm sorry about that," smiled Omni, "but as I mentioned to your sister, that's quite out of the question."

"Well, then can you at least use the radio to let them know we are safe?" asked Shauna.

"No way," said Anthony quickly. "That could ruin everything!"

"This is not being some'sing I am feeling very much good about," agreed the Russian, whose name was apparently Vladimir.

Mr. Omni smiled. "I suppose we'll have to settle for taking good care of you. Your parents will just have to wonder for the time being. But I would imagine that you're hungry, aren't you?"

"Starved!" answered Jeff.

"Good!" said Mr. Omni. "Let's show you to your stateroom first and then we'll get you all something to eat."

"What's a stateroom?" sighed Shauna. She was still unhappy about their refusal to contact our parents, but she seemed resigned to it. "We didn't see any room down here with four beds," she explained. "We did use the bathroom off of a room that had just two beds."

"Ah," smiled Mr. Omni at Shauna. "Come with me, Shari, and bring the others." We all gave each other puzzled looks when he called her *Shari*, because he just kept talking. "A stateroom is just a fancy name for a bedroom on a ship or a train. The room you found is the stateroom that I was referring to. There are actually two more beds in the wall above the beds that you saw. They just fold up when they are not needed."

Jeff and I brushed ourselves off the best we could and followed Mr. Omni back to the bedroom. The Russian and Dr. Anthony disappeared, but Leonard, the bodyguard, stayed within a few feet of Mr. Omni at all times. Jeff got to shower first, probably because it was my fault that he was a mess. But I was okay with that, because the rest of us went to what Omni called "the galley" to eat. I couldn't believe all the food they had. We had fresh fruit, granola bars, and oatmeal made in the microwave from individual packages. It was like a real kitchen. Jeff was showered and dressed before I had finished, so I climbed into the warm shower with a half-eaten apple. Shauna showered when I was done.

"Come and see the rest of the boat," invited Mr. Omni, after we had finished our food and showers. "You will not believe everything that this little, 120-foot yacht has."

He was right. We could hardly believe it. There were four levels and at least two staircases went between each of the levels—I think there were about ten in all. We already knew the lowest level very well. Mr. Omni called it the lower deck. It had the engine room, the cargo hold, the servants' galley and the servants' stateroom. It also had the two staterooms that were being used by Dr. Anthony and Vladimir.

The next level was called the main deck. This is where we originally boarded the boat and climbed down the spiral staircase to the lower deck. The main deck was open on all sides with a railing that went all the way around. There was mostly just a walkway along the sides and front, but the back was large enough for a dining table that seated 12 and several lounge chairs. This area was covered by the deck above. Inside on the main deck there was another dining table for 12, and a lounge with lots of couches and chairs. The main deck also had a master stateroom with a king-size bed (where Mr. Omni slept) and a smaller stateroom with a double bed (for Leonard). Again, each stateroom had its own attached bathroom.

The master stateroom was much nicer than the Marriott Hotel rooms where we stayed the previous year. It was finished with dark wood on all the walls and there was a huge skylight in the shape of a ship's steering wheel right above the bed. I wondered how it could have a skylight with two other decks above it, but we found that this was at the very front of the yacht and the upper decks didn't come as far forward. The master bathroom looked like it had marble floors and marble walls all the way around. It had a huge tub that could have easily fit four or five people. All I could figure was that maybe the guy had a stash of toy boats or something.

The next level was called the boat deck. It didn't cover the front third of the boat, which is how the master stateroom ended up with a skylight. The back part of the boat deck was open to the sky and on all sides, except for the front. There was a large Jacuzzi tub in the middle, with several sunbathing chairs around. The front part of this deck had another indoor lounge and also contained the pilot house that gave me the impression I was in an air traffic control center with a bank of windows along the curved front part of the room, continuing down both sides. There was a large desk that curved around under the windows with all sorts of various TV monitors and gauges and gadgets.

A large, leather captain's chair was mounted in the center of the room right in front of the control desk, with several other leather lounge chairs around the room. Vladimir was sitting in the captain's chair, and Dr. Anthony was sitting at a large table at the back of the pilot house, poring over a map. He hardly glanced up when Mr. Omni brought us in. We learned that all the men had been in the pilot house when the boat first left Seward, which is probably why no one heard John when he was yelling for them to stop.

The highest level only covered the middle third of the yacht. It was called the sun deck and was open on all sides, but had another dining table sheltered by a roof of clear plastic. Once more, the rest of the deck was littered with various squishy lounge chairs.

Once I saw all the details of this crazy, 120-foot yacht, I got the impression that the only thing rich people do is eat and sit around. *Boring!* Oh, I guess they sleep and shower, too, but probably only because those are required for life and good manners.

After our tour, we went back to the pilot house where we had seen the others. Of course, Leonard had followed wherever Mr. Omni had gone. He never said a word the entire time, but kept his arms folded across his large chest (except for when he was climbing stairs), while his long, curly hair remained perfectly in place. Bodyguarding seemed like a pretty boring job to me.

"How do you like our little home away from home, Stephanie?" asked Mr. Omni.

"It amazing!" said Shauna. "But my name is *Shauna*." Mr. Omni just smiled at her as if he thought she was just a little bit touchy, but he was willing to be patient with her.

"If you didn't see all the water," said Jeff, "you would hardly even know that you're on a boat."

"Is it all yours?" asked Meg.

"Well," replied Omni, glancing at the Russian, "for the time being, it is."

The Russian looked back thoughtfully at Omni and said, "It is being my property very soon."

I decided to tell the truth the way I saw it. "It seems like the perfect place for people who only like to eat and sit around," I said. "But people like that often have a hard time climbing stairs."

Mr. Omni laughed with a wide grin. "And right you are!" he said in loud voice.

"So are you buying this?" asked Jeff, turning to Vladimir.

"You might say that," interrupted Anthony. "But not with dollars . . . or *rubles* either. We're sort of making a trade."

"This is being truth," Vladimir nodded. "We will be trading my expert knowledge of Lena River as a boat captain for many years, for which I am receiving this beautiful yacht, which is—how you say it—being for people who are liking nothing more than eating and sitting around!"

"Well said," laughed Omni.

"The Lena River?" I asked.

"Yes," said Anthony. "After interviewing most of the people that were with you last year and studying many maps, we have decided that it was the Lena River in Russia that you floated down when you returned to the Arctic Sea." He looked at us with that sicky-sweet smile that had made me despise him two years earlier.

"How did you even know about it?" asked Jeff.

"Well," Anthony smiled again. "I just got lucky, you might say. A little more than a year ago when I discovered that I suddenly had a little more freedom than I had been used to . . ." He paused as Omni laughed at his joke. I was starting to get a little tired of Omni's gapped-tooth smile. Anthony continued by saying, "I thought I might look up some old friends—a *family*, actually. One that had been very close to my thoughts for the previous year."

"How did you get out?" I dared to ask. "I can't believe you only got sentenced to a year after all you did."

Omni laughed again.

"A technicality," sneered Anthony. "That bumbling sheriff in Iowa made such a mess of things that they really had no choice."

"What did you want? Why did you come looking for us?" I asked. Then I quickly added, "We don't have that book anymore."

"Oh, yes," Anthony nodded. "I know that now. You gave it to the Church and they probably locked it deep in that granite vault under the mountain. Your neighbor—what's her name? Geri?—she told me *all* about it."

I rolled my eyes when I thought about who he meant. Brother and Sister Stemmons lived next door. Brother Stemmons had been my deacons quorum advisor and we all thought he was great. He told great stories during his lessons and a lot of them were about his crazy wife, Geri. I don't know the first names of a lot of the grown-ups at church, because they all usually call their husband or wife Brother so-and-so or Sister so-and-so, which I always thought was kind of weird. But Brother Stemmons always referred to his wife by the name he called her: Geri. And she was great, too, of course. She always had cookies or something else for us and she would talk to us about stuff that we were interested in, like soccer. She would even come to our games once in a while. But if there's one way I would describe Sister Stemmons, it was that she was a *talker*. She could talk for*ever* about *anything*. And she would go out of her way to talk to anybody she saw. And she didn't care if they seemed interested in talking or not.

"How did you meet her?" asked Shauna.

"After a few days of *observation*," said Anthony, "it was starting to become apparent that no one was home. So I took a little stroll down the street for a closer look. I hadn't even gotten halfway along the sidewalk in front of your house when dear, sweet Geri came scurrying down her front walkway calling to me."

I could see it all. She probably had that three-legged dog limping along behind her. Every stray or injured dog for miles around seemed to find their way to her house.

"I told her the truth, of course," continued Anthony. Glancing at Mr. Omni, he added, "That's what we do here, right?" Omni laughed. Smiling, Anthony looked back at me and said, "I told her that I was interested in that first edition copy of the Book of Mormon of yours, but that you didn't seem to be home. She told me right away what you had done with the book. I knew immediately that there would be no chance of studying the book anymore." I shook my head, because every one of us knew that "studying" the book was not what he had had in mind. Anthony just smiled and went on with his story.

"That's when she told me the horrible news!" said Anthony, pretending to be shocked and afraid. "That you had been lost somewhere in Asia for several weeks and that your family and the others had only recently been rescued. She told me you were due home any day. When I got a little more detail about exactly what had happened to you and what you had discovered, I was delighted beyond imagination! Being the experienced and trained historian that I am, I quickly realized the potential value of this discovery to be much greater than that silly book of yours that was not even two centuries old."

I remembered that Dad had called the Stemmonses the first chance he got, so that everyone at home would know we were okay. It sounded like he had maybe given them a little too much information. I felt my eyes narrow as I stared at Anthony. This guy made me sick. A glance toward Jeff and Shauna told me they were feeling the same as I. Meg, on the other hand, who had snuggled up with Shauna on a lounge chair, was apparently asleep.

When I turned back to Anthony, I saw that his expression had now changed to be distant and dreamy. He was staring somewhere off into space and slowly shaking his head back and forth. "Just imagine it," he whispered. "Living, *breathing* history."

Vladimir said what we were all thinking, "I am being sure that you are imagining the dollars that will be coming to you from such a discovery of breathing history."

Anthony's dreamy look slowly turned into that slimy smile again. Vladimir was right, and Anthony wasn't denying it.

"That's when I began learning as much as possible about your experience," said Anthony, "and many of the others who were with you have been quite helpful to me."

"Of course Dr. Anthony didn't have the means to make his dream come true on his own," said Mr. Omni. "That's where I came in. Because I am so disgustingly rich, I was able to bring it *all* together." He really emphasized the word *all*. He laughed again and then asked us, "Do you know what the name *Omni* means?"

Jeff had a small smirk when he said, "It means *all*, doesn't it?"

Mr. Omni snapped his finger and pointed at Jeff with excitement all in the same motion. "That's right, Josh!" he said to Jeff, slowly nodding his head. "A name is a *very* important part of a person! It says a lot about who that person is and what they are about!"

What a joker this guy was! He's sitting here telling us the importance of names and he hadn't yet gotten any of ours right. Of course he hadn't even tried mine yet, but I could just imagine.

"My name was not always so meaningful," Omni continued. "But since I have unlimited means, I took the opportunity to make a change in that regard. *Omni* is now my legal name—Russell Omni, to be precise. I sign most documents *Mr. Omni, Esquire.* But you may call me Mr. Omni." I tried not to stare at the gaps when he smiled. "Do you know how the word *Omni* is used?" he asked.

"Of course," said Shauna, acting a little disgusted. "It means 'all' which is why we say that God is omniscient, which is all-knowing, and omnipotent, which is all-powerful."

"That is correct, Shirley," said Mr. Omni. "But as you said, I am simply *All.*"

I was feeling a little nauseous, and it wasn't from the motion of the boat. The yacht was so big that you could hardly even tell we were on water. Anthony looked like he was a little worried about Omni's mental health as well.

"So how do you know each other?" Shauna asked in an obvious attempt to avoid any more discussion about Omni and the importance of names.

"I met Leonard during my extended stay at that government resort we spoke of earlier," said Anthony. "He and I were both guests of the judicial system for a time. All expenses paid, of course." Anthony looked over at Leonard who still stood, arms folded across his chest, just a few feet from Omni. "He looked a lot different then, because his hair was much shorter," Anthony mused. "I have an almost uncontrollable urge to call him 'Curly' now."

This was the first time I'd seen any reaction from Leonard that showed he was in any way comprehending the conversation going on around him. He definitely flinched. There was just a hint of a sneer developing on his face as his lips began to curl back slightly. But almost as soon at it happened, he immediately regained his composure and stared off into space again. Anthony just chuckled slightly under his breath. I had the impression that to Leonard, Anthony was nothing more than a bothersome mosquito that he could destroy with a single, swift swat any time he felt like it. As usual, Anthony was in no way connected with reality.

"Leonard," said Mr. Omni, "was in my employ before that unfortunate time in his life, and so we were well acquainted."

"Yeah," said Anthony, "and Leonard was a little more talkative back then, and I got to hear all about Mr. O. So when this little venture came up, I knew just who might be able to help me make it happen."

"And I was happy to help," Omni agreed, "especially since the project held the promise of benefiting so many people of the world." He smiled widely again, showing off those ugly, gapped teeth once more. I was starting to wonder why he didn't spend a little of his fortune on an orthodontist.

"While taking advantage of a few people who have no interest in being acquainted with the rest of the world," I said.

"Only because they don't know what the world has to offer!" said Omni with both arms stretched out wide.

"Whatever," I mumbled. "You'll never find them."

"We sure will," said Anthony. "Vladimir has shown us that there are very few tributaries leading into the Lena River and only one that is the right distance from the Arctic Ocean to be the one you found next to the mountain pass you apparently came through. Based on the descriptions from the others who were with you, I have no doubt that we will find your little tribe quite easily."

"Does Vladimir know the mountains, too?" I asked.

"Vladimir will not be leaving from boat," said Vladimir of himself. "I must be traveling up the river for to be getting more fuel and to be taking riders on trip with new boat. This is how I am making my living: the taking of riders on river in boat."

"We only need his help getting to the tributary," said Anthony. "The three of us will be just fine from there."

"But enough of this talk," interrupted Omni. "You must all be tired. I'm sure you didn't sleep well in the engine room last night.

You are free to return to your quarters and rest or sun yourselves on one of the decks or simply roam about the boat as you please."

Both Anthony and Vladimir spun around and stared at Omni with disapproval for that last part. But he just smiled and said, "We trust the children. They are good children." Turning to me he asked, "We can trust you, Brad, can't we?"

"My name is Brandon," I said flatly.

Mr. Omni nodded at me as if to say he understood my problem. Then he turned back to Anthony and Vladimir and said, "See? They'll be fine."

"They are staying within their stateroom at the time of refueling," demanded Vladimir. "I will be having nobody seeing them on this vessel."

Mr. Omni soon left the pilot house with Leonard right behind him. We didn't really want to hang around with Anthony and Vladimir, so after waking up Meg we left as quickly as we could and closed ourselves in our stateroom. We talked for a while about what we could do or what we should do, but we couldn't agree on much of anything. I suggested we all keep an eye on the pilot house whenever we could and maybe we could sneak onto the radio and let someone know where we were. Shauna thought that was risky, but agreed that it was worth a try.

"When are they going to take us back to Mom and Dad?" asked Meg.

"It's not going to be for while," said Shauna with a sad face. "Probably not for two weeks."

Meg looked like she was going to cry.

"We're going to be okay," Shauna reassured her. "This is just something it looks like we're going to have to do."

"Why do we have to do things we don't want to?" asked Meg.

"That's just the way it is sometimes," said Shauna. "But do you know what? Even Jesus had to do something he didn't want to."

"He did?" said Meg.

"Yes, He did," nodded Shauna. "When it was time for Jesus to perform the Atonement in the garden, He told Heavenly Father that if there was any way He didn't have to do it, then He didn't want to."

"Really?" said Meg, her expression changing from sad to amazed.

"Yes," continued Shauna. "But then Jesus said He would do whatever Heavenly Father wanted Him to do, no matter what. If we had scriptures, I would read it to you."

Meg's expression now changed to excitement as she sat up straight on the bed. Without even the thought of removing the straps, she pulled her pink backpack up over one shoulder and began to fish around inside it. "Didn't you know that I brang my tiny scriptures?" she asked.

"Brought," I corrected her.

"You brought them!" smiled Shauna with excitement. "Meg, you're the greatest!"

"Didn't you know?" she asked again as she triumphantly pulled them from the backpack, letting it fall behind her again. She got this set when she was baptized a couple of years earlier. When Mom took her to choose scriptures, Meg thought the small ones were "so cute" that she just wouldn't be happy with anything else.

"Here it is," said Shauna after a moment. "It's easier to find in my own scriptures, because I marked it in seminary the year before last. Luckily I remembered it was in Luke 22." She read parts of verses 41 and 42 where it states that Jesus "kneeled down, and prayed, Saying, Father, if thou be willing, remove this cup from me: nevertheless not my will, but thine, be done."

Thinking about what started all this, Meg's face got concerned again and she asked, "But what if it's really hard, what we have to do?"

"If we pray for it," Shauna said, "Heavenly Father will send us all the help that we need. He even sent help to Jesus!"

"He did?" Meg's eyes were wide again. Shauna read the next

verse aloud, which states "and there appeared an angel unto him from heaven, strengthening him."

"Will Heavenly Father send angels to us?" asked Meg.

"If we need them, He will," said Shauna. "And whether we can see them or not, we will always have each other to help us be strong, okay?" That seemed to be good enough for Meg, because she gave a contented smile and a determined sigh before snuggling next to Shauna on the bed again. No one said anything for a moment or two until Meg broke the silence.

"Are we going to say a prayer?" she asked.

It was my turn to pray. We all kneeled around one of the beds, and I tried to say the same kinds of things that Shauna and Jeff had said in their prayers: things like keeping us safe and helping Mom and Dad not to worry. Then I added a couple of things that had to do with what Shauna and Meg had just talked about. I thought it would be a good idea to reassure Meg, but it turned out to make me feel a lot better, too. After our prayer we got distracted for just a few minutes with deciding who was going to sleep on which beds. Soon our conversation turned back to what was ahead of us.

"Do you think those guys will be able to find the tribe?" I asked.

"Who?" asked Shauna. "The Three Stooges? I doubt it!"

"The three what?" laughed Jeff. "What's a stooge?"

"Phew! I don't know," said Shauna with a big smile. "But don't you remember that show? It was one of Granny's favorites. She used to just sit and giggle whenever she would watch it."

"What was it about?" I asked. There were quite a few different favorites of Granny that would just make her giggle whenever she watched. But I didn't remember anything about stooges.

"It was in black and white and it was about these three guys," Shauna explained, still smiling, "and they were all really dopey and would always have some crazy scheme going. But they would always be fighting between themselves and could never get anything right. Granny would just sit and giggle when she watched." Shauna began

laughing just at the thought of Granny. Shauna's laugh was conta-
gious enough that Jeff and I started to laugh, too. We could all
imagine Granny doing exactly what Shauna had described.

"Oh, I think I remember," said Jeff. "Weren't their names like
'Curly' and 'Joe' and something else?"

"Larry, Moe, and Curly," said Shauna, still giggling a little bit.

"Hey!" I said, "Did you hear Anthony call Leonard 'Curly' that
one time?"

"That's right!" laughed Jeff.

"Oh, no!" breathed Shauna. "Didn't Mr. Omni say that Dr.
Anthony's first name was 'Larry'?"

"No way!" I laughed. "That must mean that Mr. Omni is the
other guy . . . what did you say his name was? Joe? Moe?"

"Moe," said Shauna, between breaths.

"M. O. for 'Mr. Omni,'" said Jeff. "They *are* the Three Stooges!"

"Almost," corrected Shauna, "but Moe is spelled with an *e* at
the end."

"Esquire," I said triumphantly. "Mr. Omni, Esquire! He's Moe!"

We laughed about the Three Stooges for several minutes before
coming back to the original question: would they be able to find the
tribe? Thinking about that cut our laughter off pretty quickly. We
started talking about Anthony's threat to bring back "something
that speaks for itself."

"Do you think he meant that he is going to kidnap somebody?"
I asked.

"I'm sure he meant that he wanted a person," answered Shauna,
"and I'm also sure that kidnapping is the only way he would be able
to get anyone to come."

"Who do you think Anthony would try to take?" I asked.

"I'm sure he knows that Levi and Aaron speak English," said
Shauna. "Either of them would be an obvious choice."

"Well, you remember what Aaron's name was when he was
born, don't you?" asked Jeff.

"Joseph," I answered.

"Oh, that's right!" said Shauna. "I forgot that his dad changed it to Aaron. That happened when he turned twelve and started helping with the priesthood responsibilities, huh?"

"Yeah," said Jeff, "but do you remember *why* his dad said that he named him Joseph?"

"No," admitted Shauna.

"Because," said Jeff, "he felt that sometime during his lifetime he would go to another land to bring salvation to his people."

"Oh, yeah!" breathed Shauna. "Just like Joseph who was in charge of the all the grain in Egypt during the famine! I remember."

"So do you think this might be what he was talking about?" I asked.

We just stared at each other in silence as we considered the possibilities.

CHAPTER 5

The Summer Home

We spent most of the rest of the morning talking about Aaron and Levi and the tribe. When we had been with them the previous year, they were at what they called their summer home. We knew that they spent only a few weeks there each year and then went back south to their main home where they spent the winter. Considering how much later in the summer it was now than then, we decided that there was a good chance the tribe might have already returned to their winter home. We were hoping that they had.

It was a six-day trip when the entire tribe went together. Most of the people walked. Many of the women and children rode on these cool reindeer sleds they had. I was completely amazed the year before when we saw that this tribe herded reindeer like cattle and harnessed them to sleds for carrying heavy loads. After we got back home, though, Dad found pictures of several groups of people in northeastern Russia who used reindeer this way. Apparently, Santa Claus didn't come up with the idea on his own. The sleds were bigger than our van and looked like a huge, fat ski made from about a dozen long poles, with the skinny ends tied together and pointing upwards in the front. They would glide pretty smoothly over the snow or grass.

After discussing it for a few minutes, we felt pretty sure that Dr. Anthony was right: the Three Stooges probably had enough information to easily make their way to the summer home. But we figured they would have absolutely no hope of finding the way to the other one.

"Do you think they will make us go with them?" asked Jeff. "I mean to the summer home."

"I doubt Vladimir will want us along while he's running the river with customers," said Shauna. "I think they'll make us go with them."

"We can't give them any help, though," I said. "If they make us go, then fine, we'll follow them wherever they lead. But we can't tell them *anything*, okay?"

"You're right," agreed Jeff. "But we might not be able to show them the way, even if we wanted to. We were only there once and we came from the other direction, so things might look totally different."

"Do you think they'll be patient, if some of us are a little slow?" I asked, glancing quickly toward Meg, who was playing quietly with a rag doll that she had brought in her backpack. I think Shauna had made it for her at a church activity a couple of years earlier. Meg had been in love with it ever since the moment she got it. She took it wherever she could, which was probably why it looked like it had spent significant time in the gutter in front of our house on a rainy day and then left on a fence post to dry. It was tattered and filthy, but she loved it.

"I don't think they will move any faster than she can," said Shauna. "Have you noticed how much time she spends outside on her bike or Rollerblades? She's in pretty good shape."

"The one I would worry about is Anthony," laughed Jeff. "He looks skinnier and wimpier than ever."

"You mean *Larry?*" I said. "You're right. And Moe is no prime specimen, either."

"I think we'll all be fine, if that's what they want us to do," said Shauna. I knew that she wasn't worried about herself, and why would she be? After all, she had played on the Orem High girls' soccer team for the last three years. She was probably in better shape than any of us.

"Well, I hope they don't find the tribe," said Jeff, "but wouldn't it be cool if *we* got to see them again? Aaron's family, I mean."

"I've been thinking about that, too," said Shauna. "It would be good to see Nawni again."

Nawni was the name of Levi's wife and Aaron's mother. Jeff and I were gone from the summer home for several days with Aaron for a feast and other things, so we didn't get to know her very well. But Shauna and Meg both spent that time with her and talked about her quite a bit during the first few weeks after we got back. Nawni didn't speak any English, but she taught Mom and Shauna and Meg how to cook some of their foods and how to pick some wild berries that were good for eating. She also taught them to sing a few songs that seemed to be required during all food preparation. They were really cool-sounding songs, too.

The mention of Nawni's name caught Meg's attention.

"Are we going to see Nawni again?" she asked with bright eyes.

"Maybe," said Shauna. "That's what these men are doing. They're trying to find the tribe."

"Do they know how to get there?" asked Meg.

"We don't know," Jeff said. "We'll have to wait and see."

"Do you think that if we're with Nawni then I won't miss Mom so much?" asked Meg.

"Nawni was like another mom, wasn't she?" said Shauna.

We talked for quite a while longer about various things. We even laughed about the fact that we apparently wouldn't be making it on our free cruise *this* year, either. Talking about the cruise reminded me that the rest of our family was probably pretty worried about us.

"Let's go see if anyone is in the pilot house," I said. "It sure would be nice if we could get a chance to use that radio."

We decided to grab some food from the kitchen for lunch and

take it up to the boat deck with us, acting like we wanted to eat in the lounge right behind the pilot house. We figured that would be a good place to wait for a chance to use the radio. We also thought that if we took food up with us, then whoever was there might see it and start to feel hungry. Mr. Omni had told us that the boat had an autopilot system, so we were hoping that maybe they would leave the pilot house empty for a minute or two; we figured that would be all the time we'd need.

Mr. Omni had bragged about all the amazing features of this boat that had been made especially for him. The autopilot worked by connecting to global positioning satellites so that the boat always knew exactly where it was. It used maps stored in computers to know where land was and would automatically shutdown and stop the boat if it got too close to any land. Also, they could set it up to beep throughout the whole yacht if the radar happened to pick up any other ships. Mr. Omni said that at 50 miles per hour the boat could run for over 24 hours straight because of extra fuel tanks that had been installed. He said that the trip from Seward, Alaska, to the Lena river would take about two and half days, so they would have to stop to refuel only twice. Both stops would be at Russian ports and, of course, Vladimir had made it clear that we would be locked in our room during each stop. That's why we figured that the radio was our best chance at contacting somebody—hopefully someone who spoke English.

When we got up to the boat deck with our lunch, we found that everybody else was there, too. Both Anthony and Vladimir were in the pilot house, while Mr. Omni and Leonard were out on the open deck. This was the first time that I had seen Leonard sitting, but he still had his arms folded across his chest. His long, curly hair was whipping this way and that in the cold wind. Mr. Omni was the one who really caught our attention. If I had thought he was crazy before, I was now completely convinced. He was sun tanning, wearing a plaid swimming suit. Even through the lounge windows we could see the goose bumps all over his arms and legs. What a weirdo. His chest was covered with short, white hair that was being ruffled by the wind. It was cold enough that we wore our coats the entire time whenever we left our room, and this lunatic was outside practically naked!

We sat in the lounge all afternoon, but Anthony and Vladimir never left the pilot house at the same time. Anthony brought food back for the both of them. Later in the afternoon Mr. Omni and Leonard went in and Vladimir said he was going to sleep in preparation for the night watch. It was pretty discouraging. I was starting to think we'd never get a chance at the radio. And the worst part was, the longer we waited, the smaller the chance that we would contact someone who spoke English. I just kept hoping that John had found Mom and Dad and at least given them some idea of what might be happening to us.

It was really hard just sitting there and watching all afternoon. We were anxious and bored at the same time. It was a pain. Finally we went to the kitchen for dinner and then back to our room, pretty much giving up on the radio idea. Of course, there wasn't much to do, because none of us had brought anything with us except for Meg. But there were several things in her pink, flowered backpack that she was happy to share with anyone that was interested. She had her scriptures, of course, and we each took turns reading from those for a while. She also had a couple of other books that didn't look anything like things I would have been reading at her age. There were also a couple of small, spiral notebooks and a large key ring with half a dozen short gel pens hanging from it, but no keys. The only other thing she had was her doll. Considering how much time she spent with it, I was glad that she had it.

We spent most of the next day and a half either talking or sleeping or taking turns with Meg's books or scriptures. Once in a while we would take a short walk around the yacht to get a little exercise or to grab some food from the galley. We pretty much tried to avoid

Vladimir and the Three Stooges. We did get close enough once to hear Anthony whining about losing his glasses.

"I'm practically blind without them!" yelled Anthony. "What am I going to do?"

"So what happened to them?" asked Omni.

"I *told* you," moaned Anthony, "I was leaning over the side of the boat and the wind caught them. They're long gone!"

We had a hard time not laughing at that one.

At one point during the afternoon on the second day we started talking about what Aaron and his family might have done with the copies of the Book of Mormon that we had left them. The man who had given them a copy of the Bible had also taught them a lot about Jesus. Some of the tribe had begun to believe in Jesus Christ as the Messiah they had been waiting for. They were trying to follow his teachings from the New Testament and were administering bread and wine to each other every Sabbath day in remembrance of the Last Supper.

"Do you think they've read the Book of Mormon?" asked Jeff.

"I'm sure they have," said Shauna. "Remember how they wanted to know everything they could about the Church and about Jesus?"

"Yeah," I said. "And they could do both by reading the Book of Mormon."

"The Book of Mormon—Another Testament of Jesus Christ," said Jeff, correcting me.

Shauna laughed. "People just call it the Book of Mormon," she said. "I think we all know what he's talking about."

"My seminary teacher was on this thing all year," explained Jeff. "Every time we said anything about the Book of Mormon, we had to use its full name."

"Who was your teacher?" asked Shauna.

"Brother Olive," Jeff replied. "I don't know how many times I've heard him say, 'they added the words *Another Testament of Jesus Christ* in 1982 for a reason.'" Jeff copied his tone as he spoke.

"What was the reason?" I asked.

"Because a lot of people don't understand that we are Christians," said Shauna. "Since we're sometimes called *Mormons*, a lot of people have no idea that we believe in Jesus Christ."

"Oh," I said, "so I guess that's why the prophets have told us to use the real name of the Church whenever we can. If everybody knew that we were really *The Church of Jesus Christ*, then they would know."

"Well," said Shauna, "not really."

"Why?" asked Jeff.

"Well, you know my friend Lynnette, don't you?" said Shauna.

"Yeah," Jeff and I both said at once.

"You know she's Catholic, right?" said Shauna, "And her dad told her that even though we say we believe in Jesus Christ that it's not the same Jesus they believe in."

"How can it be different?" asked Jeff. "We both use the New Testament."

"I know," Shauna agreed, "but you have to remember that the Catholic church has been around for almost 2,000 years, and they have a lot of traditions and beliefs that they follow that aren't necessarily spelled out in the Bible." She paused while Jeff and I thought about this for a moment. "And in our church, we know things about Jesus Christ because of modern revelation that aren't necessarily spelled out in the Bible, either."

"But it just adds to it," said Jeff, "it doesn't change anything! It just helps us understand it."

"Well, I know," said Shauna, nodding her head, "but there are lots of things in the Bible that can be understood in different ways. So they understand things a certain way and have been following that tradition for as long as they can remember, and we understand things in a different way because of the prophets that we believe in."

Jeff and I nodded our understanding.

"We all think we're consistent with the Bible," Shauna continued, "but some people think that our understanding of Jesus Christ is so different from the traditions of most Christian churches that we shouldn't be called Christians."

"Even though we all believe that Jesus is the Son of God?" asked Jeff.

"And that He performed the Atonement?" I added.

"And we all try to follow His teachings about charity and forgiveness?" said Jeff.

"I know," said Shauna. Her face was sad. "I think most people agree that that's what really matters. Lynnette does; she's a good friend."

"So like what sorts of things are they talking about?" I asked.

"Well, the biggest thing," said Shauna, "is that in Joseph Smith's first vision, he saw that Heavenly Father and Jesus are two separate Beings."

"Oh, yeah," said Jeff, "but they believe in the Trinity."

"Right," said Shauna. "So that's a huge difference. You can see why some people make a huge deal out of it."

"So is everything we know about Jesus from revelation?" I asked.

"No!" said Shauna with excitement. "Oh, that's right! You didn't get to take seminary last year: our study course was the Book of Mormon."

"Yeah," said Jeff. "It was great! We talked about all sorts of stuff that the Book of Mormon teaches us about Christ. My favorite was how after His resurrection when He visited the people in ancient America, He told them that they were the other sheep that He said in the New Testament he would visit."

"So that's something that Aaron and Levi might have found,"

said Shauna, bringing us back to where the whole conversation had started.

It was fun to talk about Aaron and his family and maybe seeing them again. Part of me hoped that we would get the chance to see them, but most of me didn't want Anthony and the other Stooges anywhere near them. If Aaron was really to go to another country sometime, I hoped it wasn't with these criminals. But fortunately, if these guys *did* manage to find the tribe, it looked like we would probably be there, too, and so we held out hope that we could at least warn them.

The morning of the third day things were very different from how they had previously been. When we went for breakfast, we happened to look out one of the port holes and saw land really close. Checking quickly, we discovered that we were no longer on the ocean, but traveling quickly upstream on a large river. There were rolling, barren hills on one side and large, rocky mountains on the other.

"Does this look familiar?" asked Anthony, who happened to come out of his stateroom as we all stood on the deck staring up at the mountains. Anthony looked weird without his glasses. There was nothing keeping his greasy hair behind his ears. He covered one eye with his hand as he squinted at the landscape with the other eye.

When we didn't answer, Anthony asked again, "So, does this look familiar or not?"

The fact was, it did. Everything looked exactly as we remembered it from the year before. I don't think he really expected us to answer him, though. It was more just a jab as he walked by. He was confident that we were in the right place and just wanted to rub it in. We were still standing there a couple of minutes later when Mr. Omni came looking for us. He informed us that we would be "putting in" at the edge of the river about lunch time and we should be ready to go.

"I have no tolerance for children," he said. "You'll be expected to keep up, do your share, and stay out of our way."

We all showered about mid-morning, knowing that this would be the last chance we would have for a while to get really clean. I was glad that we each had our coats. Luckily, too, we had each put on tennis shoes when we went for our walk at the dock. Boots would have been really nice, but we had been planning on a cruise, not a hike. We were getting anxious about things and so we went up onto the boat deck for the last hour or so. The forest of pine trees on the river banks was getting more dense the farther we went up the river. It was starting to look very much like the place where we had jumped into our raft. As we waited and watched, Mr. Omni brought three backpacks out onto the deck where we were. Apparently, the yacht had been stocked with these backpacks to be used by Vladimir's customers.

"This is for you, Jared," Mr. Omni said to Jeff, handing him a backpack. "And Brian," he said, turning to me, "this one is yours."

"It's Brandon," I said with exaggerated lip movement. He just smiled like always and gave the last one to Shauna. "Here you are," he said, without bothering to call her someone else's name.

Turning to Meg he said, "Now, Melissa, I have noticed how much you love your beautiful, pink backpack, so I did not bring one up for you. But do you think you would have enough room in there to carry a few things?"

Meg stared at him for a moment as if trying to decide if she should say something about her real name. Finally she just asked, "What are they?"

"Well," said Omni, "we have some dried fruit that is not very heavy at all, but is quite bulky. I thought that might work well for you. And each person is to have a flashlight. I brought the smallest one for you."

Without a word, she reached past her shoulders and opened the zipper. Then she turned her back to Omni so that he could put the fruit and the flashlight inside.

"Thank you," smiled Omni, "I think we will have a wonderful time, don't you?"

Without waiting for an answer he left to finish preparations. We took the opportunity to investigate what was inside our backpacks. In the large center sections, we each had a flashlight, as Omni had said, and the rest of the space was filled mostly with various kinds of lightweight food. We also had space-age looking sleeping bags that were in tight bundles about the size of a bowling ball. Jeff actually had two of those—we figured the second one must be for Meg. The small side pockets had things like first-aid kits, matches, collapsible drinking cups, and all the cool things that we always tried to talk Dad into buying for us whenever we had a Scout camp-out.

A few minutes later Mr. Omni returned with four canteens that we were expected to carry. He said that Leonard would be carrying a water pump that we could use for purifying water along the way. Jeff and Shauna and I just stared at each other as we realized that we hadn't bothered with purifying water the year before, but it apparently hadn't been a problem.

"Come and eat now," said Mr. Omni. "As soon as the boat stops we'll want to be on our way immediately." As we followed him down to the kitchen, he said, "Vladimir tells me we'll be putting in about thirty minutes from now."

Just as we finished our meal, we felt the boat begin to turn gradually to the left side of the river. We went back up to the boat deck and into the pilot house to see where we were. Everything on shore looked very familiar.

"Are you seeing the mountain passageway that I am talking to you about?" asked Vladimir. He was pointing up at the side of the mountain. Sure enough, there it was. The mountains were high on either side, but there was a thin crack that seemed to cut almost halfway down from the top. We knew from experience that the pathway at the bottom of that crevice would lead us directly to the hills above the tribe's summer home. And it didn't look very far away, either.

"You will be arriving to this place of passage in, I am thinking, perhaps one hour," said Vladimir.

"Perfect," beamed Omni.

"It looks to be a more difficult hike than I expected," said Anthony. I don't know how he could tell, though, the way he covered one eye and squinted with the other. Leonard seemed annoyed by Anthony's complaint, but didn't bother to even look in his direction. He just stood with his arms folded across his chest.

"And how far down the other side do we have to go?" asked Anthony weakly.

"Well, according to the pilot," Mr. Omni answered, "it took less than four hours to climb uphill along with those reindeer sleighs we've heard so much about, so I figure only about three hours down."

"I sure wish I had my glasses," mumbled Anthony.

Mr. Omni smiled at me again, with those gaps in his teeth that were growing larger and creepier each time I saw them. I realized that I was glaring at him. I was glaring because of all the information that these bozos had about the location of the tribe. It made me mad. As I turned away, the boat slowed to a crawl and then came to a complete stop. Mr. Omni and Leonard quickly climbed down to the main deck and jumped to the bank of the river, each holding a rope tied to the yacht.

"You will all be jumping off now," said Vladimir as he pointed at Omni and Leonard.

The only one who had any trouble getting from the boat to the shore was Anthony. He was almost whimpering as he muttered something like, "They ought to make this easier." He had thrown his backpack and another bag onto the bank ahead of him. Meg, on the other hand, had absolutely no trouble climbing down the ladder and jumping to the shore with her backpack in place the whole time. The rest of us kept ours on as well. As Anthony picked up his bags, I noticed he was already winded just from the climb out of the boat.

The next hour was a pain. Not because the hike was difficult, but because of Anthony. His whining continued all the way up to the mountain pass. The trees were thicker close to the river, but within a few minutes they were much more sparse. At first Anthony complained about the trees, but then when they weren't as thick anymore he started acting exasperated about his second bag. Anthony was the only one of us carrying more than a backpack and a canteen. He had the strap from his other bag slung over one shoulder and he would stop every few minutes to adjust the strap or try to attach it to his backpack somehow, only to grunt in frustration and scurry after us again.

"I've got to rest and have a drink," said Anthony halfway up the mountain as he slumped down next to a tree and opened up his canteen. After sloshing some water into his mouth and accidentally down the side of his neck, he added, "It's not that easy carrying two bags."

"Why do you even *have* that bag?" asked Mr. Omni, after taking a drink from his own canteen. We were all drinking large gulps of water, except for Leonard. He just stood, as always, with his arms folded across his chest. "What is in it?" continued Omni. "I had all the supplies we needed distributed among the backpacks."

Anthony's reaction reminded me of a little kid who had gotten caught with his hand in the cookie jar just five minutes after being told to not to eat anything until dinner. His eyes immediately got large and he stared back at Mr. Omni with his lips pressed tightly together. After a moment or two he quickly mumbled, "Never mind," and clumsily moved his backpack on top of his other bag. After another quick drink, Anthony pushed himself to his feet and said, "Well, that's enough rest. Are you all out of shape or something? Let's move." It was a strange thing to say, because as far as I could tell, he was the only one who acted out of breath. Without another word, he climbed slowly ahead of us toward the mountain pass. The rest of us just watched with puzzled looks as he plodded away, his gasping clearly audible.

"There goes a man," said Omni, "who lives by the philosophy that misery is its own reward."

We followed Anthony a minute later, but within a couple of minutes he fell back to the rear of the group of climbers. When we reached the mountain pass, Mr. Omni first checked to be sure that Anthony wasn't too far behind, before deciding to walk through to the other side to rest. Anthony was practically dragging himself up the last part of the climb. Even as far ahead as we were, I could hear him gasping for air so badly I thought I was about to witness my first real heart attack. After the ten-minute walk through the pass on mostly level ground, we all stopped and rested where we could clearly see the quiet valley below. Anthony was nowhere to be seen or heard.

At least ten minutes later, Anthony finally joined us. It took him so long that I figured he must have stopped to rest, but even so, he seemed to be doing only slightly better. His face was covered with sweat and his loud wheezing announced his arrival at least two minutes before we could see him. Without a word, we continued to rest for a while until his breathing seemed to return almost to normal. As we waited, we all stared out over the valley. Things looked different, though. It wasn't as green as I had remembered it. I figured it must just be the changing season. I remembered from the previous year that from this location, the tribe's huts were hidden by the thick trees near the bottom of the mountain. We would be nearly upon them before we would know if they were still there or if they had already left for their winter home.

Omni was right about how long it would take us. The next three hours passed extremely slowly. The closer we got to the bottom of the mountain, the more tense I felt. I kept trying to convince myself that the tribe would surely be gone, but at the same time I had this huge fear growing inside me that wouldn't go away.

We made a single rest stop on the way down the mountain, pausing for just a moment to catch a quick drink of water. This part of the hike was easy. Even Anthony seemed to be doing much better now. That's when Mr. Omni said something that made us all turn and look.

"Where's your other bag?" he asked.

Just as he had before, when Omni asked him about the bag in the first place, Anthony's eyes immediately grew large. He glanced nervously from person to person. We were all staring at him.

"I . . . I," Anthony grunted. "I decided that I didn't . . . uhh . . . didn't really need it after all." He quickly looked away and suddenly became very interested in the hook on his canteen strap.

"So did you just drop it somewhere, or what?" I asked.

Anthony looked extremely annoyed at being questioned. "I can pick it up on the way back," he snarled, returning to his investigation of the canteen strap. He took several small swallows of water and glanced at us again, quickly checking to see if we were still staring. We were.

"What?" said Anthony abruptly in Omni's direction. "Like you said, we already had everything we needed in the backpacks. I . . . I just didn't need it." With that, he stood, hoisted his pack onto his shoulders, and again led the way down the mountain. We all followed, but because he moved so slowly, Anthony was soon in the rear again.

When we emerged from the trees at the bottom of the mountain slope, my heart was practically in my throat. Each breath was short and my face felt hot. I was anxious to see what I *knew* would be an empty meadow, but at the same time, I was scared to death of being wrong. To my complete relief, however, the place was deserted. It looked still and peaceful, almost like no one had been there since the beginning of time. Looking at Shauna and Jeff, I realized that they had probably been feeling exactly as I. We exchanged small grins of relief and took the opportunity to grab another quick drink.

Omni and Anthony, on the other hand, seemed to be quite upset by what we found.

"Where are they?" yelled Anthony at the top of his lungs. He directed his question to no one in particular. His fists were clenched and his face was intense. We could hear the sound of his voice echo back to us a couple of seconds after he yelled.

CHAPTER 6

The Reunion

Anthony turned to Omni and yelled again. "I thought your people had this all figured out."

This was the first time I had seen Omni speak without smiling. He waited until the echo died down. "Believe me," he said softly. "I wouldn't have spent this much money or come this far without being sure of my investment."

"Did they go to their other place already?" asked Anthony in frustration. Then he turned toward us and asked, "Are we in the right place? We are, aren't we?"

None of us responded.

"I sure wish I had my glasses," said Anthony, looking around at the landscape.

"Of course we are," said Omni, "but it's much later in the year now. They surely must have gone back already."

"Okay," said Anthony quickly. "Let's go."

Omni laughed, but he wasn't smiling. "This will take a little more time, Larry. None of the people who talked to us had ever been to the other place, remember?"

"What *I* remember," said Anthony, throwing his pointing finger at Jeff and me, "is that *these* two kids were there." He glared at us. "How about it, boys? Care to exchange a little information for a ride home?"

Jeff and I simply responded with determined stares and closed mouths.

"Well," sighed Mr. Omni, "it's a several-day trip at best, so I suggest we camp here for the night. And while we're resting, we'll give these kids a chance to decide how much they are willing to cooperate." He managed half of a gapped-tooth smile.

I probably should have kept my mouth shut, but I couldn't resist. "What do you want from these people?" I asked. "Why can't you just leave them alone?"

"What do I want?" repeated Anthony with passion. "I want to discover the answers to the greatest mysteries of our time!" His eyes were wild with excitement. "These people—this tribe—oh, the things they could tell us about ourselves and our past!" Then he looked directly at me and asked, "Haven't you ever wanted to solve the world's greatest mysteries?"

I just stared at him. What a nut case. The only mysteries that had occupied *my* mind recently were things like "Who shuts the door on the school bus after the driver gets out?" or "Why do hot dogs come in packages of ten when you can only buy buns in packages of eight?"

No one really said much of anything else to us for the rest of the evening. Leonard's backpack contained two tents that were quickly and easily assembled: one was for the Three Stooges and the other for the four of us. A hot soup was made for dinner, using a small gas burner that Omni carried in his pack. It reminded me of the Bunson burner my science teacher used at school. As the sun moved lower into the northwestern sky, I was surprised at how quickly the air turned cool.

Supper was quickly made and eaten with hardly a word by anyone. Once all had been cleaned up, Shauna asked, "Do you mind if the four of us go to bed now?"

"Go right ahead, Sharon," Mr. Omni replied flatly.

As we turned toward our tent, Anthony said, "Don't think

we're not serious about leaving you here. Going to bed early might give you just the time you need to think about that." We looked at him, but none of us spoke. "I expect *full* cooperation in the morning," he concluded.

We still didn't respond, but climbed silently inside our tent. If we were tired, it wasn't obvious—the choice we had been given sent our minds spinning. It wasn't long, of course, before Meg reminded us to pray, which we did. I was glad that we had been praying together regularly; it seemed to be the only thing that could keep me calm. Though the tent fabric was thin, it was also black, cutting out all of the dim light of the evening. We knew from having been here the previous summer that the sun would be down for at least three or four hours during the night. It had only been down for a couple of hours the night we had left this place the previous year, but that was a month earlier in the season.

Much later, as I lay restlessly in the dark, I kept wondering what the next plan would be. Vladimir wouldn't be back with the boat for two weeks. As I continued to think about everything, I heard a discussion between Anthony and Omni that got louder and louder.

"We have the time and we're going to use it," said Anthony. "There's no point in going back to the river until *Captain Vladimir* returns." He said *Captain Vladimir* like he was sick of the guy.

"We can't force the children to show us the way," said Omni.

"Of course we can," insisted Anthony.

"How can we possibly force them?" asked Omni.

"Are you joking?" said Anthony with disgust. "Use Leonard, you ninny! What's the point in having a body guard if all he does is follow you around all the time and stare into space?"

I couldn't tell if Omni said anything in response or not.

Anthony's next comment was clear enough, however. He said, "I have no doubt that he can get whatever information we need out of them!"

They argued for a few more minutes before agreeing that they would try to "persuade" us in the morning, using whatever means they had available.

I was still unable to sleep quite a while later when Shauna whispered very quietly, "*Jeff!*"

Without a moment's hesitation he whispered back, "Yeah?"

"What would you think about getting out of here?" asked Shauna.

"I was thinking the same thing," he answered.

"All *right!*" I said, probably a little too loud for the circumstances.

"Shhh!" said both Shauna and Jeff at the same time.

"Are we just going to hide out until Vladimir gets back?" I asked.

"That works for me," said Jeff. "We have enough food and other stuff to last long enough."

Shauna agreed and so, after waking Meg, we squished our sleeping bags back into our packs as quickly and quietly as possible and crept out of our tent. The sky was dark, but the moon was bright. Meg was only half awake and so she stumbled a bit, but we quickly moved into the cover of the trees, intent on getting as far away from there as we could before they discovered us missing.

"What do we do now?" asked Jeff.

"We head south," I answered.

None of us had said anything for at least twenty minutes as we made our way through the trees away from the Three Stooges' campsite. We had stayed close to the edge of the meadow, regularly looking back toward the two black tents that were dimly visible in the moonlight. Now we sat huddled in a small semi-circle where we could all watch the tents. Meg had no interest in watching the tents or doing anything other than sleeping. She lay quietly on her back on the ground in front of us. Her body was arched comically over her pink backpack that she was still wearing. Both her arms lay outstretched from her body. Her mouth was partially open with her chin touching one shoulder. I think she was asleep before she even hit the ground. I figured it was entirely possible that she had never actually woken up at all, but just allowed us to direct her as she sleepwalked.

"Don't you think we should go back to the river?" asked Shauna. Before anyone answered, she added, "I do."

"What are we going to do at the river for two weeks?" I asked.

"Watch for boats!" hissed Jeff. "It would be nice to have a ride home, don't you think?"

"But Vladimir won't be back for two weeks!" I said. "I don't want to just sit around for two weeks."

"Vladimir?" questioned Jeff. "Why would we wait for Vladimir? Don't you remember him saying that he just wants to 'dump us somewheres'?" Jeff did his best to copy Vladimir's accent when he said the last three words.

"That's right," agreed Shauna. "And Anthony and Omni didn't seem too interested in helping us get back home, either. If we get back to the river, then we might see a different boat and maybe we can get their attention and get a ride."

"Don't you remember," continued Jeff, "when Levi told us that there were boats going up and down the river pretty often?"

"I don't know what you mean by 'pretty often,'" I said, "but did either of you see any other boats the last two days?" They just stared back at me. "Neither did I."

"Well, what do *you* suggest?" asked Jeff.

"Look," I answered. "Those guys are here to find the tribe. They knew they might have to try to find the tribe's winter home long before we were around. They were already on their way, remember? That means they're going after the tribe with us or without us. I think they just figured things might be a little easier with our help. C'mon, think about it. They had no trouble coming straight here— they even knew how long it would take. I'm sure they also think they know exactly how to get to the winter home."

84

"They knew how to get here because *everyone* was here," said Shauna. "That's not true about the other place. Only you and Jeff and Dad ever went there, right?"

"And Tom," I reminded her. Tom was the one person from the trip the previous summer that we really got to know and like. He hung out with our family most of the time and even joined us for our devotionals. He was amazing. He knew everything about animals and mountains and everything else that came up.

"Did they talk to Tom?" asked Jeff.

"Anthony said they talked to everyone except our family," I reminded them. "So that must mean they talked to Tom, also."

No one said anything for a moment. Finally, shaking her head slowly from side to side, Shauna said, "I just can't believe that Tom would tell them how to get there."

"And even if he *did*," added Jeff. "We all only went there once and it was a four-day trip and half the time it was night." Jeff was now shaking his head from side to side, just like Shauna. "I can't believe they'll be able to get there on their own."

"What about the tracks?" I asked.

"What tracks?" asked Jeff.

"Don't you remember?" I said. "When we came back, there were tracks from the reindeer sled that were way easy to see and to follow—even at night. And those were from a *single* sled. Together they probably have *dozens* of sleds and most of the 300 or 400 hundred people we're talking about would have been walking. Do you really think they won't be able to find the way?"

I had a point and they knew it, but neither of them seemed willing to admit it for a moment. I was sure that we would be able to find their trail with no trouble at all—even in the dim moonlight. I was about to suggest that we go look for ourselves, when Shauna finally said, "Okay, they will probably be able to find their way down there. Fine. But don't you remember how we were received when we first showed up? They were not exactly that excited to see us. We were practically prisoners."

"That was because of Esau," I said. "He's not in charge anymore—Levi is."

"At least we hope so," said Jeff. "We can't know for sure."

"Okay, okay, okay," said Shauna. "I think all we can agree on at this point, Brandon, is that almost anything is possible."

"We also agree that those bozos down there will be able to follow them to their winter home," I corrected her.

"Yes," she conceded, "we agree on that, too. So why do you want to go down there, too? Wouldn't you rather stay as far away from them as possible?"

"If that's all there was to it, then yes," I nodded. "But to answer your first question, I want to go down there for two reasons: first, to warn them and second, to get their help."

"Help with what?" asked Jeff.

"Help with staying protected from those guys," I said as I pointed toward the tents, "and help getting to a boat to take us home." Jeff and Shauna acted like they were thinking about this as I continued by saying, "I'd sort of like the guys with spears on *my* side for once."

Shauna sighed. "It just seems like a really long way to go when we're just going to have to come right back." She paused. "I worry about Meg, too," she added.

We all looked down at Meg, who still lay sprawled, face-up across her backpack.

"Worrying be not necessary," came a voice from the darkness. "Being everything well." This was a voice that we all knew very well, though none of us had heard it for over a year: It was Aaron. In fact, this was the very first thing he had ever said to us in English. When we first met him, he mixed up his sentences, always putting the verb first, but by the time we had left, his English had improved a lot.

"Aaron!" we all said at once as he came close enough for us to see him. We all stood with excitement. Levi, who was Aaron's father and Moses, who was Aaron's friend who lived with them, were both right behind Aaron. It was like a big family reunion. We each gladly hugged those we hadn't seen for so long and asked how each of them had been during the past year. Levi and Aaron looked pretty much the same as I remembered them, but Moses seemed to be significantly bigger than the previous year. He had to be about 17 now. He looked both wider and stronger.

In the year since we had last seen them, I had almost forgotten how they dressed. They each had thick leather shoes that came up well past their ankles. They wore thick woven robes and hats that were mostly brown or dark green in color. They each had a wide, leather belt.

Levi, Aaron, and Moses each called us by name and seemed to still be able to communicate in English without any problem. They had obviously been practicing. Moses, who had not spoken very well or very much the previous summer, seemed now to be much better with English. He probably spoke more in greeting each of us and saying, "I am well," than we had ever heard from him before.

It was such a relief to see them. I immediately felt *so* much safer now that they were with us.

"Where is the rest of the tribe?" asked Shauna.

"How did you find us?" asked Jeff.

"We sitting and speaking and resting," Levi suggested. We sat on the ground encircling Meg, who was completely unaware of anything going on around her. "Tribe making way to home of winter," said Levi.

"We finding ye because of noise of man speaking with much loudness," said Aaron. "Others being also with ye?" he asked.

"Being father and mother from your family also in our land?" asked Levi.

"No," said Shauna with sadness. "It's just us." She indicated the four of us with a small gesture of her arm.

"We hearing voice of man," said Aaron with obvious confusion.

"Yeah," nodded Jeff. Speaking slowly, he added, "There are three men who brought us here."

"But they are not good men," continued Shauna. "They want us to help them find you, but we didn't want them to find you."

"They want something from you," I explained. "We don't know what it is, but they want something."

Levi and Aaron and Moses all listened intently as we spoke. They seemed to understand what we were saying.

"Ye coming to this place for what reason?" asked Levi.

"We didn't mean to," said Shauna. "We were trapped—caught—on their boat on the water, and after they found us, they wouldn't take us back to the United States."

"Three men coming to this place for what reason?" asked Levi.

"They learned about you from the others," I said, shaking my head back and forth. "We didn't tell them about you—our whole *family* didn't tell them about you, but these men spoke with the others who were here."

"And they told them how to get here," continued Jeff. "And they think the whole world should know about you. They said they want to take evidence back with them that tells the world you are really here."

"These men taking *evidence?*" asked Levi. "I knowing not what this be."

"Proof," said Shauna. "A sign, a witness." Levi nodded his understanding.

"They lied to the others," I explained. "They told them they were bringing a lot of salt to you for your sacrifices. Salt to make up for the salt that was ruined—but it was a lie. That's how come the others told them how to find you. But it was not true. They don't want to give you anything, they just want to take something from you."

"Three men taking what evidence from us?" asked Aaron.

We all hesitated. "We don't know," I said. "Not for sure, anyway."

"They talked about maybe taking your ancient writings," confessed Shauna. She paused with her mouth open before slowly adding, "Or maybe even taking a person."

Aaron's and Moses' eyes both grew large at this comment. I knew they had understood.

"We're very sorry," I said. "We escaped from them because we didn't want to help them. They already knew how to get here—to your summer home—so we were happy to see that you had already left for the winter home."

"Three men finding the trail of sleds to winter home," said Levi.

"That's what we were afraid of," I said.

"These tents being resting place of three men?" asked Moses.

I couldn't help smiling a little at the fact that he could now speak English. "Yes," I nodded.

"Did you say that you heard the man shouting?" asked Shauna.

"Yes," answered Levi. "We hearing loud voice at time of evening meal. We seeing from mountain the preparing of tents for sleeping. We coming to this place following lowering of sun."

"Why aren't you with the rest of the tribe?" I asked.

"We preparing for return of tribe following winter," said Levi.

"We preparing the *Path to Jesus Christ*," added Aaron.

We all stared blankly at him, not having a clue what he might be talking about. Levi turned to Aaron and mumbled something we didn't understand. He then turned back to us and said, "We speaking no more of troubles of our tribe." That took us by surprise. What troubles? We all wanted to know, but Levi wouldn't talk about it.

"We leaving this place," said Levi, standing and reaching for Meg. In the most amazing move I've ever witnessed, he slipped her backpack straps from her arms, picked her up and laid her across the back of his own neck in one, smooth motion. Her legs hung over one of his shoulders and her arms over the other. Meg seemed to have not been disturbed in the least in the process. As Levi trudged up the hill, Aaron scooped up the pink backpack and Moses insisted on carrying Shauna's. I would have been happy to give him mine, but I knew full well that men and teenage boys did all the work in this valley. Women, girls, and children were never asked to carry any burden of any kind.

Either I was really tired or their campsite was a lot farther away than I expected. We must have walked for at least an hour. It was mostly uphill, too. I found myself wondering how they could have heard Anthony from so far away. It wasn't until later that I realized there were no other sounds to be heard around here. That fact, along with the shape of the mountains on either side of the valley, probably made it fairly easy for Anthony's shouting to echo as far as it did.

We did talk a little during the hike, but we were all pretty quiet most of the time. We found out that Levi was still the leader of the tribe, for which we were grateful. The lunatic who had been in charge when we first got there wasn't too happy about our being in his land. Levi had been made the new leader right before we left.

Levi, Aaron, and Moses had a single hut set up within the trees part way up the side of the mountain. We were quite a bit farther south now than where the pass went through the mountain to the other side. Their shelter looked something like a teepee made with half a dozen long poles and covered with a thick, dark hide. We had slept in a hut like this the previous summer when the sun never went down all night. The dark hide made it almost pitch black inside. We also knew the size limits of these huts. For a while, our family of eight made it work because we had to, but later we discovered that we were much more comfortable with only four in a single hut. In fact, it was the same four of us, now that I think of it. We tried to tell them that we would be warm enough just using our sleeping bags—something they'd never seen before—but Levi insisted that the seven of us all sleep in the tent.

Shauna and Jeff and I only protested for a moment before smiling and all climbing inside. Meg didn't argue, of course, because she was still unconscious. I wondered if I had slept like that when I was her age. We enjoyed a prayer together with them and, unlike previously, we immediately fell asleep. I know for me, I hadn't felt so relaxed in days. Yeah, we were still more than a thousand miles from home, but we were with friends. And it felt great.

It didn't last long, however. Well, I guess it lasted for a few hours, but I was asleep the whole time, so it didn't seem very long. I was awakened by a sound that I almost could *not* believe was really there. At first I thought it *had* to be a nightmare. But it wasn't. I was indeed hearing a conversation between Dr. Anthony and Mr. Omni just outside the tent.

"Wake up boys and girls," came Anthony's voice. He was practically singing the words. "Time to get u-u-up," he continued. He was obviously feeling very happy with life right about now.

"Come on out, won't you?" said Omni. "We would all like to meet your friends."

We stumbled to our feet and out into the blinding light. The tribe had a tradition of always facing their tent doors to the east, making the flap-opening time in the morning especially painful.

"How did you find us?" I croaked.

"Ever hear of a homing device?" asked Omni through a gapped smile. "Every millionaire should have one." He laughed slightly and then corrected himself, "Or perhaps I should say 'every backpack loaned out by a millionaire should have one.'"

"What's a homing device?" asked Meg.

"Ah, Melanie," said Omni. "I'm happy to explain. It's a little electronic device that sends out a signal that no one can hear. All I have to do is look at this little receiver in my hand here and I always know exactly where each of these backpacks is."

CHAPTER 7

Types and Shadows

"No way," I said, shielding my eyes from the sun. I shivered in the cool morning air and pulled my coat tighter around me, zipping it all the way to my neck. I figured the sun had been up for at least a couple of hours. Because it made almost a complete circle, passing through the east, south, and west each day, it was still low on the eastern horizon.

"Please introduce us to your friends," said Mr. Omni.

Leonard was standing behind him as always. Anthony was also slightly behind. He had inched farther back when Moses had emerged from the tent carrying a long knife. Apparently he could see well enough to recognize a weapon when he saw one. Levi immediately said something to Moses which caused him to drop the angle of the knife somewhat, but his fist was still clenched tightly around the handle.

Levi introduced himself. "I being Levi," he said. "This being Aaron. Aaron being my son. This," said Levi, turning to Moses, "being Moses. Moses being son by adoption." Levi paused after speaking and stared down at the knife still clearly visible in Moses' hand. Moses didn't do anything for a moment, but then slowly he moved the knife to his other hand, holding it by the back of the blade instead of the handle. Levi seemed satisfied with this and turned to face the Three Stooges again.

Anthony was still halfway hidden as Omni spoke to Levi. "I am

Mr. Russell Omni, Esquire," he said, carefully pronouncing each word. *Moe*, I thought. "This is my colleague, Dr. Lawrence Anthony," he said, moving to the side so that Anthony was in full view. Anthony's eyes widened a bit, and he stepped back half a step more. Gesturing to his bodyguard, Omni said, "And this is my associate, Leonard." Jeff and I looked sideways at each other in response to the word *associate*. Turning back to Levi, Omni extended his hand and added, "It is an honor to meet you, Levi."

I was shocked that he got Levi's name right. As far as we could remember, he had yet to get any of *our* names right even once, let alone the first time. Levi understood the idea of shaking hands, so he stepped forward and grabbed Omni's hand for a moment. Omni seemed surprised by the strength of Levi's grip. Levi then momentarily grabbed Anthony's hand, followed by Leonard's. I wasn't sure whether Leonard would be willing to unfold his arms long enough to shake Levi's hand or not. Aaron and Moses each followed Levi's example and briefly squeezed each person's hand. Anthony was staring at the long knife in Moses' other hand.

Levi mumbled something to Moses that Moses seemed a little unsure of, but after a brief hesitation, Moses stepped inside the shelter just long enough to deposit the knife. When he came into view again, Anthony seemed to be feeling much better about his personal safety.

"We have heard so very much about you," said Omni with his trademark smile. "It is wonderful to actually be able to finally meet you."

"Ye coming to this place for what reason?" asked Levi.

"For you," said Anthony. "I . . . I mean to *meet* you and to *learn* about you." Levi just looked at him. "There are people like myself in the world—perhaps tens of thousands of us—that spend our lives studying and learning about those who have lived in the past. I'm an historian, and you and your people are part of history. When I learned of your existence, I simply could not deny the great urgency

I felt to find you and learn all about you. I believe we can learn much from each other that will benefit us both—as well as the rest of the world."

"We desiring not for knowledge of rest of world," said Levi. "I desiring not for providing knowledge from us to rest of world."

"Oh-h-h," breathed Anthony with passion, "but you have no *idea* what the world has to offer! It's a beautiful world with many advances in medicine and science and music. It's a world of comforts and pleasures and learning and knowledge."

Wow, I thought. This is the Anthony that I remembered from when he was trying to talk my Aunt Ella out of her original edition Book of Mormon. He certainly knew how to turn on the charm when he wanted to. For me, though, it didn't really work. Combined with his long, stringy hair, his oily personality made him seem all the more slimy.

"We having already some knowledge of these things," said Levi. "We having also knowledge of many wars and of wickedness and of selfishness of peoples of the world."

"Well," said Anthony, still using his silky voice, "there is good and bad *every*where!"

"This being true," admitted Levi. "Each place having measure of good which is being matched by measure of evil." He paused before adding, "We having perhaps less many comforts and knowledge, but we also having less many wickedness and wars."

"Yes! Yes, of course this is true and you are very wise," said Anthony with excitement. "So if you are not interested in what the world can offer you, then will you consider offering to the world this great wisdom that you have just shared with me? May I study you and your people? May I return and report to the people of the world the great benefit that has come to you because of your simple and sheltered lives here?"

I was getting nauseous again. Why did that happen whenever Anthony got any significant amount of talking time?

"We will be returning to our home in two weeks," continued Anthony, "that's just fourteen days. May we stay with you and speak with you and learn from you during this time?"

Levi hesitated for a long time before answering. We had made it clear that these guys were up to no good—I knew he knew they were bad men. That's probably why I was so shocked by his answer.

"Ye remaining with us for these fourteen days," said Levi. "Ye coming with us to winter home."

"Wait, *what?*" said Shauna.

"Are you sure?" asked Jeff.

"Why?" I asked in total disbelief. Then out of the corner of my mouth I whispered, "*These* are the *guys* we were *telling* you about."

"I understanding this," Levi assured me. "Everything being well. We being waited—" he began. "We being expected at winter home five days after this day. We leaving this day."

"Wonderful!" beamed Omni. He raised one hand and seemed to be silently counting on his fingers. "That will give us plenty of time to make the round trip and even spend a couple of days with your people at your winter home."

"Thank you *very* much for the invitation," agreed Anthony. "And will you bring us back, also, to this valley so that we don't get lost?"

"Yes," said Levi.

Shauna, Jeff, and I just stared at Levi in amazement.

"Everything being well," Levi said to us again. He obviously didn't want to hear anything more about it.

We agreed to eat breakfast and be on our way as soon as possible. Anthony, Omni, and Leonard pulled out their little gas burner and heated some water for oatmeal or something like it. The rest of us preferred to eat with Levi's family. They made a quick fire and cooked small cakes on the hot rocks. They were delicious. I remembered liking them a lot, but this morning they seemed better than ever. As was their custom, Levi made plenty of extra so that we could have some cold for our midday meal.

Levi had a reindeer sled stashed in the trees not too far from their tent. Moses and Aaron retrieved their four reindeer and harnessed them with leather straps in two pairs to the front of the sled, while we stayed behind to help Levi get everything else ready. Mr. Omni informed us that he was not interested in cleaning up after us anymore, so we would be responsible for carrying our own tent from now on. Shauna put it in her backpack.

Jeff and I had gotten pretty good at disassembling the huts the year before, but you never would have known it to watch us this time. The animal hide that covered the tent poles was held in place by pinching it between two poles that were right next to each other on one side of the tent doorway. You were supposed to just lift one of the poles away from the other to get the hide to release and fall to the ground in a spiral motion around the base of the poles. For some reason we just couldn't make it work and ended up just pulling the hide down by grabbing on tight and bouncing with all our weight. Levi gave us a very strange look when we did it, but it worked.

The hide was spread out on the ground and the tent poles were laid across and rolled up inside of it. We put the tent bundle on the sled when Aaron and Moses returned with it. The sled also had quite a supply of food and water as well as a couple dozen birds in small cages of various shapes and sizes made from tree branches.

"What are the birds for?" I asked. "You don't use them for sacrifices anymore, do you?"

"No," said Levi quickly, "we being still your brethren in the Lord—Jesus Christ."

I did a double take when he said that because it sounded just like one of my favorite scriptures. It had become one of my favorites when Aunt Ella first gave me her old Book of Mormon. I noticed that Levi's words caught Shauna's and Jeff's attention, too.

"You're quoting Alma chapter 17 verse 2," I smiled, remembering that we had left our scriptures for them the year before. I had given mine to Moses. Jeff gave his to Levi and Aaron had Shauna's copy.

"This being correct," smiled Levi in return. I was surprised because he rarely smiled. "Jeff and Brandon and Shauna making important words covered with color of red," Levi said.

"Oh, that's right!" Jeff said. "You have our old copies of the Book of Mormon. They were probably *full* of markings—red markings."

"Yes," said Levi. He bowed slightly with his eyes on the ground and his hands open toward us. "We thanking family of Jeff and Brandon and Shauna and Meg for these kind and generous gifts."

"You're welcome," we all said.

It turned out that all three of them actually had the scriptures there with them. I was amazed at how worn they had become in just one year. They had been well-used.

"We're happy that they have been useful for you," added Shauna.

"How much of it have you read?" I asked.

"We reading all one time," said Levi. "We reading many times The Book of Mormon—Another Testament of Jesus Christ."

"Many times?" asked Jeff. "It's only been a year."

"We finding much teaching about Messiah in The Book of Mormon—Another Testament of Jesus Christ."

Levi was starting to remind me of Jeff's seminary teacher, the way he kept using the full name of the Book of Mormon.

"Yes," said Shauna. "It's my favorite book of scripture, too."

At this point the sled was loaded and ready to go. Levi had insisted that everyone put their backpack on the sled instead of carrying them. Levi led us in a kneeling prayer, requesting safety and speed for our journey, and then we left for their winter home. Of course, Shauna and Meg were invited to ride on the sled while the rest of us walked.

"Can I lay down?" Meg asked Aaron when he hoisted her onto the sled.

"You sleeping now," answered Aaron.

Aaron and Moses and Levi walked along the sides of the reindeer, gently guiding them down the slope. Jeff and I walked behind them, next to the second row of reindeer. Shauna sat near the front of the sled where she could easily hear our conversation. I figured she sat there partly so she wouldn't have to be so close to the Three Stooges who were bringing up the rear.

"So if you aren't doing burnt offerings anymore," I said, "then what are all the birds for?"

"We *eating* birds," said Levi, as if there couldn't possibly be any other reason.

Jeff laughed at me when Levi said this. "Well, I didn't know," I complained. I looked back at Shauna, who had the same look on her face that Jeff did.

"Did you think they might be pets?" asked Jeff with a huge smile. I ignored him.

"Does anyone do burnt offerings anymore?" I asked.

"Esau yet performing burnt offerings with sons and with two other families," said Levi.

Esau was the one who had been the leader of the tribe when they first found us. Apparently, there were four groups, each with their own leader, but one of them was also the leader over everyone in the tribe. The other three leaders decided that this guy wasn't following the Law of Moses in the way he was treating us and they really demoted him big-time because of it. There may have been some other reasons, too. They were calling him Jacob at the time, but in keeping with their tradition, they changed his name along with changing his position in the tribe.

"Is Esau the leader of these families?" asked Shauna.

"Yes," answered Levi. "Esau leader of all who believe not in Messiah Jesus Christ."

I wanted to ask something else, but I didn't want the Three Stooges to hear. As carefully as I could, I slowly glanced backwards over my shoulder to see what they were up to. Anthony had already fallen quite a distance back from the group, while Mr. Omni and Leonard seemed to each be lost in their own little daydreams. They were looking around at all the trees and plants, apparently completely oblivious to us and our conversation.

This seemed like as good a time as any, so I asked Aaron, "What troubles are you having?"

"Sky bringing rain and snow to us not many times," answered Aaron. "We searching for Living Water."

"Oh," said Shauna, "this is what we call a drought."

Aaron nodded his understanding.

"We walking with silence now," said Levi.

We all immediately understood that there was to be no more talking. What wasn't clear to me was whether this was a place on the trail where Levi just wanted to be able to listen for animals or something, or whether Levi just didn't want us "talking about their troubles" anymore.

About midmorning we stopped to rest for a few minutes and to fill any water bags and canteens that were partially empty. Leonard pulled out the small hand-powered water pump to use for filling his and Omni's canteens. Mr. Omni pulled out something, too, but I had no idea what it was for. It looked sort of like a cell phone. Omni looked at it for a moment and then carefully wrote something in a small notebook. Did he really think he could get phone service out in the middle of nowhere? Whatever.

We were almost ready to leave again by the time Anthony finally showed up. Levi suggested that he ride on the reindeer sled. If Anthony had had any breath left at all, I'm sure he would have thanked Levi from the bottom of his heart. As it was, his expression said it clearly enough and he simply flopped onto the sled next to the tent bundle. I would have thought his pride would have kept him from taking Levi's suggestion, knowing that only girls and women usually got to ride, but I guess for some people, self-preservation is a stronger motivation than pride.

When Meg woke up some time later, she was not too excited to be sharing the sled with Dr. Anthony, even if he was several feet away. By this time he was sitting up, glancing lazily around at the trees and the mountains—with one eye covered and the other one squinting, of course. I just shook my head. Meg decided she would rather be someplace else and so she and Shauna both jumped off and walked with us for the rest of the morning. Meg looked tired when we stopped for lunch, but—unlike Anthony—she had no trouble keeping up. She even managed to ask a few questions as we walked. I didn't catch her coming up with any answers, though.

Unfortunately, by the time we stopped for lunch Anthony was back to his old self: creepy and a serious pain. While everyone else was resting and eating lunch, Anthony was moving back and forth between the two groups and jabbering away the whole time about nothing worth mentioning. Omni and Leonard made up one of the groups, obviously, and the rest of us were the other. We kept hoping that Anthony would just stay with the other two.

At one point Anthony asked, "So why are you three *braves* not with the rest of your tribal brothers? Or I guess one chief and *two* braves, right?"

What a fruitcake he was. I gave Anthony a disgusted look and said, "They're not *Indians*."

"I wasn't talking to you," he snarled.

"We preparing for return of tribe," answered Levi.

"When?" asked Anthony. "Next summer?"

"Yes," said Levi. "We making preparations for next summer."

Anthony got this goofy look on his face. "But wait," he said. "I thought you were the leader of this tribe." Levi just stared at him. "What kind of chief gets left behind on KP duty," said Anthony, "when everyone else takes off for home?" Anthony laughed at his own words.

"I being leader who believing teachings of Jesus Christ," Levi said slowly. Anthony seemed a little surprised by his response. Levi then said, "Jesus Christ teaching 'so the last shall be first, and the first last.'"

"I . . . I knew that," said Anthony after a moment.

"Leader being servant of all," Levi said. Then he asked, "Anthony believing in Messiah Jesus Christ?"

"Of course," Anthony said quickly. He was acting embarrassed now and his face was red. All of a sudden he ran out of things to say, so he went and joined the Bunson Burner boys for the rest of lunch time. What a relief.

The next day and a half went pretty much the same way. Levi regularly informed us it was time to "walk with silence." When we took time to rest, Aaron would tell us some of his favorite parts from the Book of Mormon. I was starting to get the impression that he knew the book better than I did.

The first evening, we traveled again for quite a while after eating dinner, before stopping and setting up tents. We four kids used the extra tent that the Stooges brought with them. The second night Levi announced that this was the Sabbath and that we wouldn't be traveling anymore that evening or the next day. Mr. Omni was furious at the news.

"*What?*" he exploded. "You want us all to just sit around for an entire *day?* And I suppose you'll expect the same on the way back, right? If we add an extra day each direction to the five days you already told us, then we've got a twelve-day round trip. That only gives a single day to get back to the river and *no* days to spend at your little winter camp, right? We've got a tight schedule here, you know. Our boat captain, Vladimir, isn't the type to just sit around waiting for us. He'll take off! I refuse to allow him to abandon me!" Omni paused to draw a huge breath. "Now," he continued, a little more slowly, "if you're prepared to spend zero time at this winter home of yours, then this will all work. Otherwise, I'd say we have the proverbial ox in the mire, here, wouldn't you? That's a teaching of Jesus, isn't it? Jesus would say that it's okay to travel on Sunday when your ox is in the mire, right? So tell me. What's it going to be?"

Levi just waited patiently until Omni was done. He already knew how to deal with a bozo like this, because Omni was acting exactly like Esau. When it was obvious that Levi would finally have a chance to respond, he said, "We traveling two days and we resting for Sabbath and we traveling two days more to winter home."

"Wait," said Omni. "You're telling me that it only takes four traveling days to get there? You are *not* trying to con me, are you? Because I know from some of your visitors from last year that it takes longer than that to get down there. You cannot fool me."

Levi sighed patiently as he explained, "We traveling six days with all people from village. Old men walking slowly. Young children also walking slowly. We traveling six days." He gestured to all of us standing around and said, "We traveling four days with those who are not much old and not much young."

Omni smirked a little as he considered this. "Okay," he said finally, "I don't especially like the idea of just sitting around tomorrow, but we'll do it your way for now. On the way back, however, if *I* say the ox is in the mire, then we are not going to be sitting around all day just watching the clock tick by."

Levi just stared at him. I don't know what Omni expected. It's not like Levi was his "associate" or something that he could just boss around. Omni acted like he was in charge of everyone and everything. *That guy has spent way too much time sun tanning in sub-zero weather,* I thought. Whatever. Levi seemed to agree with me. He just waited until Omni went away.

Sunday was a great day. This part of the world was a day ahead of us because we had crossed the international date line, so it was still Saturday in the United States. Aaron took the time to show us his translation of the Book of Mormon that he had been working on during the winter. He only had about a third of it done. Levi and Moses had been helping, too. That probably explains why their English was so good even after a year of not having any native English speakers around. They were translating it so the rest of the tribe could read it for themselves.

We spent a lot of time during the Sabbath talking with Aaron and Levi and Moses about the Book of Mormon. They were really into types and shadows of Christ. It reminded me of the time that we watched for types and shadows of Christ when we were reading the Book of Mormon for family devotionals.

In our family, we would read the whole Book of Mormon out loud together pretty much every year. But each time we started it again, Dad had some idea of what we could be watching for this time through. One year it was names for Jesus Christ—there were like *eighty!* Another time we looked for types and shadows of Christ. I didn't even know what Dad was talking about when he first suggested it, until he explained to us that a type or shadow was something that represented Christ.

We came up with quite a list that year with our family, but the four of us seemed to be having trouble remembering very many of them when we got into the discussion that day. Aaron liked Abinadi a lot. He liked how Abinadi refused to let the wicked priests kill him until he had delivered his message, but after that it didn't matter. Aaron said that was a type of Christ.

Moses said his favorite type of Christ was the serpent on the staff that Moses (from the Old Testament) had used to heal the people who were bitten by snakes.

Levi really liked the Liahona as a type of Christ. Levi said Alma was right when he asked his son, Helaman, "Is there not a type in this thing?" Levi also pointed out to us that the word *Liahona* only shows up one time in the whole Book of Mormon. I couldn't believe it, so I looked up *Liahona* in the index. There were quite a few references listed, but Levi was right. Alma used the word "Liahona" when he was talking to Helaman, but every other place just calls it the "ball" or "director."

Shauna said, "Brother Parker, my seminary teacher last year, told us that the Book of Mormon itself is a type of Christ."

I stared blankly at her. Nobody else said anything, either. I finally blurted out, "How?"

"Because," she beamed, "the plates came out of a stone box in the ground just like Jesus came out of the stone sepulcher when He was resurrected. And the plates contain the word of God, just like Jesus is the Word. And . . . and . . . I know he told us like six other things, too, but I can't remember them all."

Jeff and I just stared in amazement. Finally Jeff breathed, "Oh, that's cool!"

"Oh, yeah!" continued Shauna. "Christ had twelve apostles to be witnesses for him and there were twelve witnesses of the Book of Mormon!"

"Twelve?" I asked. "I thought there were just three!"

"There were three," Jeff corrected me, "and then there were eight others—but that's still only eleven."

"Plus Joseph Smith," smiled Shauna. "That makes twelve."

We all thought that was pretty cool. For the rest of the afternoon I kept pestering her for what the other things were, but she couldn't think of anymore. She finally promised me she'd find the list when we got home. Mentioning home made us all quiet for a while.

Late in the afternoon, Levi, Aaron, and Moses prepared bread and juice for us to take as the sacrament. They asked Jeff and me if we wanted to perform the ordinance. They reminded us that they didn't have authority and they believed that we did. The previous year we had explained to them how the priesthood was restored to Joseph Smith and passed on until we got it. Jeff explained that we had to have permission before we could do it and so they should just go ahead like they usually did. It was really cool to be a part of their ceremony.

The only thing that was hard about that Sabbath day was the fact that Meg seemed to really be missing Mom and Dad. We tried to keep her mind occupied, but there was only so much we could do given the circumstances we were in.

When we went to bed, I was exhausted and fell right to sleep. Sometime much later, though, I was awakened by a conversation between Anthony and Omni that filtered through the thin tent fabric. I figured they were still in their tent, but we were quite close together. Their voices kept growing louder.

"I didn't say they have *no* value," hissed Anthony.

"That's what it sounded like," said Omni.

"I just said," continued Anthony, "that the only writings the boy has with him now are a translation of the Book of Mormon."

"What's wrong with that?" asked Omni, obviously growing more and more irritated. "It will show their language, and you will have the translation!"

"Yes," agreed Anthony wearily, "having a translation to an unknown language has value. I'm not arguing that! But I'm convinced that they must have writings of some of the lost books mentioned in the Old Testament! Now that would be *really* valuable! I want as much as I can get!"

Omni said something that was too quiet for me to understand.

Still sounding a little frustrated, Anthony said loudly, "We've *got* to get his other writings, too."

"We?" asked Omni, suddenly loud again. I got the impression he wanted to just be done with this conversation. "Don't say *we*, say *you*. That's your problem, Larry. I've got my own evidence gathering to worry about."

"Well, just remember that if I can't manage to get hold of any writings, then I just might need Leonard's help," said Anthony, still irritated, "and we both know that Leonard won't do a thing to help me unless you tell him to."

"Help with *what?*" asked Omni.

"*Living* proof!" said Anthony, as if it should be obvious to anyone with half a brain.

CHAPTER 8

Honor among Thieves

I could hardly sleep the rest of the night. This was the second time Anthony had implied that kidnapping was one of his options. I had to tell somebody as soon as possible—not because we could do anything about it right away, but just because we had to decide how we were going to make sure it didn't happen. But I didn't think Jeff or Shauna would appreciate being awakened in the middle of the night. We had two more long days of hiking, and so I decided I had better let them sleep as long as possible.

My mind was churning so fast, it was hard not to wake them up, though. At first I was afraid that my tossing and turning might accidentally wake them. Then, once I realized that waking them was *exactly* what I wanted, I got frustrated when my tossing and turning didn't seem to have any affect on them at all.

"*Jeff!*" I hissed in the darkness. "Are you awake?"

No reply.

"*Shauna!*" I said as loud as I dared, knowing that the Three Stooges were close enough to hear almost anything if they were awake, too. No answer from her, either. There wasn't even a change in the rhythm of their breathing. I heaved a heavy sigh (which also went unnoticed) and lay staring up into the darkness a little while longer.

I repeated my vain attempts at getting somebody's—anybody's—attention every half hour or so. By the second or third time

I called their names, I noticed the color of the tent fabric gradually growing lighter in the early morning sun. It was quite a while later, however, before there was enough light to actually begin seeing anything inside the tent.

By the time it was two or three hours after I first tried to get their attention, I was starting to get really impatient. I hissed Jeff's name and then Shauna's name, this time much louder than any of the other times. Finally, I got some response.

"Why do you keep doing that?" asked Meg without moving.

"How long have you been awake?" I asked.

"Didn't you know that I heard you say Jeff's name and Shauna's name *five* times?" she asked.

"No, I didn't," I said. "I just wish they would wake up."

"Why?" asked Meg.

"Because I want to tell them something," I said. I knew full well that this wouldn't satisfy her—but I was willing to hope.

"Tell them what?" she asked.

"Just something," I said. "It doesn't matter."

She was quiet for a moment before asking, "Brandon, do you know that Mr. Anthony wants to take Aaron's writings away from him?"

"How do you know that?" I asked.

"Didn't you hear him talking to Mr. Omni?" she asked.

"Yes, I did," I said, "but I didn't know that *you* heard it."

She was quiet again for a minute before asking, "Do you think that Mom and Dad are looking for us?"

"Yes," I said. "I know they are doing everything they can to find us."

"Do you think they miss us?" she asked.

"I'm sure they're frantic about us," I answered.

"What's frantic?" asked Meg.

"Really worried," I said.

Meg was quiet for a moment or two before asking, "Are we going to go back to the motel on Mr. Omni's boat?"

"I'm not sure," I admitted, "but we're getting back there somehow. If these guys won't take us back, then Levi will help us find someone who will."

"Are you sure?" asked Meg.

"Yes, I'm sure," I said. "You don't need to worry about it at all."

"She doesn't need to worry about what?" asked Jeff with a yawn.

"Finally!" I hissed. "You've been sleeping forever!"

"I've been awake for a while," mumbled Jeff.

"*What?*" I breathed. "You're joking, right? I've been trying to get your attention for hours." Jeff didn't respond. Still trying to whisper in spite of my frustration, I said, "And if you had been awake, then you wouldn't have had to ask me what Meg and I were talking about, now would you?"

Jeff smacked his mouth and sniffed a couple of times. "Whatever," he mumbled.

"I need to talk to you and Shauna," I whispered. "I heard Anthony and Omni arguing last night."

"I heard it, too," said Shauna.

"*What?*" I said. "You heard what?"

"I heard Anthony say," yawned Shauna, "that he wants all of Aaron's writings and that maybe he'll need Leonard's help to kidnap somebody."

"Why didn't you say anything?" I hissed.

"Because I thought everyone else was asleep, and I figured it could wait till morning," Shauna yawned again.

"I heard that, too," Jeff said. "And I figured the same thing."

My eyes narrowed as I whispered to Jeff, "You did not!" I wanted it to be obvious that I didn't believe him for a minute.

"Yes, I did," Jeff said in a tired voice. "Omni told Anthony that it was *his* problem and that he was worrying about getting his own evidence, right?"

109

"And you didn't say anything?" I asked. "Why not?" I couldn't believe what I was hearing.

"I told you I didn't think anyone else was awake," Jeff said.

"Well I'm about as awake as I can get," I said, "and I'm going to tell Aaron and Levi." I quickly kicked my way out of my sleeping bag and pulled on my coat. I noticed that it still had some powdered sugar patches on it, which annoyed me even more at the moment. When I got out of the tent, I found Levi, Aaron, and Moses all sitting around a small fire some distance from the tents. They were preparing cakes for breakfast. I took the opportunity right then to tell them what I had overhead—what apparently *all* of us had overheard. Shauna, Jeff, and Meg all came out and joined us as I was repeating what I remembered from Omni's and Anthony's conversation. Jeff and Shauna helped.

"The last thing we heard," said Shauna, "was that they might use Leonard to get some 'living proof' of your existence."

Levi thought for a moment before asking, "What being living proof?"

"I think it means they want to take a person back with them," I said.

"And another time," added Jeff, "before we got here, we heard Anthony say that he would like to have some evidence that 'speaks for itself.' When he first said it, I thought right then that he meant somebody from your tribe."

"I thinking no person from tribe wanting to be going to United States America," said Levi.

"Well, I think they're talking about forcing somebody to go," I said. "It's called kidnapping."

No one said anything for a moment until Meg asked, "But didn't you say that Aaron might be going away someday . . . to help you?"

Levi just looked thoughtfully at her. Then she added, "Isn't that why at first his name was Joseph?"

Shauna, Jeff, and I all seemed to lean in a little closer as we waited for Levi's response. This was something that we had all talked and thought a lot about in the year since we had last seen them. Levi seemed to really be thinking hard about it. Actually, I had been convinced that Aaron was coming with us last time, but it didn't work out. I got the impression from Levi's reaction that he was seriously considering it.

Finally, he began shaking his head back and forth ever so slightly. He heaved a small sigh and said, "I believing now is not time for Aaron leaving."

I didn't realize what Aaron must be thinking about this discussion until I saw his reaction to Levi's words: he looked completely relieved. And grateful.

"Aaron performing still many . . . important works for our people in this land," said Levi. "Aaron translating still words from The Book of Mormon—Another Testament of Jesus Christ. Aaron copying still words from ancient prophets."

The cakes were ready to be eaten now, and so Levi offered a prayer to begin our meal. It tasted as good as ever.

"Well," I said between bites that practically burned my tongue, "just remember that Anthony definitely wants your writings. He just talks about kidnapping someone as another option if he can't get your writings."

"Or as an extra bonus," Jeff corrected me. "He'll take both, if he can get them." Aaron and Levi looked at each other. They seemed to understand.

A few minutes later as we were finishing our meal, Anthony came out of the Stooges' tent, stopping just outside the flap for a huge stretch and yawn. He spotted us and shuffled in our direction. He seemed tired and sore. Aaron immediately took advantage of the opportunity. He said something to his father that we didn't understand. Levi gave him a short reply that seemed to be exactly what Aaron was looking for. As Anthony continued to approach us, Aaron stood and met him face to face about ten feet from our dying fire.

"You wanting my writings for what reason?" asked Aaron.

Anthony was stunned by the question. He tried to force a smile several times, but he just didn't seem to be able to keep it on his face. Then he looked nervously at the rest of us before looking back at Aaron.

"Whatever do you mean, young man?" asked Anthony. He was trying the charm approach again. I felt a case of nausea coming on.

"I hearing from my friends you wanting my writings," said Aaron. "I writing many years the writings of prophets. I preparing writings for myself and for my family following me. You wanting my writings for what reason?"

Anthony knew he couldn't deny it. He stole a glance in our direction again, but this time his scowl clearly said that he intended to make us pay for what we had done. He tried one more time to force a smile as his gaze returned to Aaron.

"I understand the great value your writings are to you," Anthony said, trying to schmooze once more. "I would never *dream* of taking them from you without your permission."

"You wanting my writings for light purposes or for dark purposes?" asked Aaron.

Anthony seemed completely confused by the question. He had absolutely no idea what Aaron was asking. "W-what do you . . . ," Anthony began. Finally he said, "*Excuse* me?"

"You are studying ancient peoples, but you are not studying writings of prophets?" asked Aaron.

Anthony just stood with a blank stare for a moment before finally saying, "Scriptures?" He paused for another moment before continuing. "Oh, yes, I've studied the scriptures! Just ask your friends here. I've spent time at . . . at their aunt's home studying a copy of the Book of Mormon. Just ask them!"

I couldn't believe it! He was actually trying to use us as

references for his spirituality! What a joke! But none of us got the chance to explain that he was really just trying to get inside the house long enough to steal the book.

"Light being truth and goodness and righteousness," explained Aaron. Anthony opened his mouth to say something, but Aaron continued before he got the chance.

"Light being from God for blessing of children of God," he said. Anthony drew a breath, but again he hesitated too long and so Aaron continued. He said, "Dark seeking for riches of world and power."

I think Anthony was surprised by how close *that* remark hit to home, because he didn't even start to open his mouth. "Before ye seek for riches, seek ye for kingdom of God," Aaron said. Jeff and Shauna immediately exchanged a knowing look.

"Scripture mastery," whispered Shauna. Jeff nodded. I learned later that "Scripture Mastery" is what they call the twenty-five scriptures that students are supposed to learn each year in seminary.

Anthony finally got himself together enough to respond. He began with the best smile he could muster. "I intended to talk with you some time later about the great benefit that your pages could be to the rest of the world," Anthony said. "The world longs for examples of men and nations that are true to the principles God has given to all men through ancient prophets." Anthony drew a deep breath. "I believe," he said, putting his hand to his chest, "deep in my heart, that these writings of yours could be the means of many people forsaking their wicked ways and returning to the true God of Israel! Returning to lives of purity and spirituality and hope and charity."

Yep. I was right: I instantly had a case of full-blown nausea. I even felt my cheeks expand slightly as I tried to hold it down. This guy was getting slimier by the minute. Thankfully, Aaron was not the least bit convinced. He just stared at Anthony for a moment and then simply said, "My writings remaining with me for blessing of my family." Aaron ended the conversation by saying, "I thanking you," and then immediately walked away to begin taking down his father's tent.

It was obvious that Anthony wasn't pleased, but I could tell that some evil plot was still trying to come together somewhere inside his little brain.

"Preparing we now for travel," announced Levi. "Everyone rising now," he said to Anthony.

Anthony understood what Levi wanted. He went back to his tent and woke up Mr. Omni and Leonard. Anthony continued to act pretty grouchy the rest of the morning, even though he was still the only one who rode the whole time. The next two days of walking were pretty much like the first two. We were silent most of the time and stopped only for short breaks. It was getting pretty tiring.

Each time we stopped I noticed that Omni pulled the same gadget from his backpack and would write something in his small notebook. I asked him once if it was a cell phone, but he just smiled and said, "I'm just taking care of business, Brett."

I'm sure he did that just to annoy us. I had noticed that he seemed to have the ability to *always* get Levi's name right. He never spoke to Aaron or Moses and though he spoke to the rest of us, he had yet to call any of us by the correct name.

We arrived at the winter home in the early evening on the second day after the Sabbath, just as the tribe was preparing for supper. We were all exhausted, but it was great to finally arrive. We had learned the year before that the tribe's winter home was a huge cave with many large caverns and passageways. Because it was still so warm, they weren't sleeping in the caverns yet and had dozens of tents set up in the meadow just down the slope from the mouth of the cave. It reminded me of how the summer home had looked when we first came to it.

We were greeted by many people from the tribe as we arrived. Nawni came immediately to embrace Levi and Aaron and Moses.

Then she turned her attention to Shauna and Meg, who managed to produce a few simple words in the tribe's language—enough to carry on a conversation for about fourteen seconds with someone who knew not a single word of English. But it didn't seem to make a bit of difference. Nawni whisked the two of them away to get cleaned up and ready for dinner. They were all smiles.

Several young men came and took care of the reindeer sled for Levi. The looks on the faces of most of the tribe members ranged from surprise to, perhaps, a little uncertainty at seeing us again. Especially since we had three strangers with us. But the face of every tribe member immediately switched to something like dismay at the sound of Esau's voice. He sounded just as he did the first time we met him. He was yelling loudly and gesturing wildly as he approached. Obviously, we couldn't understand a word of it, but we got the general idea from the way he was looking and pointing at us as he yelled in Levi's face. Esau also gestured violently toward the Three Stooges.

Levi waited for a pause and then responded calmly. This was repeated several times before Levi finally spoke very firmly to Esau, who then abruptly stormed away in obvious anger. Esau looked at us with complete disgust and hatred in his eyes.

"You said that he's not in charge anymore, right?" said Jeff to Aaron once Esau was out of hearing range and everyone seemed to relax a little.

"Yes," answered Aaron.

"Whoa," said Anthony with huge eyes and sunken cheeks. He came closer to us to get a little more information. "What was *that* all about?"

Aaron and Levi just looked at each other. Several others from the village stood silently watching what was going on.

"Esau wanting us to be killing you all," said Aaron. "Esau saying it is past time for killing you." Anthony's eyes got even bigger. Even Omni looked a little uneasy.

115

"Past time? What does *that* mean?" asked Jeff. "That he thought you should have done it last summer?"

"Yes," answered Levi.

"So what did you say to him?" I asked.

"I saying our people not murdering strangers," said Levi.

"That's a relief," said Omni. "I'm glad you're the one in charge and not him."

"Esau wanting to be leader once more," said Moses.

"Yes," agreed Levi.

"What did he say?" I asked.

"Esau saying tribe needing strong leader," said Levi. "Leader protecting us from danger and leader killing enemies of tribe."

"It sounds like this guy wants his old job back," said Omni.

"Yes," answered Levi thoughtfully.

"So where did he go?" I asked.

"Soon being time for burnt offering," Aaron said.

"I didn't think you people did that anymore," said Anthony.

"Esau performing burnt offering with only three families," explained Aaron. "All others believing and following Messiah Jesus Christ."

Anthony's eyes lit up as he said, "And these are the offerings that require salt, right?"

"Yes," answered Aaron.

"You know . . ." said Anthony very slowly. His mind seemed to be racing. I could tell that he was working seriously hard on putting something together. And I knew it couldn't be good. " . . . I think I can help," he said after a moment. "Aaron, will you come with me to talk to Esau?" asked Anthony.

"Talking for what reason?" asked Levi.

"Because," explained Anthony, "as I understand it, all the problems between you and the people—the strangers—from last summer started when they contaminated your salt deposit, right?" Everyone waited as Anthony paused. I could tell that Aaron wasn't sure what "contaminated" meant, but Anthony continued without seeming to notice. "*That's* why we came: we're here to help with that! We brought you lots and lots of salt!"

"*No, you didn't!*" I said with disgust. "Are you completely delusional? That's a total lie!" Perhaps I should have restrained myself a little, but I didn't figure our relationship with him could get any worse anyway.

Anthony looked at me the same way Omni did each time I told him my right name. "You didn't see it," said Anthony impatiently, shaking his head from side to side. "The salt I'm talking about is in the other storeroom."

"*What* other storeroom?" I challenged.

Now Anthony acted really annoyed. "It's there, believe me," he insisted. Turning back to Levi he said, "I think this could go a long way toward establishing a little more peace between our peoples, don't you? I want to tell Esau that we have all this salt for you. I want to invite him to come to our boat with that reindeer sled. It's a lot of salt, but I'm sure it would all fit on the sled."

"Yeah," I agreed, "I'm sure it would all fit *under one arm!*"

I could tell that Anthony heard my comment, but he refused to look in my direction. Turning to Aaron, he said, "Come with me, please. I think this could turn out *very* well for all of us."

Aaron looked at Levi as if to ask what he thought about it all. Levi looked back and forth between Anthony and his son several times before finally saying to Aaron, "Moses going also with you." Looking at Anthony he said, "Ye speaking with Esau of salt on boat."

I don't think I've ever seen a grown man so giddy in all my life. Anthony giggled slightly and then practically skipped down the slope in the direction that Esau had gone. "Well, let's go then," smiled Anthony, beckoning for Aaron and Moses to follow. I knew right then that something really weird was going on. Aaron and Moses eventually followed Anthony—rather reluctantly, I might

117

add. We all just watched them for a minute as they walked down the slope toward the tents. Anthony chattered with excitement as they left about how happy he was to be able to help.

A few minutes later as Jeff and I were setting up our tent next to Levi's family's tent, we continued to talk about what Anthony might be up to. Shauna and Meg had washed up and looked like they were already feeling tons better. Meg was helping Nawni with dinner, and so we took the opportunity to tell Shauna all about everything she had missed. First we told her that Esau was just as bad as ever and how he seemed to be campaigning for Levi's job. Then we told her about Anthony wanting to talk to Esau. He and Aaron weren't back yet, as far as we knew.

"What do you think he's up to?" asked Shauna.

"I don't know," I said. "But there is no other storeroom on that yacht. There's no way they have any more salt to give Esau than what we saw."

"I wouldn't trust either one of those guys as far as I could throw them," said Jeff, "so how much can they possibly trust each other?"

"Do you think maybe Anthony just wants an excuse to get Esau on the boat so he can kidnap him?" I asked.

Shauna and Jeff both thought about this for a moment. Jeff said, "I'm pretty sure he wants somebody who can speak English. If he kidnapped Esau, he would have to kidnap Levi or Aaron or Moses as a translator. He would do better just to get one of them in the first place."

"Yeah, you're right." I agreed thoughtfully. "I guess it's a really good thing that Esau *doesn't* speak English. And it's a good thing that neither of them knows how untrustworthy the other one is, otherwise they might come up with a plan that would work for both of them."

"I think that's what they call honor among thieves," Shauna said. "They'll cheat everyone but each other."

We all just stood there, shaking our heads, when all of a sudden Shauna gasped so loud that it made me jump.

"What?" asked Jeff.

Shauna's mouth and eyes were all about as wide open as you could imagine. "Do you know why thieves work together?" she asked. We just stared as she answered her own question. "To help each other both get what they want when they can't do it on their own."

"What do they both want?" I asked quietly.

"They both want *Levi*," she said.

Our blank stares made it obvious that we had no idea what she meant.

"Think about it," Shauna continued, "Anthony wants to take somebody to the United States. And Esau wants Levi *anywhere*, but here."

CHAPTER 9

The Writing Room

"But Aaron's not going to translate *that* for Anthony," I guffawed.

"He wouldn't have to," said Shauna. "If Esau comes back with us, Anthony would have four days—five counting the Sabbath—five days to get his idea across to Esau. He could make it work."

Jeff and I just stared at her.

"So do you think that's what he's up to?" asked Jeff finally.

"I don't know," Shauna admitted. She sounded defeated and discouraged.

The conversation ended when Nawni reappeared and motioned for Jeff and me to wash up for dinner. We took turns in the tent with a shallow bowl of warm water and a small rag, putting back on the same dirty clothes we had now been wearing for over a week.

Dinner seemed especially good this evening. I was even more pleased by the idea of not getting up early the next morning just so we could spend the entire day walking again. I don't think I even realized that I was thinking along those lines until Mr. Omni announced near the end of the meal, "I guess we'll be heading back first thing in the morning."

"What?" asked Anthony in obvious surprise. For once, I agreed with him.

"Well," replied Omni, "I'm done here, aren't you? I have what I came for."

"Well, *I* certainly don't!" said Anthony. "And there's no reason to be in such a big hurry; Vladimir won't be back for more than a week!"

"Well," smiled Omni with those signature teeth, "I plan on being at the river in plenty of time and jumping on the yacht as it comes by. As far as I'm concerned, Vladimir won't even have to slow down!"

Anthony looked at Omni like he thought he was insane. Obviously, Omni was joking, but Anthony could find no humor in the comment whatsoever. I knew why, though. Anthony had enough trouble getting on and off when the yacht was standing still.

"We leaving for river on morning following next," Levi announced. "We remaining here two nights."

"I guess I can wait a day," sighed Omni, managing an insincere smile.

"I hope that will work," mumbled Anthony. "It may not be enough time."

"Enough time for what?" asked Omni. "To find your glasses?"

"Enough time to convince Esau to come with us," said Anthony, as if it should be obvious.

"What difference does it make?" asked Omni. "If he comes, he comes, and if not—big deal!"

"I need his help," said Anthony. After a short pause he quickly added, "to get the salt."

Omni just stared blankly at Anthony for a moment before saying, "R-r-right." Omni rolled his eyes and smirked as he looked away.

"See!" I said to Jeff and Shauna later, as soon as we had climbed into our tent for the night. "Even Omni doesn't believe that Anthony wants to give him the salt."

"Yeah," agreed Jeff, "but Anthony said he needs his help for something."

"But apparently," added Shauna, "he still hasn't even convinced

Esau to come with us—let alone made any kidnapping plans with him. He may have a harder time than I thought."

"Or maybe we still haven't figured out what he's really up to," I suggested.

"Good point," agreed Shauna.

In our family prayer that night, Shauna asked, as always, that Mom and Dad wouldn't be too worried and that we would all be safely back together again as soon as possible. But this time, she included quite a bit about keeping everyone in the tribe safe, too. We all agreed.

The next day turned out to be a really fun day—at least it was fun for Meg, Shauna, Jeff, and me. Mr. Omni pretty much just walked or laid around the whole day, looking majorly bored. Leonard, of course, followed him around wherever he went and looked pretty much just like he always looked. Anthony, on the other hand, looked more and more uptight each time we saw him. Two times before breakfast he asked Aaron to go with him to see if Esau had decided whether he was going with us or not. Each time they came back it was obvious that Esau had not made his decision yet. Anthony paced back and forth, wringing his hands nervously. He looked terrible.

Right after the morning meal, Aaron wanted to show Shauna, Meg, Jeff, and me what he and Levi had been doing with the copies of the Book of Mormon that we had left for them the previous summer. He had already told us they were translating the book into their language. Aaron was also working on his own copy of the Old Testament writings that his people had kept with them for thousands of years. He had started this huge project when he turned twelve and was planning to finish before his eighteenth birthday. But now he said he was spending about half of his writing time each day, working with Levi and Moses on translating the Book of Mormon.

"We going in cave to place of writing," said Aaron.

Just outside the mouth of the cave was an open fire with a large metal pot hanging over it. The thick soup inside the pot was gently boiling. Aaron stooped down next to the fire and held a small clay bowl close to it for a moment. The bowl looked sort of like a gravy boat with a handle on one end and a spout on the other, but the top was almost completely closed except for a hole about the size of a nickel. A short piece of burnt cord stuck out of the spout. After the cord had caught fire, Aaron stood and motioned for us to follow him into the cave.

"What's that?" asked Meg.

"I think it's a lamp," said Shauna.

When Jeff and I had been here before, we had only come a short way into the cave and had only seen a couple of the chambers. This time we walked for several minutes down several passageways and past various caverns of different sizes. It was dark at first, but as my eyes adjusted, I was surprised out how much light came from the small lamp. Aaron spoke more about the Book of Mormon as we made our way deeper into the cave.

Apparently Levi had been using the Book of Mormon to teach the tribe about Jesus Christ—at least everyone except for Esau and his small group of followers. Levi truly seemed to understand why it's called *Another Testament of Jesus Christ*. Levi wanted to keep the Book of Mormon teachings in their own language, and so he and Aaron would carefully read and discuss each verse and then they would write down the translation as well as they could understand it. They had already finished First Nephi and most of Second Nephi. Apparently the work had gone much slower at first, but they were now getting better with English. We agreed. Their translation of Second Nephi had been going a lot faster, partly because it has so many quotes from Isaiah in it. They had already known the writings of Isaiah because of the English Bible that Levi's father got from an American years earlier.

As we came into a large cavern, Aaron said, "This being place of writing."

It smelled wet. The damp smell reminded me of a cave on the west side of Utah Lake where our Scout troop went camping one time. Only here, the smell was a lot stronger. There were several lamps hanging from the rocky walls inside this cavern. They were much larger than the one Aaron was carrying. Aaron used the lamp he brought with us to light five or six of the large lamps that were closest to the entrance of the room. The area where we stood was now filled with light, but it didn't reach either the ceiling or the back of the cavern.

"We writing here," said Aaron.

Along one wall of this cavern was a flat ledge of smooth rock that jutted out from the wall about knee height. It was several feet wide in most places and was just about as flat and level and smooth as a tabletop. The ledge stretched deep into the blackness. In the lighted area we saw large, brownish pages in stacks of various heights. Each sheet was thicker than construction paper and about twice the size of regular notebook paper. Some of the pages were rolled into thick bundles. I remembered that this was how Aaron had carried his copy of ancient writings with him—the writings that had matched some of our Old Testament. I also recognized Jeff's and my scriptures, which we had left with them the year before. They were lying open in the center of everything else. Levi and Aaron had had them as we traveled, so the two of them had obviously already been in this room since we arrived the night before.

"Ye sitting with me," Aaron said as he pointed to the ground in front of the writing area. He knelt down facing the writings. The four of us either knelt or sat next to him.

Pointing to a small stack of the sheets, he said, "This being the words of The Book of Mormon—Another Testament of Jesus Christ in the language of my people."

The pages were covered with symbols that didn't mean anything to us.

"Prophet writing much of Jesus Christ," said Aaron. Then, pointing to the open set of scriptures that he was translating from, he asked, "Ye saying name of prophet in what way?"

"Nephi," said Jeff. Aaron repeated it back two or three times to make sure he got it right.

"That's right," said Shauna.

"Are you copying *all* of the Book of Mormon?" asked Meg. Pointing to the stack of pages, she added, "With these funny words?"

"Yes," answered Aaron.

"Why?" she asked.

Aaron looked thoughtfully at her for a moment and then said, "We following words of Prophet Ne-phi." He broke the word *Nephi* in two, still trying to get used to the way Jeff told him to pronounce it. Meg just stared back at him until he continued. "We talk of Christ," Aaron said, "and we rejoice in Christ and we preach to our people of Christ and we prophesy of Christ and we write of our prophecies."

Shauna quickly added, "that our children may know to what source they may look for a remission of their sins."

Aaron nodded.

"That's one of my favorites," Shauna said. "I think it's so important to remember that the only way we can overcome our sins is through the grace of Jesus Christ."

"Yes," Aaron agreed.

"Where did you get this funny paper?" asked Meg.

"We making this paper," answered Aaron as he stood up. "Ye come with me." He picked up the small lamp and worked his way back deeper into the cavern, lighting more of the wall lamps as he went. We soon saw that the rock ledge they were using for writing got wider and wider as we went farther back. We also saw that it was covered with several dozen single sheets of the paper in various stages of drying.

It took a while for him to explain it all, but we learned that they took small twigs and branches from a certain type of plant and ground them to powder between rocks. Then they would slowly boil it for many days, along with the sticky sap from another type of tree. When it was thick enough, they would bring it into this cavern and pour the liquid out onto the smoothest parts of the rock and use really smooth logs to roll the sheets thin and leave them to dry. That's what was boiling over the fire outside the cave.

"That's why it's so damp in here," said Shauna.

"I was wondering," I nodded.

"That is *so* cool!" Jeff said.

"Can we make some paper?" asked Meg.

"Cooking not finished," said Aaron. Then gesturing back toward the entrance, he said, "Ye come to place of writing. Ye writing words on paper."

"Oh, no!" said Shauna. "Your paper is valuable! It's so hard for you to make it. We couldn't. . . . We don't want to use . . ." She couldn't decide how to say it so she finally just grunted and said, "No, thank you, Aaron."

"Shauna's right," agreed Jeff. "We shouldn't."

Aaron smiled. "Everything being fine," he said, leading us to the front of the cavern. Reaching for a small stack of pages with writings on them, he said, "We using these pages many times." Then, pointing to the stack of pages with the translation of the Book of Mormon, he said, "We using *these* pages only one time."

Hanging on the wall not far from where we stood was an animal skin pouch filled with water. Taking the water bag from the wall, Aaron untied the opening of the bag and allowed a few drops to spill onto the top page in the first stack. He then picked up what looked like a piece of animal skin that was covered in thick dark fur and rubbed the page. The writing immediately smeared and was gone.

"It washes off?" I asked in disbelief. "How come it's not permanent?"

"Aren't you afraid of losing all your work?" asked Jeff.

Aaron smiled and said, "Everything being well." As he said this, he flicked some water from the water bag onto the Book of Mormon pages and we all gasped as a few drops of water splattered onto the paper. I felt my heart jump into my throat. I thought, *He's ruined his work!*

Aaron immediately picked up the dark animal skin and rubbed the page. To our surprise, the ink didn't smear. "This being different," smiled Aaron. "Everything being well."

Aaron then showed us that they had two different types of ink. They looked exactly the same on the paper, but one would wash away with water and the other wouldn't. Once we saw that we could practice writing with the water-based ink, we each tried it out. They had several sticks that were about twice as long as pencils. They had been hollowed out part way up one side so that when we dipped the end into the small bag of ink, the little trough would hold a supply of ink. The pen held enough ink to write two or three letters before we had to dip it again. We quickly found that the ink flowed onto the paper whenever the end of the stick was touching it, so we had to keep the stick moving.

Aaron handed me the first page of his Book of Mormon translation, and I began to copy what was written there. I didn't want to quit until I had copied the entire page. I had no idea how long we were there, but it was just so cool to think that these were the words of Nephi written in some ancient language. Meg tried to copy things for a while and then just started drawing pictures. She went through quite a stack of paper in the process.

After putting out all of the wall lamps, Aaron picked up the lamp that he had carried into the cave, and we all headed back to the cave entrance. We hadn't gone far when I noticed another light coming toward us. But this light was different from Aaron's lamp— it looked more like a modern flashlight.

"Hello-o-o!" came Anthony's voice. "Anybody there?"

Aaron stopped dead in his tracks.

"That's *Anthony!*" hissed Jeff.

"Hello-o-o!" he said again, more intensely this time. He was coming closer and shined his light on us.

"Who is that?" asked Anthony. Then, with anger in his voice, he said, "Oh, it's *you!* Where have you been?"

"You leaving now," said Aaron to Anthony and he started moving again. "You leaving with us."

Anthony followed, but was still angry. "What have you been doing?" he asked.

I didn't want him to know, but it didn't matter anyway because he never gave us a chance to answer. "I've been looking all over for you!" he continued as we walked. "Aaron, I need you to go with me to Esau and find out what he's planning to do!"

"I think Esau will not be telling us," said Aaron.

"Well, we can at least *ask,*" Anthony spat.

"I think Esau becoming angry," said Aaron, following slowly. "I think Esau will be telling us not until after evening sacrifice."

"I don't care what you think," snarled Anthony. "We're going to ask him. Now, c'mon!"

It was obvious that Aaron didn't want to go, but it was also obvious that Dr. Anthony was not going to be satisfied until they asked him again. I would have thought that from what Anthony saw of Esau the night before, Aaron's warning about Esau getting mad might have made him think a little. But apparently not.

Once we got outside the cave I was shocked to learn that it was already lunch time. We had been in the writing room the entire morning. Anthony refused to let Aaron eat, insisting that they visit Esau first. In less than five minutes, Anthony and Aaron returned.

128

They both now wore very different expressions than before. Aaron had a look that said, "I told you so," and Anthony looked like he realized that he had just come within an inch of losing his life. His eyes were huge and his skinny cheeks were sunken even more than the night before. He walked unsteadily up the slope. One of his eyes seemed to be twitching slightly. I thought, *I hope that's not his good eye.* I could see his hands shaking as he pulled back the flap and disappeared inside his tent.

"I guess you were right about Esau being angry," said Shauna to Aaron.

"Yes," Aaron answered.

"What happened?" asked Jeff.

"We speaking nothing," explained Aaron. "Esau seeing us and yelling with much noise. The sons of Esau are running very fast to us with knifes and screaming."

"What did Mr. Anthony do?" asked Meg.

Aaron had just a hint of a smile on his face as he answered her, "Mr. Anthony is screaming and running, also," said Aaron. "He is screaming and running away to here."

We all laughed at the thought.

"I wish I'd been there to see *that!*" I said.

"Esau is yelling to us," continued Aaron, "not to return. Esau is telling us his determination not until this night."

"Did you tell that to Anthony?" asked Jeff.

"Yes."

"What did he say?" asked Meg.

"Anthony is saying he having no more hurry," answered Aaron with a smile. "He saying he can be waiting for much longer."

We all laughed again. I figured that Anthony could probably hear us laughing, but I didn't care. After all, Aaron had warned him. He didn't even bother to come out for lunch. I thought he was nuts; when we were hiking, we pretty much ate the same thing for every meal, but in the camp we always had great food. I wasn't

129

always sure what it was, and the tribe's explanations didn't usually help—but it always tasted fantastic!

After lunch Meg and Shauna went to help Nawni with some chores, while Levi and Aaron invited Jeff and me back into the writing room. They had questions they wanted to ask us.

"We are not always understanding the words of English," said Levi as we made our way through the dark passages back to the writing room.

"I know what you mean," I agreed. Jeff hit me like I was making a joke, but I was serious.

"Do *you* understand every word in the scriptures?" I asked Jeff.

"Well," he paused. "No."

"That's all I was saying," I defended myself.

"But there's a way that I use that helps sometimes," Jeff said.

"How is this way?" asked Levi.

"I use the Topical Guide," Jeff explained.

Levi nodded like he knew about the Topical Guide.

"Sometimes," Jeff continued, "if I look up a word in the Topical Guide, it will give a list of other words to look up, and so it gives me a good idea about what the word probably means."

"I understanding," nodded Levi.

When we got to the writing room, Levi immediately picked up one of the sets of scriptures and turned to 2 Nephi 31. He read the first part of verse 20 aloud:

Wherefore, ye must press forward with a steadfastness in Christ, . . . "I knowing not what is being *steadfastness*," said Levi.

"I think I know what it means," Jeff said, "but I'm not sure I can explain it." After a short pause he added, "That's one that I would try looking up in the Topical Guide."

At Jeff's suggestion, Levi turned to the Topical Guide and began searching for the word. He obviously knew exactly what the Topical Guide is.

Before Levi found the reference Jeff said, "It's like being firm in working toward a goal . . . or keeping a promise."

Aaron looked at Jeff as if that still didn't help him a whole lot. Levi nodded silently.

A moment later Levi said, "Here is being *steadfastness*."

"Good," said Jeff. "Sometimes the words I look for aren't in there." Looking over Levi's shoulder, Jeff pointed to the line just below the reference and said, "Look where it says 'see also' right there?"

"Ah," nodded Levi.

"Now look at all the words that come after," said Jeff. "Commitment; Courage; Dedication; Dependability; Diligence; Endure; . . ." He didn't read the whole list.

"These are being words I am knowing," nodded Levi again. "This being much good."

"Too bad we didn't bring them a dictionary," I said.

"We have dictionary of Bible," said Levi, turning quickly to the Bible Dictionary just after the Topical Guide.

"Don't go there," said Jeff to me with a hint of disgust in his voice.

Levi immediately stopped turning pages, glancing quickly up at Jeff with a questioning look.

"No—" grunted Jeff. "I'm sorry. Yes, go there. What I mean is that last year our family had a huge discussion about the Bible Dictionary not really being a true dictionary and . . ."

"This being not true?" asked Levi in dismay.

"No—" Jeff grunted again. "Yes. I'm sorry—that's not what I meant. Yes, it's true, but we have other . . ." Jeff's voice trailed off as he shook his head slightly back and forth. Finally he simply said, "Never mind. It's good. Go with it."

When Levi looked away, Jeff used the opportunity to glare at me as if it was all my fault for mentioning the word *dictionary*.

"Whatever," I mumbled.

Levi and Aaron both looked over at me. I just smiled back.

Once we got past the meaning of *steadfastness*, Levi wanted to talk about what the whole verse meant. There were quite a few other words that Levi and Aaron also wanted to talk about. The Topical Guide trick didn't always work, so Jeff and I just had to do the best we could. As we spoke, Levi would make marks in the margin of our scriptures. I noticed that he used the permanent ink and not the wash-away-in-water stuff.

We ended up spending the rest of the day in the writing room. It was fun, but my brain hurt by the time we finished.

"Any sign of Anthony?" we asked Meg and Shauna when we returned to the tents. Nawni was just finishing up the preparations for dinner. I wondered how Levi knew exactly the right time the food would be ready. I figured either there was a wall clock in the writing room that I hadn't noticed or else Levi must have the nose of an animal.

"We haven't seen him since lunch time," said Shauna.

"What are you asking her for?" asked Meg.

It turned out that Shauna had gone somewhere with Moses for most of the afternoon. It was a place that Shauna described as "Oh, nowhere."

Nawni had been very interested in Meg's rag doll, and so the two of them had spent most of the afternoon making about a dozen of them out of some thick cloth that Nawni had. When Shauna finally returned, the three of them walked through the village, giving the dolls to some of the young tribal girls.

No one really knew where Omni and Leonard were all afternoon—we were just glad that none of us had to deal with them. That's probably why we were all in such a good mood. That changed quickly, though, when Anthony made his way out of his hut. He looked like he was going to pass out.

"Do I smell food?" he asked weakly with eyes half shut. "I haven't eaten since this morning."

He acted like he was going to faint. Jeff and I just smirked at each other. I don't know what Jeff was thinking, but I thought about saying that even Meg went without food for twice as long every Fast Sunday, and she never acted anything like Anthony did.

"We eating now," Levi said.

Anthony nodded slowly as if he just didn't have the energy to give anything more than that. I saw Jeff roll his eyes. Omni and Leonard showed up about halfway through the meal.

"It looks absolutely fan*tabu*lous!" drooled Mr. Omni, reaching for a cake.

I didn't know Levi had it in him, but his hand flew so fast that I couldn't even see it. He grabbed Omni's wrist and held it tightly, keeping him from touching the food. Omni looked at Levi with shock.

Levi simply smiled at Omni and said, "Ye are praying with us before eating."

Omni closed his mouth, swallowed loudly, and nodded his understanding. Levi slowly released his grip and then bowed his head in prayer, asking Heavenly Father for His blessing on the food for Mr. Omni and Leonard. Even after the prayer, Omni didn't dare make any moves toward the food until Levi gestured and nodded.

Omni hesitantly picked up a cake, but just held it in his hand for at least two minutes without taking a bite. Finally he asked weakly, "Didn't you pray at the beginning of the meal?"

"Ye being gone away at time of praying," said Levi.

Again, Omni just nodded and went without speaking for the rest of the meal. Leonard didn't speak, either, but that was nothing new.

Toward the end of the meal, Esau approached. I think Anthony was the last to see him, because he was staring at the ground the whole time. Esau spoke a couple of short sentences and then just stared at us all for a moment. Levi said something very short, and then Esau immediately spun on his heel and left.

"What did he say?" asked Jeff. It was obvious that Anthony and Omni both really wanted to ask the same question, but neither of them seemed up to it.

"Esau and sons of Esau coming on morrow with us to river for fetching of salt," said Levi.

I think that's the happiest I've ever seen Dr. Anthony get. His face lit up as a smile slowly crept across it until it practically reached his ears. "*Wonderful!*" he whispered. His eyes darted about after he said it. I could tell that he was trying to hatch something in that puny, little brain of his again. Anthony seemed to get both more nervous and more excited over the next couple of minutes.

I noticed that Anthony had also apparently had a miraculous healing after being so near death just before eating. The rest of the evening he spoke with excitement about the trip back to the river. He kept asking the same questions over and over again about what time in the morning we would be leaving and who was going with us and what we would be taking and how long it would take. I decided that if an adult could act like that, then I needed to be a lot more patient with my younger brother and sisters.

At one point, not long before we all headed to bed, Anthony asked, "So you never did tell me what you were doing all morning, did you?"

No one seemed to want to answer him.

"Oh," said Anthony, "so it's a big, dark secret, is it?"

"I showing them our place of writing," Aaron finally responded.

Anthony immediately looked very interested. He nodded his head thoughtfully for a moment before asking, "And will you be taking your writings with us on our little trip tomorrow?"

"No," answered Aaron.

"That's probably best," nodded Anthony with a sick smile. "I'm sure you will want them to be here where you know that they will be safe and sound." He nodded a couple of more times and then added, "And then you can just check on them as soon as you're back, can't you?"

Aaron didn't answer. But I don't think that Anthony really expected him to. He just smiled and walked away. The rest of us continued cleaning up the campsite and making sure that we had everything ready to leave first thing in the morning. It was only a few minutes later that I overheard Anthony and Omni talking. They were inside their tent with the flap closed, and they didn't know that I was walking nearby as they spoke.

"So are you ready to go?" asked Omni. "Do you have everything you wanted?"

"I have all of the puzzle pieces," said Anthony, "but now I just need to start fitting them together."

CHAPTER 10

A Thief in the Night

"Guys!" I said, crawling into our hut where Shauna, Meg, and Jeff were. "Guess what I just heard." Shauna and Jeff each had their flashlight on. I told them what Omni and Anthony had said to each other.

"What do you think he's talking about?" asked Jeff. "What are all the pieces?"

"I don't know," I admitted, "but so far, nothing that we have guessed has been proven wrong."

"What do you mean?" Jeff asked.

"I mean Shauna's idea about Anthony trying to get Esau to help him kidnap Levi," I explained.

"And you know what else?" asked Shauna. "Did you hear what he said about it being good that Aaron was leaving his writings behind?"

"Yeah," I nodded. "Weird, huh? Do you think that means that he's not going to try to steal them? Did he say that just to try to make Aaron think that he's not so bad?"

"I don't know," said Shauna. "I don't get it."

"Can we have our family prayer now?" asked Meg. She was leaning against her backpack, and her eyes were looking pretty droopy.

"Sure," said Shauna gently. "You're tired, huh? I'm sorry we were talking so much."

Shauna said the prayer. She asked that we might have a safe trip and that we would all be protected from anyone or anything that might want to do us harm. She asked Heavenly Father to comfort Mom and Dad and let them know that we were all okay. She prayed especially for Moses and Aaron and Levi, that they would be able to continue to teach the people the gospel of Jesus Christ and that they would be blessed by it. As always, she even prayed for the others who were coming with us.

After she had finished her prayer and the flashlights were turned off, we lay in silence for a few minutes. Finally, I whispered, "Shauna?" I wasn't sure if she was still awake.

"Uh-huh," she said.

"How can you pray for Dr. Anthony and Mr. Omni and Esau when all they want is to hurt other people and take advantage of them?"

"That's what Jesus taught," she said softly, "both in the New Testament and again in the Book of Mormon. He said we should pray for our enemies and for those who despitefully use us."

"I know," I said. "But how can you do it? I just don't see how you can do it."

"Well," she sighed, "it's hard sometimes. But I just try to remember that Heavenly Father loves them even though they're doing bad things. I try to remember that He loves me, too, even when I do things that I know I shouldn't do."

"I guess," I said, "but the things that you might do can't be near as bad as the things that these guys are doing."

"We're not judged against other people," Shauna said. "We're judged by the things that we know are right and that we should do."

I knew she was right, of course, but I still didn't get how she could do it.

The next morning I was awakened by the sound of reindeer hooves stomping not far from our tent. As I lay still and listened for a few moments, I also heard the sounds of birds flapping their wings.

There was also an occasional squawk. We came out to find that everyone else was just about ready to go. Levi and Esau each had a reindeer sled ready. Esau had his sled loaded with the altar they used for burnt offerings when they traveled. He also had several bird cages with a dozen or so birds in them along with a tent bundle. His sons looked like they were standing guard over the sled and its supplies. This was the first time I had seen these guys since the previous summer, and they looked exactly the way I remembered them. One always looked completely disinterested in what was going on and the other one always had his mouth hanging half open. We had named them Tweedle Dee and Tweedle Dum. (Obviously, Tweedle Dum was the one who left his mouth hanging half open all the time.)

Levi's sled was loaded with several tent bundles and some animal skin bags that I figured probably had food and water in them. The Three Stooges' backpacks were also loaded on and ready to go. Anthony looked positively giddy this morning.

"C'mon, everyone," Anthony said with excitement. "We don't want to be losing any daylight, now. We had better be moving!"

Who was he kidding? The sun was up for almost 20 hours a day around here!

Aaron helped us take down our tent, and we soon had it and all of our backpacks loaded onto Levi's sled. Nawni had breakfast ready for us, and we took the time to enjoy the meal despite Anthony's impatient whining.

"Let's not spend any more time here than we absolutely must!" he encouraged us.

Near the end of the meal, Levi said something to Aaron and Moses that we obviously didn't understand. Aaron looked surprised, but pleased by what Levi had said and then he and Moses immediately stood up and left. It looked like they were headed in the direction of the cave, but I couldn't be sure. I noticed that Anthony looked very interested in what they were doing and started to act even more nervous.

"Where are they going?" Anthony asked Levi.

"Aaron and Moses are fetching one more bag in preparation for journey," explained Levi.

Anthony's eyes widened. I could tell that he wanted to ask what it was, but that he didn't dare. He was looking extremely nervous now.

"Well," he grunted, "why didn't they do it before? Or last night? We need to be going."

"Everything being well," said Levi calmly.

Esau seemed to be as impatient as Anthony. He said something to Levi and then immediately began moving his reindeer sled northward. His sons, the Tweedles, went with him.

"Are we going or not?" asked Anthony nervously. He was torn between going with Esau and watching for Moses and Aaron to return.

"Everything being well," Levi said again.

For several seconds, Anthony looked back and forth between the two sleds. Suddenly he grabbed his backpack from Levi's sled and started running after Esau. It was the funniest looking run I have ever seen in my life! If I didn't know better, I would have thought he was trying to make us all laugh. Jeff and I had huge grins as we both tried not to let anything burst out. It was all I could do to hold my lips together. Anthony put his backpack on the front of Esau's sled as soon as he caught up with him. Then he leaned over with his hands on his knees for several seconds, panting like he had just finished a marathon. I couldn't decide whether to laugh or just feel sorry for him. He had only run for about 30 seconds and yet he was ready to die!

We finished eating within five minutes, and Nawni wanted to hug everyone as Levi's sled began to move. Meg held onto Nawni the longest. I got the feeling she was going to miss having someone around to act like a mom while we were so far away from our own mom. When Meg finally let go, Levi invited her to ride on the back of the sled.

"What about Aaron and Moses?" I asked Levi. "They're not back yet."

"Moses and Aaron coming soon," said Levi.

As we started to move I noticed Esau was already quite a distance ahead of us. I was surprised Anthony hadn't already planted himself on the back of Esau's sled. It was obvious that he preferred being with Esau for some reason, but I figured he didn't have the guts to ask him for a ride. Omni and Leonard moved out ahead of Levi's sled.

"Ahh," beamed Omni, "what a gorgeous day to be in the great outdoors!" Looking at Meg snuggling in next to the tent bundles, he said, "Don't you agree, Melinda?"

She responded by stretching her mouth into a straight line across her face.

As we walked, I noticed that Anthony kept looking back every couple of minutes. He would look at us for a moment and then look back in the direction of the tribe's huts. I figured he was watching for Aaron and Moses. Why was Anthony so uptight about them? It made me think that maybe he was really interested in kidnapping Aaron after all.

Levi was right. Moses and Aaron caught up with us within a few minutes. They were carrying a single, large animal skin bag. Aaron looked a little upset. He immediately went to Levi and whispered something. They stared at each other for a moment and then, almost at exactly the same time, they turned their heads and stared at Anthony. He seemed to be having trouble keeping up with Esau, as he was now about halfway in between the two sleds. Because he was quite a bit ahead of us, he hadn't seen that Aaron and Moses had returned, but it was as if he could feel their eyes boring into his back. His head turned slowly and nervously around as he continued to walk. His eyes grew larger as they locked onto everyone staring at him. He didn't move for at least two full seconds. It was as if his feet were riveted to the ground.

"What?" he called defiantly back to us.

Levi and Moses and Aaron simply stared back at him, continuing to walk forward. Then, with a jerk, Anthony finally managed to force himself to face forward and start moving again. He was walking noticeably faster now than before, and he was well out of hearing range.

"What is it?" Shauna asked Levi. Turning to Moses, she asked, "What did you go get?"

"We wanting writings," said Levi. "We wanting to speak with you of the Book of Mormon writings concerning Jesus Christ."

"So you sent them to get the writings?" I asked.

"Yes," nodded Levi.

"But something is wrong, isn't it?" asked Shauna.

"We finding not all writings," said Aaron intensely. "Many pages missing from writing room."

"No way!" said Jeff. "Do you think Anthony took them?"

"Yes," said Aaron.

"How could he find them?" I asked. "He didn't see where we came from when we left the writing room, did he?"

"Maybe he went back during the night and just wandered around till he found it," suggested Jeff. "He wasn't that far away from it when he found us."

"Maybe he saw where the light was coming from," said Shauna, "before we put out all of the lamps on the wall. It's so dark in there, he probably could see the glow a long way."

"Are you sure they're gone?" I asked.

"Yes," answered Aaron firmly.

"That would explain why Dr. Anthony was so happy last night," Shauna said. "I mean when you said that you weren't going to bring the writings with you. He probably thought he could steal them during the night and that you wouldn't know until you got back from the river."

"And by then," I agreed, "both he *and* your writings would be long gone."

"But if Anthony's got them," Jeff said, "then they would have to be in his backpack, wouldn't they?"

"I can't imagine where else he could put them," agreed Shauna.

"The guy is a wimp," I said to Levi. Then, hesitating, I added, "I mean at least compared you, he is. So if he has them, you can just take them, right?"

"Mr. Anthony being guest of my people and me," said Levi. "We showing respect and kindness."

"But wait," I said, "do you think he stole the writings?"

"Yes," answered Levi firmly.

"So you don't think he can be trusted then, right?"

"Yes," said Levi.

"So if you don't think he's trustworthy," I said, "then *why* are you trusting him?"

"I trusting him not," said Levi. "I showing respect and kindness."

I didn't get it. Was Levi just willing to let Anthony rob him in the name of kindness? It didn't make any sense to me.

"Everything being well," Levi assured me.

Anthony had almost caught up with Esau's sled by this time. But even from as far away as we were, it was obvious that he was about ready to die. I saw him stumble several times and almost fall flat on his face. He was sort of leaning to one side and couldn't seem to walk in a straight line. He finally reached the sled and just flopped down on the back of it. Esau and his sons didn't even bother to look at him.

I turned back and was about to say something rude and laugh at him, but I was distracted by Shauna and Moses. He was helping her onto the sled. And it's a good thing he was helping her, too, because she certainly wasn't helping herself. Instead of watching what she was doing, she was just watching him. He caught her as she almost fell, but she didn't seem the least bit bothered by it. Instead, she just waited until he looked into her face and then gave him this really weird smile. Strange.

Once Shauna was settled on the sled next to Meg, nobody really said much else for a long time as we followed some distance behind Esau's sled. Leonard and Omni stayed to themselves somewhere between the two sleds the whole time. About mid-morning we saw Esau's sled come to a stop. Esau and his sons immediately sat on the ground near the sled with bags of water and food. It didn't look like Anthony was stirring on the back of the sled, though. I figured he must have fallen asleep.

When Leonard and Omni reached Esau's sled, they immediately sat down and began snacking with the others. Leonard didn't miss the opportunity to kick Anthony's foot as he walked past, though, making him wake up with a yelp. It looked like he grumbled something in Leonard's direction before remembering where he was and looking anxiously down the path toward the rest of us. He then took the opportunity to quickly go and sit with the others, trying not to be noticed.

It took us another minute or so to join them. I watched carefully to see what might be said to Anthony, but Levi acted like there was nothing wrong. Anthony was careful to look anywhere but at us, and he spent time thoroughly examining all sorts of things that happened to be near where he was sitting.

"We resting short time," announced Levi.

I knew from experience that we would only get a couple of minutes to rest here and that this would be our only stop before lunch. I had forgotten that the trail going northward was slightly uphill the whole way, so I was feeling much more tired today than I had felt any day on the way down. It was also a little more intense, having "Esau and Company" with us. Probably because they had done everything in their power to keep our family and others from leaving. The year before, we were in the process of being kidnapped and dragged back to the tribe's summer home when, with the help of Aaron and Moses, we managed to barely get away. It wasn't until now that I remembered how that felt.

"Do you think they will try to keep us here again?" I asked Shauna and Jeff as we all munched on some kind of jerky.

"Esau's not in charge anymore," Jeff reminded me.

"Yeah," I said, "but he's trying to get that back, remember?"

Aaron overheard our conversation and said, "Esau not stopping you from returning to United States of America. We helping you. Everything being well."

I nodded, knowing that Aaron and Moses and Levi would do everything they could to protect us. But I was still really unsure about where the Three Stooges stood. I had the feeling that not one of them would think twice about us if we somehow didn't manage to make it back on the yacht. Vladimir would probably just laugh and say something like, "I see you are dumping the childrens somewheres!" And that would be the only time we were mentioned or even thought about. They would then go on their merry way to lie to the "men of the Coast Guard of Russia."

"How are you going to get your writings back?" asked Jeff.

"Are you sure it couldn't be someone from your tribe?" asked Shauna.

Aaron looked about as sure as I'd ever seen. "Yes," he said firmly.

Moses, who was sitting right next to Shauna, agreed by nodding his head.

"So are you going to ask Anthony about the writings?" asked Jeff. "Or should we just check out his backpack really quick sometime when he's not looking?"

That was the idea that I thought sounded the best.

"My father saying we waiting," said Aaron. "God will provide."

"I don't think any of us will ever get a chance to get close enough to even touch it," I said, looking over at Esau's sled. It looked like Anthony's backpack was now wedged in between a couple of the bird cages. We all munched in silence until it was time to go again.

Just as he had that morning, Esau just left when he felt like it, mumbling something to Levi as he stood. Levi responded briefly to Esau and then announced, "We traveling now." We weren't all quite ready yet, but Esau obviously didn't care, and it looked like Levi intended for us to stay together. I just shook my head as Anthony limped dramatically over to Esau's sled as it began to move and flopped down on it. His face made it seem like he was in terrible pain. Apparently his last bite of jerky had caused him to twist his ankle or something.

Meg and Shauna rode on the back of Levi's sled again. This time Moses helped Shauna get on before it was actually moving, so things went a little better. I noticed that she smiled at him the same way, though. I don't think a single word was spoken by anyone the rest of the morning. The tribesmen walked next to the lead rein-deer as always and would simply push or pull the harness one way or another if they needed a slight change in direction.

We were all getting pretty used to this traveling routine by now. Mr. Omni continued to look at his whatever-it-was that he claimed was *not* a cell phone, but on the way back he didn't write anything in his notebook—instead he would just look in it and nod his head. I wondered what he was up to, but I didn't care enough to want to ask him about it again.

My favorite part of traveling was always the lunch breaks. They were long enough to get a pretty decent rest, and we didn't have to go to all the work of setting up or taking down the tents. After we had finished eating, Levi asked Aaron to get the animal skin bag of writings from the sled. Levi pulled two rolls out of the bag and then the two sets of scriptures they had gotten from Jeff and me.

"We giving thanks to God daily for the blessing of these writings," Levi said.

"We're very glad that we could give them to you," said Shauna.

Levi, Aaron, and Moses spent the next thirty or forty minutes carefully organizing and sorting through the writings they had brought with them. They discovered that most of the Book of Mormon translation pages were missing, as well as quite a few from Aaron's copy of the Old Testament. Aaron and Moses had brought with them all the rest of the pages from the cave, including those that we had practiced on the day before. Luckily, we learned, Levi had kept his copy of their original writings with him in his tent, so those were all still safe with Nawni.

Part way through the sorting, Anthony saw what they were doing and got very nervous again. Two or three times, I saw him act as though he wanted to come over for a closer look, but then he would chicken out.

"Anthony was watching you with your writings," I said to Aaron.

Aaron looked over in Anthony's direction, but didn't say anything.

"He admitted that he wants them," I said. "You should just tell him they're gone and make him show you inside his backpack."

Aaron nodded, but didn't say anything.

The afternoon went along as always. I was more than ready for a hot meal when we finally stopped for the night. Of course we had to unharness the reindeer and make sure they were taken care of before anything else—including food. But, luckily, dinner came next, and it was well worth the wait. Once we had finished eating, the tents were set up, and everything else was taken care of, Levi wanted to talk about the Book of Mormon some more.

"Much writings of Jesus Christ found in The Book of Mormon—Another Testament of Jesus Christ," Levi nodded. "Much good."

"The Book of Mormon is my favorite," agreed Shauna.

"The Book of Mormon—Another Testament of Jesus Christ," Jeff said with a smile.

"My favorite scriptures in the Book of Mormon," said Shauna, ignoring Jeff, "are the ones that tell us to feast upon the words of Christ. I love the word *feast* because it makes me realize that there is so much there and enough for all—and more than you can enjoy all at one sitting."

Moses was watching her intently as she spoke.

"And I like where it says," Shauna continued, "that the words of Christ will tell us all things that we should do."

"This being much good," agreed Moses.

"Because it's so true," Shauna said. "We can find everything we need in the teachings of Jesus Christ."

Just as he had done with Jeff and me in the writing room, Levi began to ask questions about particular verses. He wrote short notes in the margins. A couple of times he wanted to look at the Book of Mormon translation that they had already made. It was obvious that he was getting frustrated by the fact that they didn't have all of the translated pages. I had watched Anthony take his backpack and put it inside his tent as soon as it was set up. He seemed less nervous after that.

The whole time everyone was having their discussion about the Book of Mormon, I was watching the Three Stooges' tent. I knew those pages had to be in Anthony's backpack, and I couldn't stop thinking about them. I kept watching for my chance to sneak into their tent and see for myself, but one of them was always somewhere close.

The next day was very much like the first one. Anthony was all fidgety as he loaded his backpack onto Esau's sled, and he acted suspicious whenever anyone seemed to be even looking in that direction. We had more Book of Mormon discussions with Levi, Aaron, and Moses after lunch and again after dinner. I tried several times to get Jeff to agree to help me check out Anthony's backpack, but he wanted nothing to do with it.

That night I didn't really listen to what anybody was talking about. I was too preoccupied with the idea of trying to get a look inside Anthony's backpack. After all, we were already halfway to the river, and nobody seemed to be willing to do anything. Finally, late in the evening, Anthony went inside his tent and stayed there. I thought, *Well, I just lost my chance*. Disgusted with the situation, I got up and started walking around the campsite, kicking at the ground. Eventually I started just pacing back and forth in front of the Stooges' tent. It was late enough and we were close enough to the side of the mountain that it was starting to get dark. I noticed a flashlight switch on inside Anthony's tent as a dim glow came through the dark fabric.

A few minutes later I stopped pacing not far from the front of the tent when Mr. Omni walked past and said to me, "I shall now be retiring for the evening, Brent."

With the same drama that he liked to use for everything, when Omni reached the tent, he unzipped the entire flap with a single swoop of his arm, letting it fall completely open. Then, standing next to the opening, he stared up at the darkening sky and said loudly to no one in particular, "Oh, what a spectacularious night."

How I got so lucky, I don't know, but I just happened to have stopped in the perfect position to see directly inside the open tent as Mr. Omni spoke. And sitting right there, in full view, was Dr. Anthony with the missing pages spread out all around him.

CHAPTER 11

The Hand Is Quicker Than the Eye

Dr. Anthony was horrified by what had happened and scrambled to switch off the flashlight as fast as he could. Because of the bright light inside and because I stood several feet away in the darkness, Anthony apparently didn't know that I was there.

"Who's out there?" he hissed, still shuffling papers.

"It is I!" said Omni, with another sweep of his arm. "The incredulous Mr. Omni, esquire." With that, he stooped and entered the tent.

"Get *in* here!" hissed Anthony as Omni was closing the flap. "I don't want anyone to see this stuff! Next time *warn* me before you do that!"

"No one saw a thing!" assured Omni with the final, dramatic zip of the tent flap opening. That was the last that I could hear clearly.

I was stunned by what I had just seen. I now knew that Anthony was the thief—I had seen the stolen pages with my own eyes. But I was more stunned by what had happened right after that. Did Mr. Omni really think that I hadn't seen anything? He had just told me that he was going to bed only half a second before he opened the flap. And I hadn't moved an inch. Was he really that dumb? Or was he just trying to make me *think* he was that dumb?

It was a good thirty seconds before I stopped trying to figure this out and ran to tell the others what I had seen. They were still in a discussion about Christ in the Book of Mormon.

I came scurrying up to the campfire and dropped to my knees right in the middle of them. I think Shauna and Jeff would have just ignored me, passing it off as my typical abnormal behavior. But Levi, Aaron, and Moses stopped short whatever they were saying and looked at me with shock. Meg was asleep in Shauna's lap.

"Guess what?" I whispered, seizing the opportunity created by my dramatic entrance. I continued before anyone could answer. I didn't want to just spill it all right out, so I offered another little teaser.

"Guess what I just saw spread out all over inside Anthony's tent?" I beamed. Then I added, "And it doesn't belong to him."

Everyone stared at me in silence.

"The *writings!*" I hissed. "He's got them!"

Everyone still stared.

"Well, c'mon!" I said. "Let's go get them. We know for a fact that he has them! It's not a matter of just not trusting him anymore. We know!"

Everyone was staring back and forth at each other, but still no one said a word. I couldn't believe it. Was I talking in *gibberish* or something?

"What?" I asked.

"I think," offered Shauna, "they're just trying to decide the best way to do it."

"What's to decide?" I asked. "We walk calmly over there, ring the doorbell, tell them what I saw, and demand he give the pages back."

Again, no one responded.

Trying to guess what they could all still be wondering about, I added, "It probably wouldn't hurt to bring along a knife or two, I suppose. That might make things go a *little* smoother."

Finally, Levi responded. Everyone was looking at him. "We will be waiting," he said.

"For what?" I asked. "The closer they get to that river and that boat, the harder it will be."

"God will provide," Aaron said, showing support for his father's decision.

I couldn't believe it. What was wrong with everybody? As soon as they saw that I was speechless, they returned to the conversation they had been having before I showed up. Shocked and bewildered, I sat back, dropped my elbows to my knees, and held my head in my hands. Every minute or so, I felt myself shaking my head back and forth slightly in total amazement.

Later, in the tent, Shauna and Jeff tried to offer some sort of explanation as to why Levi might be so reluctant to take his pages back from Anthony.

"Maybe Levi doesn't want to give Anthony any reason to think he needs to be worried about him," Shauna said.

"Yeah," Jeff agreed, "or maybe Levi thinks that it would be better to let him have the pages and hope that then Anthony won't try to kidnap anyone."

"Or maybe," Shauna said, "he doesn't want Anthony to know that he doesn't trust him, 'cause it might make it harder to get away when they drop us off."

I just stared at them, shaking my head some more.

"Whatever," I mumbled. I didn't really have any desire to talk about it anymore.

After we had prayed and lay quietly in the darkness for a few minutes I asked, "Do you think that Leonard would switch the pages for us?"

"You're crazy," mumbled Jeff.

"I agree," said Shauna.

"Well," I defended myself. "I thought about asking Moe, but he's not interested in anything that doesn't directly involve some advantage to himself. So Leonard is the only choice we have."

"Did you hear me say that you're crazy?" Jeff asked.

I didn't answer, but instead I tried to think about how I might be able to talk Leonard into it. I'm sure I was awake for at least another two hours trying to come up with a plan. By the time I fell asleep, I had a smile on my face. I thought my argument just might work—at least if Leonard was slightly more intelligent than he looked.

The next morning I asked Aaron if I could have the extra pages he had brought with him from the writing room. He gave me all the pages we had used to practice with as well as quite a stack of blank papers. To me it looked like just about the same number that I had seen spread out in Anthony's tent. I put them into my backpack.

Next, I waited for a chance to speak to Leonard when Mr. Omni wasn't nearby. As far as I could tell, the only time this *ever* happened was when Mr. Omni went to take care of nature's call in the trees for a few minutes after eating. The Stooges ate pretty much by themselves, using the food they had brought in their back-packs. I noticed that Anthony usually ate quickly and was off some-place else by the time the other two finished eating. I was hopeful it would be that way again this time.

As I sat near the fire at breakfast, I didn't even notice what I was eating. I was far too wrapped up in my stakeout of the Three Stooges, quickly glancing in their direction every few seconds. I stopped eating altogether when I saw Anthony leave the other two by themselves and climb inside the tent. I still held half of a cake in my hand, but I completely forgot to do anything with it as I stared, just waiting for my chance. Then it happened.

"I shall return," Omni announced with his gapped-tooth smile, as always, to no one in particular.

I quickly stood and moved over to where Leonard sat on a large rock with his arms folded across his chest. I didn't say anything until I sat down right next to him on the rock. I decided to stare off into space the same direction he was looking, thinking this might make him feel more comfortable.

"Hey, Leonard," I said. "How's it going?"

He didn't respond.

"Good," I said. "I'm glad you don't want to bother with wasted words because I don't have a lot of time to say what I need to say."

No response.

I continued. "Any idea how much prison time somebody would get for stealing ancient artifacts from a foreign country and carrying them through international waters back to the United States?"

I glanced over at him, but he showed absolutely no reaction.

"You already know, of course," I said, "that Anthony—what do you call him? Larry?—Well, Larry has quite a few *ancient* writings on *ancient* paper that belong to Levi and his people. You know that, don't you? And I'm sure you know that he didn't get permission, either. So since you're all going back together, I guess that amounts to basically what I said—stealing ancient artifacts from a foreign country and carrying them through international waters back to the United States."

I glanced over at him again. There was still no reaction.

"According to my friend's dad, who's an archeologist," I continued, "you can get about as much prison time for something like that as you can for—say—*kidnapping*."

Still no response. I was starting to wonder if the rock I was apparently talking to was harder than the rock I was sitting on.

"Now *you* know and *I* know," I said, "that we weren't kidnapped on purpose by you three—but who's going to believe that? Especially from a group of guys who've already been to prison. Well, wait a minute. I guess both you and Larry have been to prison—but now what about Mr. Omni? Has he ever been to prison?"

I didn't bother to look over at him this time.

"Seems to me," I continued, "that you were working for him right before you went to prison, weren't you? I've had the pleasure the last few days of watching the work that you do for him: this bodyguard thing. As I said, it seems to me that it would be nearly impossible for you to do *anything* that would land you in prison unless the guy you're bodyguarding is right in the middle of it, too."

Now I looked over at him and didn't look away.

"The only other thing that I can figure," I said thoughtfully, "is that maybe you didn't do anything wrong at all, but maybe you just went to prison to protect Omni—like it was some kind of extension to your bodyguard job or something."

Leonard's eyelids fluttered ever so slightly.

"So what happens next time?" I asked. "I mean—if the three of you are caught either kidnapping or in possession of stolen arti-facts—or both—is it going to be Omni's turn to go to prison? Is *he* going to cover for *you* this time? He's a great employer, isn't he? And a pretty nice guy, too. He would take his turn in prison, wouldn't he? For your sake?"

Leonard's eyelids fluttered again, and I kept looking straight at him.

"I can hear it all now!" I said. Since Leonard hung out with Moe so much, I figured he might appreciate a little drama. So I said, "I can just hear him saying, 'Oh, Leonard, *you* went last time! It's *my* turn to go. Now don't worry about a thing! I'll cover for you this time!'"

Leonard's stare fell from the top of the trees to the ground in front of him.

"I'll tell you what," I said, "I just came over here to ask you a small favor. I've got a stack of blank and unimportant pages in my backpack that look a whole lot like the pages that Anthony has. When I go to sleep tonight, I'm going to leave my backpack wide open, just inside our tent door. If you, uh—happen to have a few minutes—perhaps you could come and grab those sometime when everyone else is asleep and make a little switch for me—with the pages that Anthony has in his backpack."

I paused for a moment. "It seems to me," I continued more slowly, "that I have never seen you threaten any of us or actively participate in their scheming plans in any way. Personally, I think if you went to prison for this, you'd be getting totally ripped off by your employer and his partner in crime. And I would be happy to say that in court—in exchange for those papers, of course."

Leonard was still staring at the ground. His expression had changed, but I couldn't tell if that meant he was actually thinking about what I said or if I had just annoyed him. I looked up and saw Mr. Omni returning from the trees.

"If you have any questions, we can talk again at lunch time," I said, hopping off the rock and heading back to our tent. I could feel myself starting to shake as I came nearer. I almost dropped the half-eaten cake that was still in my hand. I hadn't realized how anxious I was until now. I fumbled to unzip the flap, then crawled inside the tent and closed the flap behind me. All of a sudden, I was freezing and could barely control my hands as I wrapped up in my sleeping bag and tried to relax.

A few minutes later I was feeling very much better. I took several deep breaths and went to go tell Jeff and Shauna what I had done.

"He'll never do it," Jeff said while tightening the harness around a reindeer's neck.

"How do you know?" I asked defiantly.

"I don't," he admitted. "I just don't think he will."

"That was really brave," said Shauna.

"That's one word for it, I suppose," Jeff said.

"What do you mean by that?" I asked. "At least *I'm* trying to do something about it."

"Hey, guys," Shauna said, "come on. We are not going to do this." Turning to me, she said, "Brandon, I'll say it again: that was really brave. I'm amazed that you did it. It would be really great if Leonard does it, too. I hope it works."

"Thanks, Shauna," I said. I was glad she was with us. Jeff could be a real pain sometimes.

"Are you going to tell Levi what you did?" asked Jeff.

"Only if it works," I mumbled.

None of us said anything more about it for the rest of the morning. As lunch time grew nearer I felt myself getting more and more nervous again as I waited for the chance to find out what Leonard might say. I would have tried to get an answer from him earlier, but as always, he was right next to Omni the whole time. As we ate, I watched the Three Stooges out of the corner of my eye and waited for my chance. These guys were pretty predictable: Anthony left first, and a few minutes later Omni said something dopey and left Leonard by himself.

I went over near him and sat down like I had after breakfast. He acted like he didn't even notice me. Neither of us said anything for a moment or two.

"Well?" I said. "Any comments or questions?" I reminded myself of a school teacher.

Leonard gave no sign that I existed. It was then, for the first time, I realized that I didn't remember ever hearing Leonard speak. After the thought hit me, I tried as hard as I could to think of *any* time that I had ever heard him speak. I couldn't come up with a single thing. Shocked and a little off balance, I finally said the first thing that came into my mind.

"Do you speak English?" I asked.

This brought the most dramatic response I had seen from him at any time up to this point in our association over the last week. He turned his head quickly in my direction and gave me a look that clearly said he thought I was the dumbest kid he had ever laid eyes on.

"I guess that answers my question," I mumbled. "Well—just so you know, I'm still planning to leave my backpack where and how I said I would."

This time he responded by returning to his previous position and staring into space again. Discouraged, I walked away without another word.

"Have you ever heard Leonard say anything?" I asked Jeff and Shauna when I got back to Levi's sled and was helping them load up the food and water bags.

Shauna scrunched up her face for moment, then slowly began to shake her head. "I don't think so." She paused a moment, still trying to come up with something, and then said, "How weird."

Jeff seemed a lot less interested. He said without any apparent thought, "Nope. But I'll be sure to let you know if I do."

"Do you think he speaks English?" asked Shauna.

I thought about giving her the same look that Leonard gave to me, but instead I just shrugged my shoulders. "If he doesn't," I answered, "I might just have to come up with a way to take care of this myself." I thought about this for a moment and then added, "I guess I might have to do that anyway."

I was feeling pretty miserable the rest of the day. The whole mess was making me tired, and I was having a hard time keeping up with the sled. I was glad when I figured out that the Sabbath would begin at sundown and we wouldn't be traveling at all the next day. Then we would have just one more day to get to the tribe's summer camp.

Because of the Sabbath, we stopped earlier in the evening than we had the previous two nights. The tribe didn't really wait until sundown to begin their Sabbath during the summer because it was so late by the time the sun actually went down. I wondered if they ignored the sun in the winter, also, when it went down much earlier in the afternoon. I was going to ask but never did get around to it.

As we ate dinner, I was dreading the thought of having to talk to Leonard again. I found myself hoping that they wouldn't leave him by himself this time, so I would have an excuse not to say anything to him. I knew he wouldn't respond, so what was the point? Deep down, I guess I was still hopeful, though, because I found myself still watching the Stooges as they ate their dinner.

I heaved a heavy sigh when I saw Omni get up and walk away,

leaving Leonard by himself once more. I knew I should go over to him if for no other reason than I told him I would, but it took me a few seconds to force myself to do it. Finally I stood up and walked slowly toward him. He responded exactly as expected—I was completely ignored as I approached. This time I didn't bother to sit down next to him like I had before.

"Well," I said hesitantly, "I just want you to know that I really hope you will help us out with this."

At least five seconds went by in silence. Just as I turned to leave I heard a voice from behind me. It was Mr. Omni. He had returned quicker than usual.

"Ahh, Brady!" Omni said. I figured he was referring to me since the name he used started with a B. "So nice of you to drop by and visit Leonard. He tells me that you've been doing that regularly today." Mr. Omni's moist smile was wider than normal. "Oh, and by the way," he continued. "Leonard told me that in English."

I looked over at Leonard who wore a wry smile, but was still staring into space. I could feel my face getting hot.

"He told me about your little request," Omni continued. He chuckled softly. "Can you possibly be serious? Did you really think that we would help you steal from our friend?"

"Are you trying to say that you're against stealing?" I asked quietly.

"What?" said Omni.

"I asked if you think stealing is wrong," I said more strongly. I noticed my breathing getting louder and faster.

"Well, I certainly do not approve of it when someone tries to steal from me or from my friend," he said. "And the amazing gall of you to ask us to help you! I am truly shocked."

"You stole from *my* friend," I said. "Am I not supposed to be shocked by that? Don't you think I should try to help my friend?"

"How you feel or what you attempt is completely beyond any concern that I might have," Omni sniffed. "The only interest there could possibly be for me is simply that I find it rather amusing. Oh, and—did you *really* think you could convince Leonard to cheat me, his best friend?" Omni laughed again, shaking his head.

I still don't know which feeling was stronger: my anger or my humiliation. It was obvious that standing there any longer was only going to give him more time to mock me, so I turned and stalked back to our tent. I could still hear Omni laughing to himself until I had climbed through the open flap and zipped it shut. What a loser. No wonder he and Anthony were friends. But *Leonard!* I really thought that I might have a chance with Leonard.

I flopped down over my rolled-up sleeping bag and fumed for several minutes, replaying everything in my head again and again.

"*Fine!*" I breathed in exasperation. "I don't need you."

From then until everyone else came to bed, I tried to think of a way to make the switch on my own. I was so wrapped up in my thoughts that I don't remember what anyone said when they finally all got there or even what Meg said in her prayer.

Hours later I was still awake in my sleeping bag, staring up into the darkness. When I figured the night was as dark as it was going to get, I picked up my backpack, unzipped the tent flap, and climbed out of the tent. I moved a few feet away from the tent to try to reduce the chance of someone hearing what I was doing. As quietly as I could, I removed the flashlight and the worthless pages from my backpack. Then I carried everything around the back side of the Stooges' tent.

As I lay planning this for the last several hours, my biggest fear was that my flashlight would give me away. I knew there wouldn't be enough light in the tent for me to find Aaron's pages and make the switch. But I also knew that these flashlights were bright enough that any number of the Three Stooges would likely wake up as soon as I lit up their tent—and since I would be holding the flashlight, they would be able to catch me easily and immediately.

I finally decided that I needed a way to dim the light quite a bit and also have it be somewhere other than in my hand!

Moving as quietly as possible, I placed my backpack on the ground right next to the back of the Stooges' tent. Then, pointing the flashlight straight up into the sky, I turned it on. I stared down at the ground and squinted so my eyes wouldn't get used to the light. Then, over the next two or three minutes, I gradually angled the light closer and closer to the tent, hoping that it wouldn't be a big enough change to wake anybody up. Finally, I laid the flashlight down on the top of my backpack and pushed the lens right up against the tent fabric. Because the tent was black, I figured it just might be a great filter. I also hoped that if somebody *did* happen to wake up, they would first concentrate on the light, long enough that I could get away without being caught.

Then I crept around to the front of the tent. I spent at least another two or three minutes slowly opening the zipper on the tent flap, pulling it only one or two ticks at a time. I was so scared, my breathing got louder and my heart was pounding in my throat. When I finally opened the flap, I was ecstatic to find that the tent was glowing perfectly; it couldn't have been better.

I could see their three backpacks stacked together right in the middle of the tent, with one person sleeping next to each of the three walls that didn't have the door flap. Leonard was lying on his back with his sleeping bag pulled up to his chest and his arms folded across it. I couldn't tell which of the other two was Anthony. Whoever was sleeping against the back wall had the sleeping bag pulled completely over his head. The other one was rolled up into a little ball, lying on his side, facing the side of the tent. That one almost sounded like he was sucking his thumb, but I couldn't be sure. I decided to look inside the backpack closest to him first.

Putting the extra pages down just inside the tent, I crawled slowly over to the backpack. The top flap was closed but not tied, so I was able to easily move it out of the way. The opening was toward the front of the tent, so there wasn't enough light to see what was inside it. As quietly as I could, I pushed it up onto its bottom and angled it toward the light. It felt like it was practically empty. When I had it turned over enough that some light shined inside, my heart skipped a beat! *The pages were inside!*

Because the pages were the only thing inside the pack, they were easy to get to, but I cringed with every little rustle they made. Suddenly, Leonard snorted in his sleep and turned his head toward me. My heart nearly stopped while I held my breath and watched to see if he was going to wake up. He smacked his lips a couple of times but didn't open his eyes. I waited a few seconds for him to settle, then put the practice sheets in the backpack, quietly folded the top flap down, and tipped the backpack over into its original position.

As I inched backward to the opening of the tent, my hands were shaking so badly it made the papers rustle, and I cringed, thinking one or all of the three would hear me and wake up. I kept telling myself to breathe deeply and relax. Finally, I reached the tent flap and made it outside. It took just as long to zip up the flap as it had opening it. Then I tiptoed to the back of the tent and switched off my flashlight. I thought about moving it gradually, as I had done before, but by this time, I just didn't have the patience. As quietly as I could, I returned to my own tent and put everything down just inside the flap and crawled inside. After zipping it closed, I put the rescued pages and flashlight into my backpack and just left them right where they were.

My heart was still pounding, but I couldn't believe how well it had gone! It absolutely, no way, could have been any better! I lay in my sleeping bag, shaking with excitement. What luck to have them all sleeping next to the walls! And to find the pages in the very first backpack I checked. Wow! I figured that meant that Anthony had to be the thumb sucker. I could hardly wait until morning to tell somebody what I had done!

CHAPTER 12

Keeping the Sabbath Day Holy

I slept the rest of that night better than I had since this whole thing began. I don't know if it was because we had just walked for three days straight, or if it was because I had stayed up half the night getting Aaron's writings back, or if it was because I had actually succeeded in getting them! Maybe it was a combination of all three. Anyway, when I finally woke up, I spent the first few moments halfway between reality and a really satisfying dream that I had the side of my face pressed deep into a very comfortable pillow in my own bedroom at home.

As I became more and more awake, my not-so-comfortable, inflatable pillow was the first part of reality to hit. Next was the fact that I was in a sleeping bag in a tent instead of in my own bedroom. Last came the memory of the excitement I had felt when I went to sleep. My eyes were still closed, but a smile crept across my face just the same. Suddenly, the inflatable pillow and sleeping bag didn't seem quite so annoying. I thought about seeing if there was anyone awake yet that I could tell my good news to, but my eyelids had no intention of releasing their grip on my eyeballs just yet. Instead I just listened for any sounds of life, thinking that might inspire my eyelids.

I was still in a fog and couldn't hear anyone in the tent making any noise. I couldn't hear anyone outside the tent, either. Next I tried my sense of smell. The yummy smell of cakes, cooking over a nearby fire had awakened me several times over the past several days. I took a deep, exploring sniff—no cakes were cooking as far as I could tell. I found myself wondering if Shauna or Meg would have been able to smell anything. They seemed to have much better noses than I did. I decided it must still be too early and that even though I was tired, my excitement over last night's great accomplishment was probably responsible for me waking up so soon.

A few minutes later I had drifted part way back to the soft-pillow-in-my-own-bedroom dream when I heard the zipper to our tent being opened.

"Do you think Brandon is still asleep?" came Meg's voice from outside the tent.

"It sure looks that way," said Jeff. It sounded like he was outside, too. Surprised, I propped myself up on my elbows and blinked a few times.

"Why?" asked Meg.

Before he could answer her, Jeff stuck his head inside the tent and saw that I was indeed awake, so he spoke to me instead.

"It's about time," he said. "We had breakfast hours ago."

"Really?" I mumbled, rubbing my eyes with my thumb and index finger. Jeff and Meg climbed inside and closed the flap behind them.

"Yeah," said Jeff. "You're lucky today's the Sabbath or no one would have let you sleep this long."

I was so busy being amazed by how late it was that I forgot why I had apparently slept so long. Otherwise I would have immediately told them the great thing I had done.

"Can I tell him what happened?" asked Meg.

"Sure," said Jeff.

"Did you know that everybody's gone?" she asked me.

I had to think about her question for a moment before answering. "Everybody who?" I asked. My voice was raspy.

"All the bad guys," answered Jeff.

"The bad guys?" I questioned. "Do you mean Esau and the Tweedles?"

"*And* the Three Stooges," said Jeff.

"*What?*" I said, blinking several times. "Where did they all go?"

"We don't know," Jeff replied. "Apparently they left without talking to anyone. Levi thinks they probably just went on ahead to the river."

I was still feeling a little groggy, but I was doing my best to wake up and think clearly. "But . . ." I hesitated, "but what about the Sabbath?" I continued before Jeff said anything. "I mean, I know the Stooges don't care about it, but what about Esau? And his sons? Are they calling this an ox-in-the-mire-type-thing or what?"

"They don't believe in Jesus, remember?" said Jeff. "He's the one who taught about the ox in the mire."

"The ox and the what?" asked Meg.

"I'll explain it later," said Jeff.

"Are you trying to keep me from finding out?" Meg asked, clamping her lips together and narrowing her eyes.

"No," grunted Jeff, slightly exasperated. "Okay, fine—but it's not the ox *and*, it's the ox *in*, okay?" He said very slowly, "the ox *in* the mire."

"What's the mire?" she asked, still acting as though she thought she was being tricked.

"It's like a really muddy place where an ox could get stuck," explained Jeff. "And Jesus taught that if your ox gets stuck in the mire on the Sabbath, then you don't have to wait until the next day to get the ox out."

Meg pulled a face, obviously confused. "Where's the ox?" she asked.

"There is no ox," Jeff said. "It's just an example."

"It means that if you have an emergency, you are allowed to

take care of it," I said, "even if it's on Sunday." Suddenly I was feeling wide awake. Meg often had that effect on me.

Once Meg seemed to be satisfied, Jeff turned back to me and said, "We asked Aaron and Levi the same thing, but they said that Esau and his people have their Sabbath the day before everybody else now."

"When did they start doing that?" I asked.

"I guess not too long after we left last year," answered Jeff. "Levi told us about it this morning. Remember how last year we thought it was weird that they had their Sabbath on Sunday?"

"Right," I said. "Because they should have still been doing it the Old Testament way—on Saturday."

"Exactly," nodded Jeff. "Well, remember, too, that when Levi's father was in charge a long time ago was when they first found out about Jesus Christ from the guy who came from the United States and lived here for the rest of his life?"

"Yeah," I nodded, sitting all the way up now.

"Well," Jeff continued. "I guess they started having their Sabbath on Sunday way back then—to be like the New Testament Apostles when they started meeting together on the first day of the week, after Jesus was resurrected. And when Esau's father took over and made everybody go back to following the old ways, they never bothered to change the day back again."

"So why did Esau do it now?" I asked.

"Levi said it was so he would be noticed," Jeff said with a smug look. "Like he was just trying to draw attention to himself or something."

"What a show-off," I said.

"Yep," Jeff agreed.

"So why did they hike along with the rest of us yesterday?" I asked. "Why didn't they do the Sabbath then?"

"Apparently Esau only does that stuff when the other people are around," Jeff said.

I shook my head, thinking about what a hypocrite this guy was. "So now that they all left, are we just going to stay here today anyway?" I asked.

Jeff nodded, "Yeah. Levi says he thinks that Esau's reindeer sled is going to have a pretty tough time getting through the trees all the way down to the river. He thinks we'll be able to catch up."

"So when are we leaving?" I asked.

"Aaron didn't want to wait until tomorrow," said Jeff, "so he talked Levi into leaving tonight, as soon as the Sabbath is over. He's really worried about his Old Testament writings and the Book of Mormon pages that they translated."

"Oh!" I said with excitement. "I almost forgot to tell you."

"You *did* forget," said Jeff. "At least until now!"

I gave him an exasperated grunt as I kicked my way quickly out of my sleeping bag. "You know what I mean," I said smugly. Then, smiling again, I said, "But just wait till you see what I have in my backpack."

Meg was sort of lying across the top of it because it was still next to the doorway.

"Meg," I said. "I need to get into my backpack. Go get Aaron! Quick!"

"Why do you want him?" she asked, making no real attempt to get out of my way.

"Me-e-eg!" I whined, "I need to show him something! Please go! Fast!"

Pouting again, she opened the zipper on the door flap before bothering to get out of my way. I had been trying to be more patient with her lately, so I didn't say anything—I just watched anxiously until she finally climbed off of my backpack and out of the tent.

"Guess what I did?" I said to Jeff as I pulled back the top flap and reached inside. Then with a triumphant smile, I announced, "I got the pages back!"

"No way!" said Jeff. "How?"

As I pulled out the sheets, I said, "I sneaked into the tent when they were all asleep and switched them with the other pages that Aaron gave me last night!" With that I plopped them into Jeff's lap, beaming all the while. "*That's* why I was so tired this morning," I continued as Jeff stared with amazement at the pages, "because I was up half the night."

That's when I noticed Jeff's face change from amazement to a smirk. He was shuffling through the pages. "Funny, Bran," he said. "I really believed you for a minute."

"What do you mean?" I asked.

"These are the pages that Aaron gave you," Jeff said, handing them back to me.

I grabbed the pages and flipped through them in astonishment. I was so shocked by what I saw that I felt like I couldn't even breathe for a minute. Slowly, I leafed through them again, one by one, trying to imagine what had possibly happened.

"I promise," I whispered. "I *promise* I switched them."

Jeff just looked at me. I could tell he wasn't sure what to think. But believing me wasn't at the top of his list.

"I went into their tent," I explained, "and I switched the pages." Shaking my head slowly back and forth, I continued to look through the pages again and again as I described what I had done. "First, I went around the back of their tent and put my flashlight against it so it would shine inside without being too bright," I said. "Then I took forever opening the zipper on the door flap. And then I pulled the pages out of Anthony's pack and put these pages in there."

Jeff just stared at me.

"Anthony was sucking his thumb!" I said. "I was there!"

That was the first thing I had said that Jeff thought sounded believable. "His thumb?" he asked. "Sometimes I've had dreams," Jeff said slowly, "that seemed *so* real to me . . ."

167

"It wasn't a *dream!*" I said firmly. "I *know* that I did it. I never even fell asleep last night until I went and made the switch!"

Just then, Meg returned with Aaron and held open the door flap. Shauna, Moses, and Levi were all close behind.

"I *had* them," I said to Aaron. Shaking my head, I added, "I don't know what happened! I *know* I had them. I switched these pages for the pages that Anthony had in his backpack."

Completely bewildered, I repeated for them what I had just explained to Jeff. I was so frustrated, I could hardly think. They listened to my story, but none of them seemed any more convinced than Jeff had been. As Aaron took the pages and slowly sifted through them, I dropped my head into my hands in discouragement. No one said anything for several moments.

"Maybe," said Shauna, trying to be encouraging, "you wanted to do it so badly, that you dreamed you did it. I've had that happen to me before. And dreams can sometimes seem so real!"

I looked up at her with a face that apparently said exactly what I was thinking, because she responded by simply saying, "It was just an idea—sorry."

"I know," I mumbled.

"You eating morning meal now," suggested Levi. "Everything being well."

I didn't feel like eating but decided to follow them over to the fire area anyway. The fire was already gone. The cakes were cold, but I didn't care. Several people tried to say things to me to make me feel better, but it just made me feel dumb. I couldn't believe it. What could have happened?

Most of the rest of the morning and afternoon was spent in talking about Sabbath day type things. We read quite a lot of the Book of Mormon out loud together and tried to explain some of the words that were difficult for Levi, Aaron, and Moses. Since they didn't have their translated pages, they just continued to make small notes in the margins using symbols that meant nothing to us.

I was amazed that they already knew very well which parts of the Book of Mormon had the most to do with Jesus Christ. That was obviously what they were most interested in. They really used it as the subtitle suggested: as *Another Testament of Jesus Christ.*

Late in the afternoon, Levi, Aaron, and Moses prepared the sacrament for all of us. I was kind of glad that everyone else was gone. It was nice to be able to just enjoy it with those who really understood its value. When we were done, I could tell that Levi was trying to decide whether to ask us something. He kept drawing a breath as if he would speak, but then he would look away and close his mouth again.

"What is it?" Jeff finally asked.

Levi hesitated before saying, "Your father returning for giving priesthood to my people?"

We had talked about this the previous year. Levi really wanted to be able to have the proper authority to do all the things he was doing for the tribe. Even though he knew he didn't have the priesthood, in the end he felt it was better to practice doing what he knew should be done—even without the authority. He had asked us before if our dad could lay hands on him and give him the authority.

"Our father said that he could only do it if he had permission to," said Jeff. "I'm sorry."

Levi nodded.

"I think that means you would have to be known to the rest of the world," explained Shauna. "Or at least to the highest leaders of the Church."

Levi nodded again. He seemed to think about what all this would mean. Finally he said to no one in particular, "Perhaps time coming."

"I think they would want to meet you," said Shauna. "So either they would need to come here or you would need to go there."

Levi continued to nod his understanding. "Perhaps time

coming." He looked over at Aaron as he said this. My mind began to reel with the possibilities. Was he thinking about the *Joseph* idea again, where Aaron might go to another land? I wanted to ask, but I didn't dare.

After the evening meal, Levi announced that the Sabbath had ended and we could prepare to leave. We took the tents down and packed everything up as fast as possible onto the reindeer sled. Meg and Shauna rode from the start, but as we continued to hike later and longer, Levi eventually suggested that Jeff and I ride also. I was very grateful to accept the offer. I had been starting to think I was going to fall over with each step. Meg and Shauna were already asleep when we climbed onto the sled with them. There was plenty of room. I asked Aaron and Moses if they were going to ride, too, but they continued to walk alongside the reindeer, guiding them along the dark trail.

The sun was bright when I awoke. I could tell that it was still quite early in the day—still a long time before breakfast. But the sun came up early around here. I quickly saw that Levi was now the only one walking. Moses and Aaron were asleep at the front of the sled. I learned later that Levi had walked all night, which I found impressive, since he was never entirely convinced that we needed to be in such a rush anyway. Levi felt that with the difficulty of getting the reindeer sled through the trees and down to the yacht, plus the time it would take to load it up, we could have just waited until Monday morning to leave. But since Aaron was so anxious, Levi was willing to do it.

I continued to ride, enjoying the gentle rocking of the reindeer sled as it made its way along this trail that these people had followed every year for hundreds or maybe thousands of years. When Moses and Aaron woke up, they each immediately got off of the sled and hiked again. I thought about following their example, but I just couldn't bring myself to do it. I'd been offered a ride, and I was going to gratefully accept it until I was asked to give it up. I continued to lay quietly, hoping to prolong the gift as long as possible.

We arrived in the valley of the tribe's summer home about breakfast time. I was starving. There was no sign of the others. Levi suggested that we should stop and eat, even though Aaron would have much preferred to keep going until we caught up to the others. While Levi and Aaron prepared breakfast, Jeff and I helped Moses unharness the reindeer so they could graze and rest.

As we ate, Aaron and Moses kept looking up toward the pass, scanning the mountainside for any sign of the other group. Just as we were finishing, Aaron excitedly said something in their language that we didn't understand—but we all knew what it probably meant. I looked up in time to catch just a glimpse of the reindeer sled as it disappeared into the mountain pass. It had been hidden in the trees on the slope until that moment.

Aaron wanted to go right then, but Levi said he could wait and that he needed his rest. They had a conversation that we couldn't understand until Levi asked us, "Boat having places of hiding for writings?"

"Yes," we all answered at once.

"That boat has *many* places for hiding things," said Shauna.

It turns out Aaron was worried that once Anthony got to the boat, Aaron would have almost no chance of getting the writings back. Though Levi didn't want to insult Anthony—his guest—by accusing him of being a thief, he desperately wanted to get the writings back. So Aaron was allowed to go. Aaron liked the idea of making a switch, if he could, so he took the useless pages with him. Levi told him that the rest of us would leave to catch up with him after lunch. Levi said he was just too tired to go then.

We all stood and watched as Aaron scurried away with nothing other than the animal skin bag holding the pages. He didn't even take any food or water with him. Once Aaron had disappeared into the trees, Levi made himself comfortable on the back of the reindeer sled and soon fell asleep. It turned out that Moses had apparently slept quite a bit less than Aaron had during the previous night, and so he curled up and soon fell asleep as well.

As if with the help of an alarm clock, Levi woke up when the sun was at its absolute highest point in the southern sky. Levi didn't think the reindeer had rested enough. He suggested we go the rest of the way without the reindeer sled, so we began the four-hour hike up to the pass on foot. We were a little worried about Meg, but for no good reason; she did fine.

As we approached the pass, I began to worry about Levi. He seemed to be getting really tired and began to stagger a little bit with each step. I figured it probably had a lot to do with staying up all night walking and then only getting three or four hours of sleep before hiking up the mountainside.

Moses and Shauna were in the lead. Meg was walking by Jeff and me, with Levi a few feet behind. About 50 feet from the pass I heard Levi trip and fall. Jeff and I both immediately turned and ran back to see if we could help him. He didn't make any sound, but we could tell that he was in a lot of pain. He was holding his ankle with both hands in a tight grip.

"Are you okay?" I asked.

"Will you be all right?" Jeff asked. "Can we help?"

Levi didn't say anything for at least a minute. By this time Moses and Shauna had joined us.

"Much bad," Levi finally admitted. He pulled his hands away and pushed his thick leather shoe down off of his ankle. We could see that it was already beginning to swell. Levi examined his ankle briefly and then grabbed on with both hands again.

Moses spoke first. "You needing medicine," he said. "I going."

"No!" called Levi, bringing Moses back. He winced. "Jeff and Brandon helping me with medicine," Levi said. "You taking Shauna and Meg to river. Boys following soon."

"Yes," said Moses. Taking Meg by both hands, he swung her

around onto his back, pink backpack and all. "Coming with me," he said to Shauna. "Jeff and Brandon being not long behind." And with that they were gone.

"What kind of medicine?" asked Jeff, turning his attention back to Levi. "Where is it? Is it on the sled?"

"Medicine," winced Levi, "for the swell in leg and foot."

"To make the swelling go down?" asked Jeff.

"Yes," answered Levi.

"Do we need to go back down the mountain to get the medicine?" I asked.

"No," answered Levi.

It turned out that we were to make the medicine by boiling the leaves of a certain plant. Jeff was sent to find the right kind of bush. According to Levi's description, the plant was supposedly not quite as tall as Jeff and it had lots of small, pointed leaves with some very small blue flowers.

My job was to start a fire and have some water boiling for the leaves by the time that Jeff returned. I was grateful for my backpack, since it had matches as well as a mess kit with a small metal bowl. I didn't have one of those nifty little stove-type burners like the Stooges, though, so I had to gather some wood. I poured water from my canteen into the metal bowl and began to heat it over my small fire.

Jeff came back once in the middle of what I was doing. He had some leaves from a plant that apparently didn't have any flowers on it, but Jeff said that the plant had the smallest leaves he could find.

"No," said Levi. "Smaller leaves. Blue flowers."

It took Jeff another ten minutes to finally come back with the right leaves.

"Yes," said Levi. "This being well."

We immediately put the leaves into the boiling water to cook.

"Ye going when leaves are ready," said Levi. "Ye taking dish when leaves are ready. I coming after ye when ankle is better."

"Are you sure?" asked Jeff. "I don't think our boat will be leaving until the day after tomorrow. We can stay with you."

"No," said Levi, shaking his head back and forth. "Ye going soon."

"Well, if you want us to go," I said, "we can go now. We don't have to wait for the dish. I seriously doubt Vladimir will notice if one of his backpacks is returned missing a dish."

"Omni can pay for it," Jeff suggested.

Levi nodded, still firmly holding his ankle with both hands. "This being well," he said. Then, taking one hand away from his ankle he gripped Jeff's shoulder and said, "Farewell." Then he did the same to me. "Ye taking greetings to family," Levi said as we stood to leave.

"Yes, we will," we agreed.

With that we scampered up to the mountain pass, anxious to catch up to Moses and the girls. Being a lot more excited than we were physically able, we had to stop and rest after running up the last fifty feet and then all the way through the pass. We ran until we could see the river below us and knew for sure that Vladimir hadn't come back yet. Then we stopped to catch our breath.

"Do you think Levi will be okay?" I asked.

"He knows what he's doing," Jeff answered.

After we had rested for a couple of minutes, I started glancing around a bit. "This is the third time we've come through here," I said. "Once last year and now twice in a week."

"It better be the last time," said Jeff.

I just nodded my reply and looked away. As I did so, something caught my eye. "What is that?" I asked as I walked over for a closer look. I had seen something long and thin and shiny that didn't look like anything that would normally be in a place like this. As I got closer, I thought it looked like an antenna sticking up out of a bush from behind a rock.

"Hey, Jeff," I called back over my shoulder. "I think I found Dr. Anthony's second backpack."

"Oh, yeah," said Jeff, coming to join me. "I'd forgotten about that."

"But it's got an antenna sticking out of it," I said, pulling the backpack out where I could get a better look. It was heavy. "Did he put a mega-radio in there or what?"

Unzipping the bag, we were shocked by what we saw. Instead of being attached to a radio, the antenna went into a small black box that had no dials or knobs or anything. But what shocked us was the stack of what looked like sticks of dynamite in the bottom of the bag. There were at least a dozen sticks, taped together with wires running between them and the little black box.

"He's going to blow up the mountain pass!" gasped Jeff.

"*Why?*" I breathed.

"How should I know?" replied Jeff. "But we've got to get out of here!" He started running for the river. I didn't follow.

"What about Levi?" I called after Jeff. He stopped in his tracks and turned halfway back around. I continued by saying, "He said he would be coming after us. And with his ankle, it will take him forever to get through here."

Jeff just stared at me.

"We have to go back and warn him," I said.

Jeff looked like he couldn't decide what to say. "Well, let's run *some*where!" he finally said. "I don't like standing around close to that thing."

Without another word we both took off running back through the pass to warn Levi. I kept trying to think about how we were going to describe dynamite to this guy. I hadn't come up with anything by the time we got back to where Levi was. But it didn't matter, because just as he was about to ask us why we had come back, a huge explosion pierced our ears, rocking the entire mountain.

CHAPTER 13

The Path of Living Water

The explosion knocked Jeff and me to the ground. We fell forward down the slope just a few feet in front of Levi, who wore a look of absolute horror. I'm sure he'd never experienced anything like that before. He was staring up the mountainside. Still on my hands and knees, I turned to look back up the slope and saw rocks flying out of the pass and clouds of dust rising above it. Some of the rocks hung in the air for several seconds before crashing to the ground. Luckily nothing came too close to where we were. Levi was still staring up at the mountain in total astonishment when I turned to face him again. A moment later he looked intently at us as if he wanted to ask what was happening, but he didn't even know what to say.

"Anthony did it!" gasped Jeff.

Levi looked like he couldn't imagine how any man could be responsible for such a thing—only God had so much power. I couldn't think of anything in his experience that might have compared with that huge blast and deafening noise, except maybe lightning.

"That's why we came back," Jeff gasped again, "to warn you that this might happen."

"How this being done?" Levi finally managed to ask.

"It's called dynamite," I breathed. "It's . . . It . . . It just *does* that. I-It explodes." I threw my hands up and out in an effort to get my idea across to him. "It just blows things apart," I said. How do you explain dynamite or an explosion to somebody who's never seen or heard of such a thing? Levi still looked completely bewildered.

"Dr. Anthony killing people," said Levi with intensity.

"I don't think so," I said, trying to reassure him.

Levi looked at me like he thought I was a total nutcase.

"I mean, yeah, sure," I said quickly, "if people were close to the explosion it would probably kill them—but I meant I don't think anybody *was* close to it."

Levi still looked like he didn't think he should believe me. I'm sure he was worried about those who had gone before us—especially Aaron.

"We saw the place where Anthony hid the dynamite, "Jeff explained. "You know—the stuff that goes boom—and nobody was near it, except for Brandon and me. Everyone else had already gone down the other side."

"That's why we came back," I added, "like Jeff said before. We came back to make sure you wouldn't go near it."

Levi took this all in for several moments before speaking again.

"Why Dr. Anthony creating this ex-plo-sion?" asked Levi, separating the last word into syllables.

"I don't know," said Jeff, shaking his head and looking over at me. "We don't know." Levi was looking for more, so Jeff tried to suggest anything that might make sense. "He definitely wanted to keep anybody from getting through that pass again," Jeff said. "Either to keep you from catching him and getting your writings back or—to keep us from getting back to the boat because he didn't want to take us back with him. Or maybe for some other reason. The guy's just crazy, that's all."

That's when it first hit me. It was like one of those flying rocks just landed right in my stomach. I gasped for air. "We can't get through," I breathed. Then louder, "How are we going to get through?!" I started to panic. My eyes darted from Levi to Jeff to the pass and back around again. "Shauna and Meg are on the other side! How are we going to get over there? How are we going to get home?" I was breathing hard now, and I could feel myself getting light-headed.

"Ye following path of Christ," said Levi, reassuringly. "Ye following the path of Living Water."

I could hear his words, but they sounded far away.

"Brandon?" said Jeff in a hollow, far-away voice. "Are you okay?" His voice drifted off.

The next thing I knew, I was flat on my back staring up at Levi and Jeff.

"Brandon, are you all right?" asked Jeff, in a voice that sounded more normal. I had apparently been unconscious for several minutes.

I blinked several times and tried to nod my head, but I don't think it moved very much.

"Brandon?" said Jeff again.

My mouth was dry, but I managed to say very slowly, "Jeff, I think you were right before—" I paused long enough to lick my lips and then continued. "About that being the last time we would go through the pass," I said. "Maybe we should have just gone down the other side."

Jeff just stared at me for a moment. Then he looked at Levi and said, "Maybe, but then Levi would have had no clue what had happened."

He was right, of course. Coming back to warn Levi was the right thing to do—but now what? Levi made me sit up and take a drink of water.

"What's the path you're talking about?" I asked, after swallowing a small gulp of water. It seemed really cold and made me shiver. Looking up at the mountain, I said, "I think it will take forever to climb over the top of this thing. And Vladimir is supposed to be back the day after tomorrow."

"Path of Living Water going not over mountain," said Levi. "Path of Living Water going *through* mountain."

I was a little confused.

"A *tunnel!*" exclaimed Jeff. "Levi told me that there's a tunnel going all the way through the mountain." I got the idea Levi had done some explaining while I was unconscious.

I thought about this for a minute before asking, "Where is it?"

"Levi says it's not too far south of here," explained Jeff. "That's where Levi and Moses and Aaron were the night we first found them last week. They had stayed behind to explore the tunnel."

"That's got to be at least *five hours* from here!" I exclaimed. "It took us four hours to get up here from where we left the reindeer, and last week it took over an hour to get from there to where they were camping!"

"We don't go back down the mountain," explained Jeff. "Levi says that if we just walk along the side to get over there, then he thinks it will only take about half as long."

I thought about this for a minute. Turning to Levi, I asked, "You said you stayed behind to explore? So is this tunnel something new that you just found?"

"Tunnel being new to me," said Levi. "Not new to my people." He picked up a stick and stirred the leaves that were still boiling over the small fire. This was the first time I noticed that Levi was still holding his ankle with one hand.

"The tribe has used it in the past to get water," said Jeff, "but the last time was when Levi was really young, so he has never been inside it before. When it's too dry on this side of the mountain, they go through, and I guess the opening on the other side is close to water coming down the side of the mountain."

"So you have to haul it back?" I asked. "I hope it's not a very long tunnel."

"What being *haul?*" asked Levi.

"Uhh," said Jeff, "it means to carry. Do you have to carry it back?"

"No," said Levi. "We *turning* water. We flowing water into tunnel. Water flowing through tunnel."

"You divert it?" asked Jeff. "With what? Like logs and rocks and stuff?"

"What being *logs?*" asked Levi.

"Trees," answered Jeff. "Big branches and tree trunks."

"Yes," said Levi, stirring his brew one more time.

"So when you don't need the extra water anymore," said Jeff, "then you go back through and move the trees out of the way or what?"

"No," said Levi. "Water moving. Water flowing different path down mountain."

"Oh," nodded Jeff, "so after a while it just doesn't come through anymore? Is that what you mean? But it still stays close enough to the opening that you can divert it—turn it again?"

"Not always the same," said Levi. "Many paths through mountain."

Jeff looked slightly stunned by this explanation. I could hear him gulp before asking, "So how do we know which path to take? Does it matter? Or are they all pretty much the same? Are you coming with us?" Jeff looked down at Levi's swollen ankle when he asked the last question.

"No," said Levi, shaking his head in a wide motion back and forth.

I wanted to ask which one of Jeff's eighteen questions Levi was saying *no* to. Did he mean, "No, it doesn't matter," or "No, they're not pretty much the same," or "No, he wasn't coming with us." Most of the possibilities didn't sound too good.

"No," said Levi again. "I going not. Ye following Path to Christ."

"What do you mean?" I asked. My head was starting to clear. "Are you saying we're just supposed to follow the Spirit?"

"No," said Levi again. "Ye following writings on walls."

I felt my eyes get wide and my mouth drop part way open as I looked over at Jeff. He looked exactly how I imagined that I must look.

"W-w-words?" asked Jeff. "We're supposed to *read* the words on the walls? We can't read your words!"

"No words," said Levi. He struggled to decide how to describe it. Frustrated, he finally just said, "No words."

"You don't mean pictures," said Jeff, obviously not thinking that could be the answer.

"Yes," nodded Levi emphatically. "Yes, pictures."

"So let me get this straight," said Jeff. "There are pictures drawn on the walls in this tunnel that we follow to go the right way to get out on the other side."

"Yes," said Levi. "Ye following pictures."

"Are there pictures only in the right tunnels?" I asked.

"Two tunnels with pictures," answered Levi.

"W-well, okay," said Jeff. "Then how do we know which tunnel to follow?"

"Ye following not *old* pictures," said Levi. "Ye following *new* pictures."

"What?" I asked in disbelief. This was not sounding like such a great idea. I mean—going by ourselves was pretty shaky even with a single, clearly-marked path, but now we were supposed to *choose* between *two* paths?

"So how do we know which ones are new and which ones are old?" I asked. I think my major doubts about this whole thing were quite obvious.

"I knowing not," said Levi softly. He seemed concerned. *No kidding,* I thought. *I'm pretty concerned, too.*

"Has anyone seen the pictures?" I asked. "I mean anyone that's still alive?"

Levi shook his head slowly back and forth. Then he said, "Christian seeing pictures."

Christian was the name of the man who had lived with these people years earlier and had given a copy of the Bible to Levi's father. We just nodded our understanding. As interesting as that little tidbit of information was, unfortunately, it wasn't very helpful.

"Christian calling path, Tunnel of Hezekiah," said Levi, as if this would mean something to us. It didn't. Neither one of us could ever remember hearing about Hezekiah before. Levi assured us that Hezekiah was in the Old Testament, but we just conceded that that was something that we would have to check out later. That didn't seem very important either at the moment.

Over the next several minutes Levi explained that the tunnel had been used several times to divert water into the valley, starting hundreds of years earlier. But, apparently, the last time they did it, they discovered that the water's path on the other side had moved far enough away from the opening that they couldn't divert the water over to it anymore. Levi's father had found a different tunnel that apparently opened up right next to the water. So, according to what Levi understood from his father, part way through the mountain we were supposed to find two tunnels that were marked with pictures—one with "old" pictures and the other with "new" ones. Since Levi had never been into the tunnels, he couldn't tell us anymore than that.

"So how new are the new pictures?" I asked, trying to get at least some idea that might help. "I mean how many years ago did your father draw these pictures in there?"

"I being young," said Levi. "Pictures being perhaps forty years there."

"And the old ones?" I asked.

"Old pictures being many hundred years there," said Levi. "Perhaps thousand years, or more."

"Okay," I sighed. "Hopefully we'll be able to tell the difference between pictures that are hundreds of years old and pictures that are only forty years old. What do you think, Jeff?"

He looked scared. "I think we don't have any choice," he said.

We watched as Levi removed his boiling leaves from the fire. The mixture now looked thick and gooey. He blew on it to help it cool faster. Over the next several minutes, Levi explained to us the shortest way to get to the opening of the tunnel. He described landmarks for us to look for and the shape of the top of the mountain that was directly above where the opening was. Neither Jeff nor I felt very confident that we would be able to find it, but we knew we had to at least try.

Levi said we should leave immediately so that we could find the opening before dark. Luckily, Jeff and I each had a flashlight in our backpacks that we could use once we were inside the tunnels. We watched as Levi stopped squeezing his ankle and scooped the warm, gooey "medicine" that he had made onto his swollen leg. His ankle had gotten really big around. Levi removed the leather strap from around his waist and wrapped it tightly around the swollen part.

"I coming perhaps in morning," Levi assured us. He was hoping that he would be well enough to travel by then. He asked us to pray with him before we left. We left him one of our canteens and gave him some jerky that I had been carrying in my backpack. We offered him some of our dehydrated food, but he had absolutely no interest in it. He had tried it once a few days earlier. I think he decided then that he would rather starve than eat that stuff again. I knew how he felt.

"Before we go," I suggested, "let's go check the pass just to be sure."

Jeff agreed and so we climbed back up to the pass and started to make our way through it. Almost immediately it became obvious that there was no way we were going to be able to get through there. Before Anthony's dynamite did its trick, the pass had been a thin crack that cut down through from the top of the mountain. In some places I was sure that it was actually wider at the bottom than anyplace else going up. We were now only able to walk a little more than halfway through it and there was no visible opening for as far up as we could see. The tunnel—this Path of Living Water as Levi called it—was our only hope.

What was Anthony thinking? Did he think he could kidnap all of them? Was Vladimir coming back with others to help trap them? The more I wondered about what might be going on over there, the more uptight I became, so I tried to just not think about it.

Ten minutes later we were back to where Levi lay resting. He said, "Farewell," to each of us again, and we headed south to find this mysterious opening that would hopefully lead us through the mountain.

It took us over three hours to get to where we camped the first night with Levi, Aaron, and Moses. Levi thought he knew how to find the opening to the tunnel based on the descriptions his father gave, but he had never actually been there himself. Because we were on the east side of the mountain, we didn't have much sunlight to help us out by the time we got there. The shadows of the trees made finding the opening a real pain, but after stopping twice to pray, we eventually found it.

We both had learned when we were younger how important it was to give a prayer of thanks after Heavenly Father blesses you with what you've been asking for. We were more than happy to drop to our knees right at the mouth of the tunnel and make it clear to Him how grateful we were to have found it. We each took a turn saying a prayer.

When we were done, we just sat in the dim light not saying anything for a few minutes. Neither one of us seemed eager to charge in there. Then my stomach growled.

184

"I'm starving," I said.

"Me, too," agreed Jeff.

"And I'm almost dead, too," I admitted.

Jeff just looked at me.

"Do we have to go through there tonight?" I asked. "Now that we found it, can we just go to sleep and find our way through in the morning?"

Jeff sighed a couple of times, trying to decide what to say. "I don't think we better," he said at last. "Let's eat something really fast and then find our way through, okay?"

I didn't respond.

"As soon as we're through, we can rest, okay?" he said.

I wasn't too excited about it, but I finally agreed.

"Don't eat too much, though," Jeff cautioned me as I began to wolf down what was left of my jerky stash. "If you get completely full, you'll be too tired to walk very far."

"I'm a *long* way from being completely full," I assured him.

After just a few minutes Jeff said we should go. He told me again that I should quit eating, so I wouldn't get so tired. I was more than slightly annoyed that he was making such a big deal out of it, but I put the jerky away just the same. I really didn't want to create any bad feelings between us. I knew that we would need all the help we could give each other if this was going to work. After one more prayer, we switched on our flashlights and headed into the darkness.

Once we got inside, we could see that where we were walking looked very much like a lot of water had flowed through there at some time. The floor was smooth and sloping. But it was completely dry now. The walls were rough and jagged, so we figured the water must not have ever reached too high up the sides of the tunnel. That made me feel a little better, after imagining what would happen to us if water suddenly started coming through while we were still in there.

For the first little while there was only one way to go, so it was no big deal. Eventually, though, we came to a place where the tunnel split in two. We shined our lights around and soon found two drawings that looked almost exactly the same. One was in the tunnel we were coming from and the other was in one of the other tunnels.

The drawing looked like there were several animals in one spot and then, above them, there was a man holding a single animal that looked like the others. If it was trying to tell us something, we had no clue what. But we were much more interested in whether it looked old or new. Unfortunately, we had no clue about that, either. But it seemed obvious which way we were supposed to go, so we just went on.

There were several places where we came across multiple passageways. Each time there was more than one way to go we looked around until we found some sort of drawing scraped into the rock. And, happily, we would always find two drawings: one in the tunnel we were coming from and the other in the tunnel that we were apparently supposed to follow.

We couldn't even tell what some of the drawings were supposed to be, but some of them seemed clear enough. There was one pair that looked like a man holding a long stick with a snake on the top of it. We figured this had to have been showing the time when Moses had put a serpent on a pole and told the people to look at it if they wanted to be healed from the snake bites. Anyone who looked was healed, but those who wouldn't look died.

In another place we saw what looked like an altar with fire and an animal standing on top of it. We recognized this as a sacrifice from the Law of Moses that was supposed to help the people remember that Christ would be sacrificed for their sins.

Someplace else we found a drawing of lots of people leaning over and touching the ground. They weren't kneeling down, it was more like they were bent in half. We had no idea what this could possibly mean.

Then came the tough one—the one we had been dreading. We had been walking for hours when we came to a place that had two new tunnels, both with pictures. The tunnel we were coming from had drawings that matched the drawings in both tunnels. Just the thought of trying to figure this out made me practically fall over from exhaustion. I was tired and hungry and my feet were killing me.

"C'mon, Bran," Jeff said with a tired voice. "Help me decide which one of these is the new one."

I was leaning against one wall of the passage staring blankly at the ground in front of me where my light was shining. Heaving a huge sigh, I eventually mumbled something and walked over to where he stood looking at the two drawings. I was so tired, I'm not even sure what my mumble was supposed to be.

"We should only have to do this once," Jeff said. "Then we should be in the right tunnel the rest of the way."

"How much farther do we have to go?" I whined.

"How should I know?" Jeff complained. He was right, of course. How could either of us know?

"Just help me," he said. "Which one looks newer?"

I stared back and forth several times. This was the first time I noticed that our flashlights might not be as bright as they were before. Speaking of being bright, I realized that if we had been smart, we would have kept one of our flashlights off most of the time to save the battery.

"I can't tell," I admitted. "There's not enough light."

One of the drawings looked like a man with a big stick. It sort of looked like there was water flowing under his feet.

"Is that just a drawing of what they use this tunnel for?" asked Jeff. "To get water?"

"I don't know," I admitted. "Maybe. So what's with the stick?"

Jeff had no guess. The other drawing was of ten or twelve people. One of them was holding out his hands toward the others.

He was holding a cup in one hand and a plate in the other. There was something on the plate. We stared for several moments in silence.

Then Jeff made a quiet gasp. "I think I know what this is," he said. He paused. "I think this is the sacrament! That's supposed to be Jesus giving the sacrament to his Apostles!"

I looked more closely at the drawing.

"Levi and his people don't have cups!" I said. "They don't have plates, either."

"But Christian would know what a cup and plate are," said Jeff. "And he was here with Levi's father, remember?"

"And if this is the sacrament," I said slowly, "then it would have to be a *new* drawing, because they wouldn't have known about the sacrament until they got Christian's Bible! They only had Old Testament writings before Christian got here!"

"All right, Brandon!" yelled Jeff. His voice echoed through the passageways.

"Let's go," I said. "Let's get out of this place."

We both walked with much more energy now, excited that we might actually almost be out of this maze. Jeff took the lead, and I followed with my flashlight off. It took probably another half an hour, but then, suddenly, we could see light coming from up ahead. Jeff turned off his light and we both ran the last fifty feet. We could hear water running as we got closer. And when we reached the end we knew why.

The opening to the tunnel was actually behind a waterfall, and there were quite a few old, thick logs jutting up out of the mouth of the tunnel toward the falling water. The ends of the logs next to the water were rotted and covered with thick green moss, so we figured the logs had originally gone all the way into the stream. That was how they must have diverted water into the tunnel and brought it through to the other side.

Suddenly, exhaustion hit me like a ton of bricks. It looked like it would be a little tricky to climb out and around the waterfall, so we agreed to rest for a little while first. Sleep came easily, since we knew that all we had to do now was hike down to the river. We had been so worried about getting to this point, that for the past several hours neither one of us thought about who was going to be waiting for us or what they might have in mind. All we thought about was the distinct possibility that we would soon be meeting up with Aaron, Moses, Shauna, and Meg again. What a relief that would be! Both of us curled up, using our backpacks as pillows. The rushing of the water quickly lulled us both to sleep.

CHAPTER 14

The Covenant

"Brandon!" Jeff cried, shaking me.

I felt myself twitch violently like what happens when I dream that I just fell off something.

"Brandon, wake up!" Jeff repeated. He was practically yelling in order to be heard above the sound of the waterfall. "We've slept all day!"

That comment woke me in a hurry.

"What?" I breathed. "No way!" Even as I said it, I knew it was true because the sun was low enough in the sky to be shining directly through the rushing water into the tunnel. It was blinding.

"Get your poncho and let's get out of here!" called Jeff, rifling through his backpack

"Forget the poncho!" I yelled, making my way to the opening. "Let's just go!"

"There's no way we can get out of here without getting soaked," he insisted. "And I'm not interested in hiking the rest of the way in wet clothes. You're nuts!"

He was right, of course, and I knew it. Without bothering to acknowledge that he was right, I quickly found my poncho and threw it over my shoulders, being careful to cover my backpack as well. Then we headed for the waterfall.

Making our way across the rotted logs, we saw that we could hug the rocks to one side of the opening and probably make it out without too much trouble and without getting any direct hits from the falling water. But there was a lot of mist that made the moss-covered rocks extremely slippery. Luckily, though, the rocks were jagged, and so we were able to get some fairly good hand-holds as we worked our way out from behind the waterfall and onto dry ground.

Once completely outside of the cave, we got our first good look at the river below. We were pleasantly surprised to find we were really close to the point on the river where Vladimir had dropped us off almost two weeks earlier. There were still no signs of a yacht down there.

"Bran!" said Jeff. "I think we're closer than if we had come through the pass!"

"What pass?" I asked. I knew what he was talking about, of course, but I was staring up the mountain to where the pass no longer was. Jeff saw where I was looking and immediately looked that way as well.

Softly, under his breath, he said, "Whoa!" as we both surveyed the damage.

It looked a lot worse on this side than the other. Anthony had really done a job, destroying the opening. We just shook our heads. Neither of us bothered to express what we thought of him.

"Let's go find everybody," Jeff suggested, removing his poncho. I followed his example, jamming the wet plastic into one of the outer pockets on my pack, in an effort to keep everything else dry. Sprinting down the mountain like we were about to get left behind at Scout camp, we let the steep slope control our speed and simply concentrated on steering well enough to miss any major trees.

About ten minutes later, the slope flattened out considerably and we slowed to catch our breath. This was the first time we talked about what we might find.

"Do you think they're all just sitting around by the river?" I asked.

"I don't know," said Jeff.

"Do you think Aaron has been able to get his writings back?" I asked.

"I don't know," said Jeff again. "Maybe."

"I wonder if Anthony and Esau ever made a deal," I said. "Do you think Esau would help him kidnap Aaron?"

"I don't know," Jeff said one more time. Hearing Jeff say "I don't know" three times in a row made me realize that I was starting to sound like Meg.

"Maybe we better be really quiet and careful," I suggested, "until we know for sure what's going on."

Jeff just nodded like that's what he had been thinking all along. I decided to quit talking. The closer we got to the place where Vladimir had dropped us off, the slower we walked. Luckily, the forest was really thick there, and so we were well hidden as we approached.

Not far from the bank of the river we spotted two modern tents and one of the tribe's animal skin huts. Esau's reindeer sled was nearby, but there was no sign of the reindeer. The Three Stooges were the only people we could see. They were gathered around their cute little gas burner, dishing up their evening meal. We crouched down behind some thick bushes and checked it all out.

"Where's everybody else?" I whispered. "Shauna's got to be here, because the Stooges only had one tent—she had the other one."

Jeff just glanced nervously in my direction and then back at the Stooges.

For at least ten minutes we waited and watched for signs of any-one else, but didn't see any. The Stooges ate in silence until Anthony finally spoke.

"Do you think anyone else is hungry?" Anthony asked. We were only about thirty feet away, so we were able to hear pretty well. Neither Omni nor Leonard acted like they had even heard him speak. "I'll ask," said Anthony. Then, yelling toward the three tents he said, "Anyone hungry?" He laughed as he added, "Come and get it!" Standing quickly, he practically ran to the animal skin hut and then to one of the other tents and slapped his hand several times on the outside. Then he returned to his seat with a huge smile on his face.

Omni looked over at him, but Leonard made no response. He had finished eating and had now returned his arms to their usual folded position across his chest.

"Stop taunting them, Larry," Omni said to Anthony. "You're getting on my nerves."

"I'm enjoying this!" said Anthony. "I have a right to enjoy this. I've worked hard for this."

Omni just stared at him.

"Just think of it," said Anthony dramatically. "I am about to reveal to the entire world an ancient language, written by descendants of ancient people who have had virtually no contact with the rest of the world for thousands of years. And as an extra, little bonus, I'll even deliver a young interpreter, who just happens to speak English as well!" He laughed with pleasure at his own words. "I'll be famous! I'll be rich!" He looked over at Omni and said, "And you'll be even richer. You can be famous, too, if you want. I'm willing to share the glory!"

Omni grunted. "You've got what you came for, so just leave it alone."

"What are you so sore about?" asked Anthony, a little perturbed now. "You got what you came for, too, didn't you? You said so days ago."

"Well, it's not quite as useful now that you've effectively destroyed that mountain pass," said Omni, gesturing toward the mountain.

Anthony looked shocked for a moment as he stared at Omni. He said slowly, "Don't tell me you intended to bring others back here? That's what you've been doing with that little gadget of yours, isn't it? You've been keeping track of the coordinates all along the way, haven't you? That's why you said that you had what you needed as soon as we reached their winter home, isn't it? What is that thing, a GSP device?"

"GPS," said Omni flatly. "As in *Global Positioning Satellite*. And yes, I used it to keep track of our position. The coordinates will still work, but now I won't be able to get through the pass."

"You fool!" said Anthony. "If we tell others how to get here, then they won't need *us!* We will not get either rich *or* famous for being the only ones in the world who have access to this ancient culture. What were you *thinking?*"

Omni glared at Anthony and said, "Just *now* I was thinking I should have thrown you overboard in the Arctic Ocean about two weeks ago. Maybe you could have become famous as a human iceberg."

Anthony looked mildly offended and just a little bit worried. "Don't forget," he said a little more quietly, "if it wasn't for me you never would have known anything about this place."

"Don't forget," Omni glared back at him, "we still have one more trip through the Arctic Ocean."

Anthony's eyes grew larger, but he had no response. He sat quietly for a moment or two and then stood and headed toward the river, saying, "I'll be back soon."

After Anthony was gone, Omni grunted with exasperation and said, "Me, too." Then he headed into the trees on the other side of the campsite from where Jeff and I were hiding.

"Sounds like he caught Aaron," I whispered.

"Yeah," Jeff agreed. "And he's planning to drag him back to the United States."

"So do you think he's tied up in the tent or something?" I asked.

"I don't know," said Jeff.

"Do you think Esau is tied up, too?" I asked.

"It almost sounded like it, huh?" responded Jeff.

"They had to get that other tent from Shauna's backpack, so do you think they're all in the tent with Aaron?" I asked.

"I have no idea," sighed Jeff.

We quit whispering to each other when Leonard stood and walked over to the third tent—the one that Anthony had not slapped with his hand—and climbed inside.

"Let's see who's in those other tents," I whispered.

Jeff agreed. Leaving our backpacks behind the bush, we scampered over to the tent that we figured was Shauna's and cautiously unzipped the door flap. Pulling the flap all the way back to let as much light in as possible, we saw Shauna, Meg, Aaron, and Moses inside. They were all gagged and had their hands and ankles tied. Meg started to whimper as soon as she saw us. She looked tiny and helpless. In fact they all did, except for Moses. This was the first time I really noticed how much bigger Moses was than Shauna, even though they were the same age.

"Shhh! Don't let them hear you," Jeff hissed to Meg. We both quickly climbed inside and closed the flap behind us.

Jeff untied the gag from Shauna's mouth. "How did you get here?" she whispered. "I didn't think you'd have a chance to get through the pass! Where's Levi? Is he okay?"

"Levi's fine," Jeff said. "He's still on the other side, but he showed us a different way to get through the mountain. We'll explain later."

As quickly as possible, we removed all the gags, then started untying the canvas straps that held their wrists. We found that not only were their hands tied behind them, but there were also sticks tied to their wrists, connecting the four of them together. There was a short stick running from Meg's wrists to Aaron's and another one between Shauna and Moses. A longer stick connected Aaron's wrists to Moses'.

"What's all this for?" I whispered.

195

"They did it so we couldn't get close enough to untie each other," Shauna explained.

"Who's *they?*" Jeff asked.

"Who do you *think* it was?" whimpered Meg angrily.

"Shhh! Be quiet," I whispered. "You'll be okay in just a sec."

"It was the Stooges," Shauna said.

"Where are Esau and the Tweedles?" Jeff asked quietly.

"They have them tied up as well," Shauna said. "In their hut."

"Why?" I asked. "What are the Stooges planning to do?"

"I don't know," Shauna replied. "When Moses and Meg and I got here, everybody else was already tied up. They grabbed us and threw us in here with Aaron." Shauna reached over and started rubbing Meg's wrists before she continued.

"But Aaron said that when he got here, they were all just setting up camp," Shauna went on. "Aaron told me he was able to switch the pages when no one was looking, but as he was running away, one of the Tweedles saw him and caught him and dragged him back."

"I being caught by Tweedle Dum," Aaron said.

"I told him that was our name for him," Shauna smiled. Jeff and I smiled, too.

"Apparently," Shauna continued, "Anthony made Aaron translate for him. He told them that he had great powers and that he would kill them all if they didn't do exactly what he said. That's when he pulled out what they said was a 'little black box.' Anthony said that he could destroy anything with that box. I guess he pointed it at the mountain and that's when it exploded. I don't know how he did it."

"We do," I said. "Remember his second backpack? Well, we found it up there, and it was full of dynamite."

"It had an antenna sticking out of the top of it," said Jeff. "The little box was obviously a detonator."

Shauna nodded. "That explains it," she said. "So, apparently, that scared them enough that they let Leonard tie them all up while Anthony pointed his little black box at them."

"Do you think he has more dynamite somewhere?" asked Meg.

"I doubt it," Jeff said. "I'm sure he's done everything that his little black box can do."

"Are they all in the hut now?" I asked.

"Yes," said Aaron.

"So now what do we do?" Jeff asked. "Did they say if they're planning on leaving the rest of us here?"

"I don't know," said Shauna. "They told Aaron he was going with them, but they didn't say anything about the rest of us."

"I guess," Jeff said thoughtfully, "that if they don't take us, we could just wait here for another boat to come by. Remember how Levi told us last year that something comes by every few days?"

"It might be our only chance to get home," said Shauna, soberly. "At least if these guys leave us here."

Jeff nodded.

"Well they're not taking Aaron or Moses," I said. "Not now. But if Aaron and Moses get away, do you think that the Stooges would take Esau instead?"

"We leaving not Esau behind," said Aaron firmly.

"What?" I asked. "You're planning to untie him? Why? He's threatened to kill you! He's threatened to kill every single one of us!"

"Bran," Shauna hissed. "Shhh!"

"We giving help one to another," said Aaron. "My father being leader of tribe. We giving help to Esau."

I had no response for that. I knew that it wouldn't be possible to talk him out of it.

"Ye speaking now of path to this place," said Aaron.

"Do you mean how we got here?" Jeff said. "We followed what you call the Path of Christ—the Path of Living Water."

Aaron's eyes broadened. "My father finding the Path of Living Water?"

"No," I said. "He just told us where to find it and how to follow the markings inside the tunnel."

Aaron didn't know anything about the drawings in the tunnel. We told him how to find his way through. We also told him where the opening was. He said he had seen the waterfall and thought he would have no trouble finding the opening behind it. Then Aaron grinned.

"Esau making covenant," said Aaron through his smile. "Esau killing not. Esau hurting not. Esau following us on Path of Living Water."

"What do you mean?" asked Shauna, also smiling. "If he doesn't covenant not to hurt anyone, then you won't show him the way back?"

"Yes," said Aaron triumphantly.

"You can't trust him," I said. "How do you know he won't just break the covenant."

"The Book of Mormon—Another Testament of Jesus Christ telling of Christian people covenanting with enemy," said Aaron. "Christians trusting enemy following covenant."

He was right, of course. I remembered reading that in more than one place in the Book of Mormon. I remembered it because I was always amazed that they could trust each other. A covenant wouldn't mean anything to bad guys these days.

"Is he still going to want the salt from the boat?" asked Jeff. "There isn't any."

"Esau taking nothing," said Aaron.

"Are you making that part of his covenant, too?" I asked.

"Yes," said Aaron.

Cautiously opening the tent flap, we saw no sign of any of the Three Stooges. Aaron and Moses sneaked out and quickly climbed inside Esau's hut, pulling the opening closed behind them. Shauna,

Jeff, Meg, and I began trying to decide what we would do if we did, in fact, get left behind. We didn't get very far, though. Within five minutes, Aaron and Moses were back. Esau and his sons were right behind them. They didn't look very happy about the situation, but they didn't act like they were going to threaten anyone either. They were spread out, looking intently around the campsite.

"I guess they agreed to your covenant," I said.

"Yes," said Aaron.

Just then we saw the Tweedles charging toward the Three Stooges' tent. Leonard was climbing out. He was caught completely by surprise, and they quickly had him down on his stomach and were tying him up with the same straps that had been used on them for the last twenty-four hours.

"I thought they weren't going to hurt anybody," Shauna said.

"They hurting him not," said Aaron. "They holding only."

"Oh," I said, with raised eyebrows. Nodding my head a couple of times, I added, "I like it."

Within a few minutes, both Mr. Omni and Dr. Anthony returned to camp. Neither of them bothered to put up a struggle, like Leonard had; they simply surrendered, allowing themselves to be tied up next to Leonard.

"What are you going to do with us?" Anthony whimpered.

Mr. Omni just rolled his eyes. His expression seemed to say that whatever they had in mind couldn't possibly be any worse than enduring Anthony.

"We hurting ye not," said Aaron.

That was the absolute wrong thing to say. Anthony's whimper immediately turned to surprise and almost delight. "You're not going to hurt us?" he asked.

"You're not worth the trouble," I said flatly.

Anthony glared at me.

"Before Aaron would untie Esau and his sons," Shauna told Omni and Anthony, "he made them covenant not to hurt anyone."

199

Anthony actually smiled at Shauna. "I knew you were on my side all along!" he said.

I felt the nausea coming back. Then, as if he just realized that Jeff and I hadn't been there before, Anthony said, "How did *you* get here?"

"We found a way," said Jeff. After a moment he added, "With Levi's help."

Anthony looked perturbed. "I suppose he still wants the salt," he said, pointing with his head toward Esau. "The boat may not be here until tomorrow sometime. You're not going to keep us tied up that long, are you?"

"You had us tied up for more than a day!" Shauna said.

"Well, that's different," moaned Anthony.

"How?" I asked, in total disbelief. What a sleaze this guy was. Omni smirked and scooted himself farther away from Anthony.

"Don't worry," Jeff said, "the way they're going, they won't be able to take the reindeer sled back with them. So no one will ever know that you lied about having a boatload of salt to give them."

Anthony scowled at Jeff.

"Oh, that's right," said Shauna. "They'll have to leave the reindeer. Are they going to be mad about that?"

"My father helping all people of tribe," said Aaron.

"The tribe will give them some others?" Shauna asked.

"Yes," said Aaron.

That's when we heard the sound of a motor. It was coming from upriver. I looked that direction and was surprised to see Vladimir's yacht approaching. But it was not alone. Behind it was a much larger ship that looked like some kind of a military vessel, with a Russian flag flying from its mast.

Everyone from the tribe seemed terrified by the sight. Without another word, Esau and the two Tweedles scrambled toward their hut, grabbed food and water bags from inside, and then disappeared into the trees.

Aaron ignored the Three Stooges, but he took the time to grip each of the rest of us on the shoulders and say, "Farewell," just as his father had. Moses did the same with everyone but Shauna. Instead of grabbing her shoulders, he took both of her hands in his and stood looking into her eyes for several seconds. Then he grabbed the food bag he had brought with him and followed Esau. Aaron left with only his bag of precious writings.

When they were gone, I looked over at Shauna. I'm sure the look of astonishment on my face was obvious.

"What was *that* all about?" I asked.

"What do you mean?" she smiled back at me. I couldn't remember the last time I had seen her try to look so innocent.

"C'mon, Bran," said Jeff. "Do you mean to say that this is the first time you noticed?"

"Noticed *what?*" I said. I honestly didn't know what he was talking about.

He just shook his head and grunted, letting a small puff of air escape from his nose. "Never mind," he said.

I noticed that Meg had a huge grin on her face. Shauna just smiled.

"Untie us," demanded Anthony.

We all turned our attention to him.

"You heard me," he said. "We're not going to do anything to you! Untie us."

We just stared at him.

"Well, if you don't, then in two minutes *they* will," Anthony said with disgust, gesturing with his head toward the approaching ships.

"We might as well," said Shauna, "because it looks like we have a ride home, even if these guys don't want to give us one. Isn't that the same type of ship that took us back last year?"

"Believe me," said Mr. Omni. "I wouldn't have let him leave you here." He sounded completely sincere. I was shocked.

"B-but, wait a minute," I said. "Wasn't it you who said you weren't going to worry about taking us back? You were going to 'burn that bridge when you got to it,' remember?"

"I sincerely apologize," Omni said. "I should never have said such a thing. I promise you, my attitude has changed during the last few days."

"I noticed," said Anthony with disgust.

"That's why I decided to help you switch the writings," said Omni.

"*What?*" said Leonard, whipping his head around, his mouth gaping open. This was the first time we had ever heard him say a single word—and, come to think of it—that's all it was.

"Yes," said Omni. "Before we left in the middle of the night, I switched the pages that Larry had with the pages in your backpack that you left by your tent door. That was the arrangement, right?"

"Oh-h-h!" I moaned. "That's what happened!" Then, realizing that I now had proof that I hadn't just been dreaming, I yelled, "See!" Jeff and Shauna stared at me. "I *told* you I had switched them."

"What?" asked Omni. "No. I did it."

"Yeah," I nodded, "but I did it first. So I ended up with the wrong ones again!"

Omni looked dismayed. "I apologize. I honestly tried to help you kids."

Leonard still had a look of total disbelief on his face. Anthony, on the other hand, looked completely smug. I'm sure he thought he still had Aaron's pages.

"C'mon, guys," Shauna said, "let's untie them."

As soon as Anthony was loose, he immediately ran to his backpack inside the tent.

"Ha!" we heard him call out. Then he came outside holding the pages. "I've still got the writings," he gloated.

"Aaron switched them before he left," I smiled. "You just have pages that we practiced on. It's *our* writing, not his."

"Look at them. Most of them are blank," Jeff added.

Anthony's face dropped slightly as he started shuffling through the pages. "So what are these characters? Are they just something you made up?"

"No," I answered. "That front page is actually the very beginning of the Book of Mormon. I copied it from their translation. But you probably have a few of Meg's drawings in there. How do you like those?"

Anthony stared at the pages. Then he shot an evil smile at me. "You're such a fool!" he said. "I still have everything I need. I have their writing and—thanks to you—I know exactly what they represent. Whether it was written by you or by him doesn't really matter, now does it?"

I walked slowly toward him. "That's true," I said, trying not to let a smile escape from my lips. "But there's something else you may not know."

Anthony started backing up, being smart enough not to trust me. "Stay away," he warned. I knew what a coward he was—and I also knew that he was pretty well blind, so as soon as he was right in front of a large rock that came about up to his knees, I lunged at him. He tried to back away but tumbled backwards over the rock, tossing the pages behind him as he tried to catch himself. After landing hard on the ground, he was much more interested in his pain than the papers, so I was able to easily run past him and scoop them up. Jeff helped.

"What are you doing?" Anthony called out, still flat on his back on the ground.

"They got a little dirty," I called over my shoulder. "I'm going to wash them off for you."

"Don't you let them float down the river!" yelled Anthony, struggling to his feet.

By the time Anthony got to where I was kneeling next to the river, I had completely soaked all of the pages, sloshing them several times in the freezing water. Seeing that all the ink was now nothing but huge smears, I stood, turned around and handed the stack to Anthony. He immediately saw what had happened. I thought he was going to cry.

"What have you *done?*" he moaned. "You fool! You—*child!*"

"Ouch!" I said with a huge smile on my face. My hands were freezing, but I didn't care.

"Good job, Bran!" Jeff said.

Vladimir's yacht pulled in close to the bank where Anthony was standing. "You will be grabbing onto the flying rope, yes?" called Vladimir to Anthony as he threw the rope. Anthony stood motionless as the rope hit him in the head and fell to the riverbank. But Anthony didn't bother to do anything about it. He just stood there staring at the blank, dripping papers in his hand.

"Vladimir, my friend," called Omni, rushing over to pick up the rope. "Wonderful to see you! It looks like you've brought some friends with you."

The bigger military ship was stopped farther out from shore, toward the middle of the river. We saw the huge anchor dropped from a hole near the front of the ship, just below the main deck line.

"Ya," said Vladimir. "They are being friends of mine, if I am leading them correctly to these lost childrens. Now, perhaps, I am being allowed to keep my new boat." He paused and then added, "However, they are not being friends of the crazy person who has been exploding these mountains."

This was the first time that Anthony showed any sign of life since I handed him the wet papers. With eyes as big as soccer balls and his mouth half open, he dropped his hands to his sides and stared up at Vladimir.

CHAPTER 15

Restoration of All Things

"One of my new friends is being very anxious to be speaking with you," said Vladimir. As Vladimir finished what he was saying, a man dressed in a dark brownish-green uniform came strutting out of the lounge on the main deck of the yacht. He looked down at the paralyzed Dr. Anthony and spoke with a stronger Russian accent than Vladimir.

"You are being Dr. Lawrence Anthony from the United States of America?"

Anthony just stared up at him. I could see the pages in his hands trembling. They were still hanging at his sides.

The man yelled unexpectedly, "You will be answering the question!" The Russian said *vill* instead of *will* and *ze* instead of *the*. Everyone jumped except for Vladimir, who was closer to him than anyone. I figured he must have been used to this by now, since the guy had obviously been on his ship for a while.

"Y-y-yes, I am Dr. Anthony," he said weakly.

"You are being in Russia illegally," said the man, returning to his calm voice. He still looked stern.

"N-no!" said Anthony. "I have a valid passport and visa." He dropped Aaron's papers on the bank of the river and rushed to his backpack. "I'll show you! Everything is in order!"

As Anthony searched frantically through his backpack, I retrieved the pages he had dropped on the ground next to the cold water. When I stood up again, I noticed a small motorboat had been dropped into the river from the huge ship and was now making its way over to where we were.

Anthony found his passport and rushed over to the yacht. Meanwhile, the man in the uniform had climbed down to the riverbank and stood waiting. Anthony handed him the passport with it open to the visa stamp.

"S-see, right here," said Anthony, pointing to the open page. "It's valid. I'm here legally."

Without even bothering to look inside the passport, the Russian closed it and put it into his coat pocket. "This visa is not being legal visa," he said. He was switching all of the Ws and Vs, so he said *wisa* instead of *visa.*

Anthony looked shocked. "Of course it is," he said frantically. Spinning and turning to Mr. Omni, he said, "Tell him! Tell him it's legal!" Then he saw us. "Hey! If you're interested in catching people who are here illegally, get those four kids! Not one of them has a passport! They sneaked onto our boat and came with us without our even knowing about it! They're stowaways! Grab them, quick, before they go hide out in the mountains with their cavemen friends!"

The Russian looked up at us. "Four childrens," he said. "Two young mens and two young ladies." He nodded slowly as he looked at each of us. "You will, of course, be having no passports or visas, yes?" he asked.

"No, sir," said Shauna. "We don't."

"This is because you are being children of the Andrews family, yes?" he said.

Shauna's face brightened. "Yes! We are!"

"Your parents will be very pleased to be knowing that we have rescued you from the kidnapper, Lawrence Anthony."

"*What!*" cried Anthony. "I didn't kidnap them! I've never done *anything* to them."

Turning back to Anthony, the Russian said, "It is being my understanding that not just two years ago you have been threatening these exact same four childrens with loaded gun, yes?"

Anthony looked stunned. He stammered, but nothing intelligent came out. (Actually, nothing intelligent *ever* came out of his mouth—but this time, nothing understandable came out, either.)

The Russian continued. "And this is to have been taking place after you kidnap them in the home of the aunt of these childrens in state of Iowa in the United States of America, yes?"

Anthony didn't even try to respond this time. He just stared with ever-widening eyes and a trembling lower lip.

"It is not being only the opinion of myself that this passport and this visa is being illegal," said the Russian, tapping the pocket where he had put Anthony's passport. "It is also being the opinion of the government of the United States of America, yes?"

Anthony now looked totally bewildered. He didn't even notice that the motorboat had arrived and two men, also in uniforms, were now standing not far behind him.

"There is question," said the Russian, "on application for receiving passport. You have been lying on application for passport. You have been writing down that you are never to have been previously in prison in United States of America. But this is being lie from you, yes?"

Anthony's whole body began to shake now. He exhaled so that he almost looked as though he was shriveling up right before our eyes.

"Perhaps you have been forgetting about this prison?" asked the Russian. Now he smiled for the first time. "I will be making promise to you, Mr. Lawrence Anthony," he said slowly. "You will *never* be forgetting about prison in Russia."

The Russian's smile quickly faded. He looked at the men behind Anthony and gestured toward their motorboat with a quick flick of his head. They immediately grabbed Anthony by each arm and pushed him into the boat. Anthony made no attempt to fight back.

"Wait!" Anthony called as if he had just remembered something. "That guy, right there," he said, pointing to Leonard. "Leonard's been in prison, too! He was there the same time I was!"

"Pardon me, sir," said Leonard, "You must have me confused with my twin brother. My name is Leopold." As he said this he handed his passport to the Russian, who opened it and began to examine it carefully. Anthony looked stunned once more.

"You're not Leonard?" he asked quietly. Then with more determination, he said, "No, you're not Leonard! You don't even sound like him!"

"As I already stated, sir, my name is Leopold," he smiled.

"Ha!" I laughed, "That's why you never said anything, huh? So Anthony wouldn't know!"

Leonard smiled—or I guess Leopold did. Maybe Leonard was smiling, too—wherever he was.

Returning Leopold's passport, the Russian said, "Everything is being in order for you." Then he asked for Omni's passport and spent a few moments examining it. "Everything is being in order for you both," said the Russian as he handed the passport back to Mr. Omni. "Very good. You will now be traveling again with Vladimir, yes?"

"Yes," said Mr. Omni, with a wet smile. It was the first time I had seen the gaps in his teeth for quite a while.

"I will be speaking with you very soonly," called the Russian after Anthony. "About the exploding of mountain. Perhaps this time you will be telling no lies to me, yes?"

Anthony didn't even look at him. Looking completely defeated, he just stared at the bottom of the boat as it sped away toward the ship anchored in the river. Once they were gone, the Russian turned to us again.

"We will be taking you very quickly back to United States Coast Guard ship to be meeting with parents," he said.

We were instructed to leave everything behind that we had not brought with us. I had sort of been hoping to keep the papers, even though they were blank, but the Russian told me to leave them inside Esau's hut. I flipped through them one more time as I slowly shuffled over to the tent. That's when something caught my eye. There was writing at the bottom of one of the pages that had not washed away like all the rest. The writing was obviously Aaron's, but it wasn't in his language. Written in permanent ink was the scripture reference: "Mormon 8:14, 15."

Why had Aaron done this? Was this a message or something? Who was it for? He had given these pages to Anthony, so was he trying to say something to him about stealing his pages? I would have to find out later because the Russian wanted us to leave as soon as possible. I repeated the reference out loud two or three times to make sure I wouldn't forget it, then I put the pages inside the hut and closed the flap.

The motorboat had returned to take the Russian military guy and the four of us back to his ship. The only thing we were to carry with us was Meg's pink, flowered backpack. Omni and "Leonard" took all of the other backpacks with them, since they belonged to the yacht.

"One of the backpacks is missing part of a mess kit," I said to Omni. "Levi was using it when we left."

"No worries, Brandon!" Omni smiled. I was so stunned that he actually got my name right, that I had no response. "I'll consider it a gift," he smiled again. He thought for a moment and said, "I think I should give them another gift as well." Reaching into his pocket, he pulled out the notebook where he had been writing down all of the coordinates from his GPS gadget. "How about you put that into the hut as well, okay, Meg?" he said as he handed her the notebook.

Meg's entire face sparkled at finally being called by the right name. She skipped over to the tent and placed the notebook carefully inside.

"Please allow me to apologize one more time, Jeff," he said, looking sincerely into his face. "I'm sure I said things that frightened you and I truly am sorry." Turning to Shauna, he said, "Shauna, you have been quite a guardian for your siblings. Your parents should be proud." Looking toward the rest of us, he added, "It was truly an honor to meet you children and to see that there are still some people in this world who care about others and about doing what is right. Thank you again."

Shauna had a strange look on her face.

"Is there something else?" asked Omni.

"I was just wondering," said Shauna. After a brief hesitation she asked, "What happened?"

"What do you mean?" asked Omni.

"Were you just joking before?" she asked. "Or what?"

"Yeah," said Jeff, "and what did you mean when we were at the winter camp and you said that you had what you came for?"

"Ah, that!" said Omni, chuckling slightly. He stopped short and shook his head back and forth. "It was at that point," he explained, "that I had the GPS coordinates so I could return at any time I wanted. But as we made our way back to the river," he sighed, "I became convinced that there really is nothing to be gained by ever returning here. Larry still thought there was money to be made, but I don't see how." Omni smiled. "It was an intriguing adventure—but that's all." After a pause, he said, "I'll say it again, though: it was an honor meeting each of you. I think I'll remember you far longer than I'll remember anything about the tribe. God bless you."

We just smiled and nodded.

The motorboat was waiting, and the Russian told us it was time to go.

"Good-bye!" we called to Omni, Leopold, and Vladimir.

As we climbed into the motorboat and sped toward the ship, Meg said, "I think Leonard is nice."

"Did you just say something that wasn't a question?" I asked in mock astonishment. "Meg! What a breakthrough! Wahoo! Fifth grade, here we come!"

Turning to Shauna, Meg asked, "Why did he say that?"

"Arrgh!" I screamed. Meg looked stunned by the noise.

Smiling, Shauna drew Meg into her arms. "I'll explain later."

Once on the ship, we were given warm food and the chance to take a hot shower for the first time in almost two weeks. They even took our clothes and washed them for us while we were cleaning up. It felt great. Jeff and I shared a stateroom, while Shauna and Meg were in the room right next door. They weren't nearly as nice as the room we had on the yacht, but it sure felt good to be going home. We were promised that we would meet up with our parents in less than two days. We were treated extremely well the entire time. We knew that Dr. Anthony was on the ship, too, but wherever he was, we never saw him.

The first night Shauna and Meg joined Jeff and me in our room, and we stayed up really late talking. The girls wanted to know more about the Path of Living Water. We told them all about the tunnel and described the drawings we had seen.

"Remember the name that Levi called it?" I asked. "Heze-something's tunnel?"

"Oh, yeah," said Jeff. "It was Heze-tation—or Heze—. Oh, I know: Hezekiah."

"Hezekiah's Tunnel?" Shauna asked. "What's that?"

"How should we know?" I said.

Pulling Meg's scriptures from her backpack, we found *Hezekiah* in the Topical Guide, and it said "*see Dictionary:* Hezekiah; Hezekiah's Tunnel." When we looked up *Hezekiah's Tunnel* in the Bible Dictionary, we learned that it was a 1770-foot tunnel created around 701 B.C., during the reign of King Hezekiah, used to bring fresh water into the city of Jerusalem. They dug the tunnel in case the city was ever attacked by the Assyrian army, to make sure Jerusalem would have a continuing supply of water.

"That's *cool!*" said Jeff.

"So," I added, "just like Hezekiah had a tunnel made so they could get water in an emergency, the tribe did the same thing!"

"Amazing," Shauna said. "Hezekiah's Tunnel." She paused and then said, "They called it the Path of Christ a couple of times, too, didn't they?"

"Yeah," said Jeff.

Shauna smiled. "Christ is the Living Water," she said. "He gives us Eternal Life."

"So do you think all of the drawings have something to do with Jesus Christ?" asked Jeff.

"Probably," said Shauna, reaching for Meg's scriptures again. Meg was asleep on Jeff's bed, and, of course, she had her backpack on.

"I found something really cool a while ago," said Shauna as she flipped through the pages. "It's in the Topical Guide. When you look up *Jesus Christ,*" she continued, "there are at least 50 different subheadings."

"Really?" I said.

"No way," said Jeff.

"Yeah," said Shauna, nodding her head. "Look! There's *Jesus Christ, the Anointed;* there are two for *Jesus Christ, Appearances,* divided up by before he came to earth and after." She continued to turn pages as she read. "There's *Jesus Christ, Authority of;* there's *Jesus Christ, Baptism of; Jesus Christ, Betrayal of; Jesus Christ, Foreordained;* and a whole bunch more."

"Whoa," Jeff and I both said, staring at page after page of references.

"But the cool ones I wanted to show you," Shauna said, "are the ones about types and shadows. Oh, here they are: *Jesus Christ, Types of, in Anticipation* and *Jesus Christ, Types of, in Memory*. The drawing you saw of a serpent on the pole and the drawing of the burnt offering are types of Christ, so it made me think of this."

"So what does it have listed in there?" I asked.

"The first one," Shauna answered, "is 'Abel . . . brought of the *firstlings* of his flock.'"

Jeff thought for a minute and then breathed, "Oh!" His eyes darted about and then he asked me, "Do you think that's what the drawing was with all the animals in one place and the man carrying one of them away?"

"Oh, yeah!" I said. "I bet you're right!"

"The next one is about a burnt offering," Shauna said, her finger running down the page. "And the next one is, too . . . and the next."

"We definitely saw a drawing of burnt offerings," I said.

Shauna paused. "Here's one, 'manna . . . the bread which the Lord hath given.' Did you see any drawings about manna?"

Jeff and I just stared at each other for a minute. Then Jeff's face brightened. "I know!" he said. "Remember the one where all the people were leaning over and touching the ground! Do you think they were picking up manna?"

I started nodding my head more and more as I thought about it. "You're right!" I agreed.

We continued to go through the scripture references listed. There ended up being a couple more that we thought matched up with the drawings, including the serpent on the pole and Moses striking the rock with his staff and water coming out.

"Living water!" said Shauna. "It all fits, doesn't it?"

"These people are amazing," I said.

When we read the references for *Jesus Christ, Types of, in Memory*, we only found one that seemed to match: the sacrament.

"But that makes sense," Shauna said. "Because all of those

others were probably there before they found out about the coming of Jesus Christ."

Jeff and Shauna continued to talk for a while, but I was getting really sleepy. I felt myself drifting in and out several times before Shauna finally said that she and Meg should probably be heading back to their own room.

As Shauna was slipping Meg's scriptures back into her backpack, she said, "Wait a second." Apparently remembering that Aaron had written a scripture reference on the pages I left in Esau's hut, she asked, "Brandon, what was that scripture reference that Aaron wrote?"

I heard her ask, but my eyes were closed, and I was already so far gone that she had to repeat the question two more times before I figured out what she was talking about.

"Mormon 8:14, 15," I finally mumbled, never bothering to open my eyes.

I was already dozing off again when I heard her laugh and say, "It was a message for Anthony!"

Jeff chuckled, too, and said, "Brandon, do you want to hear this?"

"Tell me in the morning," I said with a groggy voice, and I snuggled into my pillow.